BRUTAL SEASON

Seasons Mystery Series
~Book Four~

Maryann Miller

To my daughter, Anjanette.

While not a police officer, she is an incredibly strong woman and can stand with Sarah and Angel any time.

ACKNOWLEDGEMENTS

It is with much gratitude that I acknowledge the officers at the Dallas Police Department who shared their experiences and expertise with me when this series was first developed. I owe special thanks to the late Tim Huskey, a former police officer and a wonderful writer. For years he was the one who kept me on the right course about how police officers work. I also want to thank Doug Grantham, a retired Dallas police officer who more recently has become an expert source I turn to for help with police procedures and policies. Any variance from the way things really work is why this is called fiction.

Many thanks to Dany Russell for all the wonderful covers she's created for the series, Audrey Lintner at Alto Editing for the precise and careful editing, and to Eeva at The Book Khaleesi for first-rate interior design and formatting. All three are a delight to work with.

PRAISE for the SERIES

Open Season

"Miller spins a tight tale that's a cut above the average police procedural… Readers will want to see more of these engaging female cops." ~ **Publisher's Weekly**

"Try this debut mystery for its open treatment of current urban problems, clean prose, and realistic depiction of women working together. For readers who enjoy Robin Burcell and fans of police procedurals." ~ **Library Journal**

"Detectives Sarah Kingsly and Angel Johnson are crisply drawn characters. The hard-edged story of racial tension in Dallas could be drawn from today's headlines. *Open Season* is a smart, spirited page-turner." ~ **Bruce Cook Tommy Gun Tango**

"*Open Season* is a solid police procedural with fully developed characters and provocative social issues." ~ **L.J. Sellers, author of the Detective Jackson Mysteries**

Stalking Season

"…gripping second mystery featuring Dallas, Tex., police Detectives Sarah Kingsly and Angel Johnson. The relationship between the women is just as absorbing as the search for the killer. Few readers will anticipate the closing twist." ~ **STARRED Publishers Weekly Review**

"Dallas Detectives Sarah Kingsly and Angel Johnson (*Open Season*, 2011, etc.) return to confront a case almost as gnarly as their relationship… So deftly plotted and paced that, although it's certainly possible to grow impatient with the protagonists' unwarranted impatience toward each other, they're appealing enough to keep the pages turning." ~ **Kirkus Review**

Desperate Season

"Hard working female cop partners, a good mystery, racial tensions. What more could one want from this great author? This riveting novel had me hooked from page one. I respect Ms. Miller on her style and ability to understand and describe the race relations difficulties with ease and accuracy." ~ **Amazon Review**

"…a well written, captivating police thriller. The author did a good job creating and crafting the characters who fit perfectly with the storyline." ~ **Amazon Review**

CHAPTER ONE

Tuesday, June 16, 2021 - Morning

Sitting at her desk in the Crimes Against Persons Division of the Dallas Police Department, Detective Sarah Kingsley heard the ping of an incoming text on her partner's phone and looked over as Angel picked it up and read the message, then slammed her phone down. "Christ! Another Black man's been killed."

Another ping. This time, from Sarah's phone. She grabbed it but didn't check the message. She was unable to tear her gaze from her partner, who radiated a growing anger like heat from an open oven door. "Was it an accident?" She asked the question, hoping, but her instinct answered before her partner.

Fury flashed across Angel Johnson's face. "No. It was *not* a goddamn accident. One of our officers shot him. In his own front yard."

Sarah couldn't recall a time that she had seen so much anger burning out of her partner's eyes, but the sight of it now stunned her into silence. She turned away, hoping that if she just gave Angel some time, the heat of that rage would dissipate.

A moment later, Sarah's phone pinged with another message. She heard the same alert on Angel's phone and glanced over, but her partner just sat there. Not moving, as if she'd become a stone replica of herself. Sarah looked at her phone, then back to Angel. "It's McGregor. He wants us in conference room B in ten minutes."

She waited, but Angel didn't stir a muscle or blink an eye. It was the longest few minutes in Sarah's life. She didn't know what to say. Or even if she should say anything to the woman who could have been a statue in the chair. Maybe it would be best not to poke a hornet's nest.

Sarah stood. "Okay, then. See you there."

Still no response, so Sarah quickly strode out of the squad room. She took a moment to relieve her bladder from too much coffee that morning, followed by a splash of cold water on her face to ease the tightness around her eyes. She hated to think of what waited in the conference room.

When she got there, she saw her immediate boss, Lieutenant McGregor; the Chief of D's, Helen Dorsett; and one of Sarah's least favorite people on earth, Price, the PR guy for the Dallas Police Department. She was sure that he'd been behind the initial pairing of her with Angel a few years ago to quell community protests over the death of the young Black teen that Sarah had shot. What a nightmare that whole time had been. Not only had she been forced to kill a kid, something she regretted to this day, Sarah had lost her long-time partner in that same undercover fiasco. Few people had lamented the loss of one of Dallas's finest. Instead, they'd come at Sarah with all the sound and fury of a marauding army. The Dallas Review Board had almost succeeded in taking her badge, and it was only the intervention of

McGregor that had saved her.

Not surprisingly, the outrage had died down to a dull roar after the partnership between her and Angel had been announced. Slick move on the part of the PR department, but not so slick for the detectives. Even though they were in a better place today than at first, too often some racial sensitivity would hit a nerve and push the two women back to square one. Sarah wondered if that would ever stop, and this latest news didn't bode well for the possibility of them cementing a working relationship any time soon.

Let alone a personal one.

Sarah barely gave Price a nod, but did acknowledge the others in the room, noting how crowded it already was, with officers standing along the back wall, almost like a line-up. Now she understood why the largest conference room had been chosen. She'd just taken a seat when the door opened and more officers filed in. Some from Vice and more from the CAPERS unit. They were followed by Burt and his partner, Simms, along with Ryan from narcotics and his boss, Lieutenant Webb.

Despite his bypass surgery a couple of months ago, he looked pretty good. He'd lost some weight, which was probably in his favor. Might keep him from having another coronary.

The door opened again and Angel slipped in, heading for the far end of the conference table. Well away from others already seated there. And definitely well away from Sarah. *What the hell?* Angel's whole demeanor still screamed anger. Was she going to be pissed at the whole department because of one idiot who couldn't control his trigger finger?

The last to arrive was Bruce Walinski from The Special Investigations Unit. Sarah wasn't surprised to see an SIU officer, although it usually took more than twenty-four hours for their unit to get involved in an officer-related shooting, whether being shot or having to use deadly force.

Things had changed in the investigative process since her face-off with Quinlin a few years ago, and for that she was grateful. Having to discharge your weapon, knowing that someone had to die to protect yourself or the public, or your fellow officers, gives most cops nightmares for weeks, or months, or often for the rest of their lives.

Piling on the guilt, like Quinlin had tried with her, did nothing to ease the trauma.

Now with the new policy and approach to the investigations of cop-related shootings, officers would be spared the same kind of demeaning third degree.

Helen stood and went to the front of the room, facing the large conference table ringed by officers in comfortable wooden chairs. "You all know the basic facts by now. There's been an officer-involved shooting. What we know so far is that the victim was Jamel Frederickson, age eighteen. The officer is Brad Smithfield."

Sarah groaned. She knew full well what that officer was in for.

"Preliminary report states the teen was not armed."

"Oh, shit." McGregor said.

Helen nodded. "As in feces and the proverbial fan."

"Do we know any more?" Sarah asked.

"Nothing official yet," Helen said. "but Price has set us up with a live feed from Channel Eight News who has a reporter at the scene." She motioned to Price who had his laptop open and connected to a large smart screen on the wall behind Helen. She took a step to the side and Price touched a key, bringing the screen to life. The scene was chaos. Lights from an ambulance and three police cars swept across yards, the sidewalk, and the front of a small brick house. The lights looked like bright yellow and blue strobes at a dance club. People milled around the area, most holding cell phones aloft, recording the moment, probably more for thrills than posterity. Several uniformed officers were doing their best to hold people back from the grassy lawn where the outline of a body could be seen under a white sheet.

Bianca Gomez stood to one side of the chaos, black hair dancing slightly in a low breeze, microphone to her lips. "Bianca Gomez, Channel Eight News, reporting from the scene of a deadly shooting that took place at 6:45 this morning. The victim, eighteen-year-old Jamel Frederickson, was taken to the hospital where he was pronounced DOA. Rookie Dallas Police officer Brad Smithfield has been taken to department headquarters where he will be questioned, then put on administrative leave pending a full investigation."

The reporter paused a moment and Sarah could clearly hear another woman's voice crying, "My baby. My baby!" The camera swung around, finally focusing on a rail-thin woman with light mocha skin, mascara running in black rivers down her cheeks. A tall, burly man with ebony skin held her upright as best he could while she wailed, "He killed my baby."

The reporter's pause was no coincidence. Sarah was sure of that. A distraught mother made for great television, and Bianca was all about great television.

Slowly the camera panned back to Bianca and she continued. "There are still only few details known about the incident. According to a neighbor, who didn't want to speak on camera, Jamel has mental health issues and had stopped taking his meds recently. Nobody was aware. Not even his mother, according to the neighbor. The mother told her neighbor that she'd come home from work and allegedly found him pacing around the house, cursing and hitting his head with a plastic spatula. He was in a crisis and needed help. The mother called 911 and told the dispatcher what was happening and requested an ambulance."

Another dramatic pause while the camera moved to show the mother being comforted by another woman about the same age. Bianca's voice came from off screen. "Even though Jamel was so big, his mother described him as soft as a teddy bear and just as harmless. As long as he took his meds."

Bianca continued the report as the camera came back to her. "Before an ambulance could arrive, a patrol car came screaming up the street. According to what the mother told her neighbor, when Jamel saw the police cars he ran out of the house before she could stop him. He was still carrying the spatula and ran toward the two officers, Smithfield and Greg Renshaw, who shouted for Jamel to stop.

"He didn't stop until officer Smithfield put five bullets into this unarmed man."

"Turn that shit off." McGregor's voice was sharp, and Helen didn't even object to the language. She often did, thinking that cops didn't have to curse like drunken sailors, but she just nodded to Price, who pushed a key on his laptop.

The screen went blank and silence reigned for just a moment, then Helen cleared her throat. "Under normal circumstances, we wouldn't be having this meeting. But, well … you all know how *not* normal things are. So, we need to look ahead and make sure we don't end up like Minneapolis."

"There are sure to be protests," Burt said.

Helen nodded. "So, we're preparing. The mayor has asked for added security around the Federal Building. That seems to be the place where protesters make the most noise."

"Are we going to be part of that security?" Simms asked, gesturing to the others in the room.

"Not at first," Helen said. "Grotelli is already pulling his uniformed squad together to hit the streets. The commissioner has authorized overtime for the foreseeable future. You will all be on standby to assist whenever needed. Nobody rests until this is over."

Sarah knew that lack of sleep included Helen, too. She never asked anything more of her team than what she was willing to do. Probably where McGregor learned that basic tenet of leadership.

"You'll be called for help containing the protestors if things escalate. And they probably will. We all know the history of this town." Helen paused then nodded toward the captains in the room. "Orders will come through the normal chain of command. We can hope the detective squads won't be needed for street safety."

Yeah. We can hope.

"Nothing goes to the press except through Price." Helen glanced toward him and Sarah swore he swelled more than a little in importance. *Prick.* "And nobody goes near the protesters unless they're assigned to help the uniforms. Got it?"

Helen shot her trademark icy glare around the room skewering each person in turn until getting a nod of assent. Anyone new to the detective squad who'd never seen this phenomenon before and wondered how this diminutive lady, who looked a cross between Mary Poppins and their own grandmother, had become Chief of Ds, no longer wondered.

"Anybody else want to weigh in before we end the meeting?" Again, Helen gazed around the room, but this time the blue ice of her eyes had melted.

"We were thinking of hitting the pause button on any current drug operations," Webb said. "Keep people in place. Just not make any moves."

"Good idea. What about you?" Helen pointed to Lieutenant Burlingham, head of the gang unit.

"I'm pulling my guys in." Burlingham hitched from one side of the chair to the other, perhaps to ease a sore back. "Going to reach out to my CIs to see if they want to be 'arrested' for the duration."

"Think they will?" Helen asked.

He shrugged.

"Okay. Go ahead. Anyone else? McGregor?"

"We're good. I got Kingsly and Johnson. Burt and Simms. And Ryan can float over from Vice if I need him since Webb is pausing stuff over there."

Webb snorted, but Ryan smiled. Sarah knew what precipitated both reactions. There was a rivalry between Webb and McGregor, sometimes friendly but mostly intense, both determined to someday stand where Helen was now. And Ryan? Well, Ryan would smile any time he was close to Angel.

"You want to add anything, Walinski?" Helen asked.

"We'll do our usual due diligence, but most of the gathering of details around the incident will go through Grotelli. Talking to neighbors. Friends. That sort of thing. Of course, one of our team will be in close touch with the family of the victim at all times."

Sarah flinched. *The victim*? Such an impersonal way to refer to another young teen whose life ended much too soon.

CHAPTER TWO

Sunday, June 21 - Afternoon

I told you, didn't I?" Each word from her father was like a stab to Angel's heart. "I said they was all against us and I was right."

Gilbert slammed his fist on the kitchen table, making his cutlery jump. "And don't you go telling me how some white folks are just fine and others are not. Your 'just fine White police officer' shot another poor Black kid—"

"But Daddy—"

"Don't 'but Daddy' me, girl. I'm right and you know it. When're you gonna wake up and do the right thing?"

"But Daddy—"

Gilbert brushed her protest away with a wave of his hand and pushed away from the table so vehemently his chair thudded against the wall. Then he stormed out of the dining room.

For a moment, it felt like he had taken all the air from the room with him, and Angel struggled to take a breath. She looked at the remains of what had started as their usual Sunday dinner. Mounds of mashed potatoes like little white mountains. Cold roast beef swimming in congealed gravy. She felt like her heart was just as congealed. Then the tears spilled out of her eyes and ran in a warm river down her cheeks. She said softly, "Oh, Mama. I don't know what to do. Please tell me what to do."

"I can't do that, child. You're a grown woman."

"But Mama—"

Martha raised her hand in a gesture identical to the one Gilbert had used to wave away Angel's protest. "No longer will I be the one to try to patch things between you and your father. You have to figure this one out for yourself."

That response stunned Angel as much as the words from her father. What would she do without her mother's support? It was always there as a buffer to her father's periodic angry outbursts. Not that there had been many throughout her childhood, but the explosions he'd had when she was in high school had been fierce. That's when she was with Bobby, and he got all messed up with drugs. Her mother had protected her, softening the anger in the room when her father railed against her boyfriend. Threatened to toss Angel out if she didn't stop seeing him.

Angel's mother would wrap her arms around the girl, who'd been left in the living room so many times trembling with tears after her father stomped out. Her mother would tell her everything would be okay. And the funny thing was, life was okay whenever Angel got around to doing things her father's way.

Today, her mother's words stripped Angel of any sense of that protection she'd always counted on, and she didn't know what to do.

Martha stood. "You need to go. Take your anger with you."

"I'm not angry, Mama."

"Oh, child. Yes, you are. I feel it circling around you like a blackbird looking for a place to roost."

Angel didn't know what to say to that, even though deep inside her soul she knew the truth in her mother's words. Finally, she looked at her mother, letting the tears roll down her face. "I'm sorry, Mama."

"Don't be sorry. Be righteous."

Angel didn't move for a long moment, while her mother locked eyes with her. Then, swiping the wetness from her cheeks, Angel stood and pushed her chair tight to the table. "Can I help clean up?"

"No."

That single word hurt almost as much as her father's tirade.

A fresh flood of tears threatened as Angel hurried out of the house and ran to her car. Once behind the wheel, she let the dam break. She couldn't remember the last time she'd felt so low. So alone. She wished her brother was here. To hold her. To pat her back and tell her this wasn't the end of the world. The same way LaVon had done so many times when life had sucker-punched her. But then, part of her was glad that he was stuck in L.A. because of the pandemic and hadn't been here to witness this humiliation.

Taking a few deep breaths to pull her emotions together, Angel realized that her parents were right. Not in being so harsh. That was never right. But in the message. Angel was the only one who could figure out what to do. For the first time since she'd made the decision to become a police officer, doubts about the wisdom of that decision were rising like grisly specters from the dead.

She'd been so young and idealistic when her good friend

Stacy had been shot and killed during a robbery at the jewelry store where she worked. The robber had never been caught, and Stacy's father was convinced the police didn't care enough to really dig into the case. Angel was still in college then, but that's when she switched her major to criminal justice. When she graduated, she joined the police force, so maybe she could do right by her people. And let's face it, they were her people. They weren't the white man's people.

Oh, shit. What am I going to do?

Grabbing a napkin from the wad in her center console, Angel mopped her face and blew her nose. She certainly couldn't sit here for the rest of the night. Some white patrol officer might come by and shoot her.

Oh, girl. Don't go there.

Angel took a deep breath and let it out slowly, hoping the ugly mood would be taken away on the exhale. She tried it a few more times before easing the car into gear and pulling away from her parent's house. She hoped she wouldn't be exiled for long.

The route back to her house took Angel through the outskirts of downtown, and she noticed more people on the streets than usual on hot summer nights. She slowed as she passed clusters of folks and noted that most of them were Black. One young woman held a sign aloft that proclaimed, Black Lives Matter.

She was momentarily stymied. As a cop, she should definitely alert the department that something was brewing. But as a confused, angry Black woman she didn't want to do that. Not at the moment, anyway. Let the people be.

Before she could make a decision, her phone pinged with an alert to a text message, and she pulled into a parking spot to read it. The text was from Isabella, a young woman she'd met last year when a local group of activists formed to protest the killing of George Floyd. It had been a chance encounter at a vigil for Floyd held at Fair Park. At the time, Angel had debated about going. Not sure if it was okay with the department that officers attend something like that, but she'd not been able to resist the pull of her heart that took her there.

After the prayer service came to a close, Angel wanted to avoid being seen by the good Reverend Billie Norton who'd led the prayer service. He was good friends with her father, and Angel didn't want him reporting that he'd seen her here, so she'd pushed to the back of the crowd, inadvertently bumping into Isabella. After apologies and quick smiles were exchanged, Isabella had slipped Angel a business card. "In case you'd like to join the movement."

The movement turned out to be a local group of activists in the Black Lives Matter organization. Angel had almost tossed the card. There was no way she could get involved. Surely that would be a risk to her job. But as the national momentum against the injustices of Black people getting killed by police grew, she'd felt a pull to take a stand. So, she'd met with Isabella a few times, even going so far as to give the young woman her phone number, but with each visit, Angel had become increasingly conflicted. Finally, the last time they met, she told Isabella about her job and all the reasons she couldn't join the local protests. Much as part of her heart wanted to.

Still, Angel hadn't deleted Isabella from her contacts. She'd admired the young woman's dedication to the cause and sense of righteousness. Was this what Angel's mother meant about being righteous? Daring to do the uncomfortable?

Angel texted back, *Where are you?*

MARYANN MILLER

At the Metro Diner.
Coming.

CHAPTER THREE

Wednesday, July 1 - Night

Fred pulled his mask tighter around his ears and pinched it tight across the bridge of his nose. He supposed that was one good thing that could be said for the pandemic. It had most people who were out for the protest wearing masks, although the leaf blower the guy in front of him had was doing a better job of keeping the tear gas at bay than the flimsy paper mask.

He, and a few hundred protesters, were headed to the Earle Cabell Federal building on Commerce Street. Not to vandalize it, or try to break in like those idiots did on January 6th in D.C. It was just a great spot to stand and get a message across. Even if the media wasn't out in the middle of the night, everyone was an amateur reporter now; cell phones always at the ready for recording.

The beauty of the digital age.

Josiah, the young man who'd come to speak at the church last Sunday had made it clear that they were going to try non-violence first. Fred could relate to that. He'd always been a bit of a pacifist, which was one of the reasons that his wife had seemed so shocked when Fred told her that he wanted to join the Black Lives Matter protest in downtown Dallas. "What? You finally grew a pair?"

She'd thrown the insult with the accuracy of a dart, and he'd ignored it, like he had so many of her recent barbs. When had their twenty-year marriage started to disintegrate to such a low point? He really didn't know. It was like it had slowly started to slip away in recent years like the land along shorelines giving way to rising water levels. They didn't spend much time together. Both with demanding jobs. But they used to be able to make the most of that time with some romance; wine and music and dancing in the kitchen. Then the good times under the sheets.

Not much of any of that for some time now.

He'd almost laughed when, in the next breath, Amelia had begged him not to go downtown and march. Not because she was so concerned about his safety. He didn't pretend to believe that. She was definitely more concerned about her standing in the legal community.

Her firm had been hired by the police officer who'd been fired for shooting the kid two weeks ago. That shooting had started all of the local protests, and Fred didn't understand why she'd accepted when she was asked to handle the case. Would it really help that White officer to have a Black attorney? Maybe. Probably. But at what personal cost? Had Amelia's loyalty to the Black community gone down the same drain as their marriage?

The killing of the Frederickson kid, whose only crime had been having mental health issues and coming off his meds, had followed too closely on the heels of the death of George Floyd in Minneapolis. Up to that point, the streets of Dallas had been relatively quiet when it came to protests. No large crowds back last May. But no longer. Every night since the teen had been shot and killed, the Black Lives Matter marches and protests had mushroomed, with hundreds of people turning out in support.

While Fred had initially tried to respect his wife's wishes to stay neutral about it all, things had changed for him after listening to the young, passionate Josiah deliver his call to action from the pulpit last Sunday. Weeks ago, their pastor, the Reverend Jedediah Daniels, had invited the young activist to preach for the next few Sundays, and the first sermon had stirred a fire inside Fred.

He'd been downtown every night since.

The crowd of protestors, who followed the guy with the leaf blower, were now within three blocks of the federal building, the July heat and humidly hanging as heavily in the air as the tear gas. Fred paused a moment to catch his breath, and that's when he felt it. A quick, sharp pain in the middle of his back. What the hell? Was he having a heart attack? He stumbled. Went down on one knee and tried to recover. But there was no catching a breath. Something wet and sticky rolled down his back. Sweat? Should he take his shirt off? Maybe. But his hands and arms refused to listen to his brain.

The crowd moved around him, following the guy with the leaf blower who was like a Pied Piper.

Then Fred's legs went out completely. He could see the pavement coming up to greet him.

But he never felt his cheek touch down.

CHAPTER FOUR

Wednesday, July 1 - Night

The incessant chiming of her cell phone woke Sarah from a deep sleep. Stretching one arm out from under the covers, she reached for the nasty intrusion on her nightstand only realizing at the last second that she was reaching with the wrong arm. She rolled off the bed with a painful thud. Finally grasping her phone, she saw McGregor's number on the screen.

Why the hell was he calling in the middle of the night?

A year ago, she would have asked why the fuck he was he calling, but she was still really trying to clean up her language.

Honest.

The slip up the other day notwithstanding.

She pressed the accept-call button. "You do realize this is like o-dark-thirty," she said, "and I'm on day duty."

McGregor didn't respond to the sarcasm. "We've got a vic down on Commerce."

"You want me to go downtown in the middle of a goddamn protest?"

McGregor's response was delivered in a low even tone that Sarah recognized meant 'cut the bullshit and do your job.'

She sighed. "Okay. I'll get dressed and get there. Angel on her way?"

"She hasn't answered her phone. Burt will meet you."

A year ago, it would've been Chad at the scene with her if Angel wasn't available, but Chad was now permanently unavailable After he'd been killed in a raid, she'd been awash in grief again. It had been so hard to work around another huge loss in the department, and to her personally. She'd grown to like the cocky young detective a lot, and she missed his ready smile and clever lines. While she had the highest regard for Burt, she'd not worked as closely with him as she had with Chad, and that made a difference. While she'd never been as close to Chad as she had her former partner, John, they'd been on enough cases together that they'd started to know each other's moves, sometimes almost each other's thoughts. Since Burt mostly worked burglary/robbery, she'd never had the opportunity to make that same kind of instinctive connection with him.

Still. Burt was a seasoned cop, and she knew she could count on him.

A half-hour later, Sarah parked her Taurus a few blocks over from Commerce, hoping that it was far enough away from the heart of the protest that it was safe. The car was still new enough that she was super protective. Her old Honda had sported so many dents and scratches, a few more hadn't mattered, but when it had rolled its last mile and stopped, she'd done the humane thing and retired it.

Skirting potholes the city was slow to fix, she walked toward the area where the most protesters were filling the streets, many of them appearing to just be walking randomly, often changing direction more than once. Others, however, seemed to have a purpose in mind and were marching closer to the barrier in front of the federal building. The metal fencing reminded Sarah of the chain-link used for dog kennels that a neighbor man in Tennessee had for the dogs he raised. The fencing stood about four and a half feet high, and the outraged mob had a similar look in their eyes as the angry dogs that had been confined in those kennels when she was a kid.

Oh, geez. This is not good for anybody.

Sarah worked her way through the crowd, heading toward the corner where McGregor said the victim had gone down. It was about a half a block ahead, and there was enough ambient light that she could see Burt standing by a crumpled body. Nearby, officers in uniform wearing gas masks were trying to form a line to keep people back. The scene was close enough to the federal building that lingering clouds of tear gas filled the stagnant air, stinging her eyes and bringing tears. Unfortunately, nothing moved in the heat and humidity that were still high enough to be close to ninety degrees. A breeze, any kind of breeze, would be a relief.

Reaching into her pocket, Sarah pulled out the facemask she'd been using for the past few months because of the COVID pandemic. The flimsy cloth wasn't as good as having a gas mask, but it was better than having nothing between her and the tear gas.

Pop! Pop! Pop!

The sudden explosion of sounds started a virtual stampede. People screamed. People shoved each other, bolting to get away from the stun grenades and creating a scene of pure chaos. Hundreds of people raced down the street, barely parting to go around the police officers who'd circled the body on the concrete. Sarah pushed on, feeling like a salmon going against the flow of a river as people bumped and jostled her. She stumbled, almost going down, but a hand reached out to steady her. Whose? She didn't know. But she was thankful for the assist, finally making her way toward Burt.

The stun grenades had been effective, forcing that stream of people down the street, away from the scene. Now only a few people milled around, not far from the man on the concrete who wasn't moving. Cell phones were held aloft, aimed at the victim and the cops. Nothing happened anymore that wasn't instantly shared on the Internet.

Realizing this could go from calm to storm in just a few seconds, Sarah took a step toward a young Hispanic teen who was brandishing his phone. "You want to put something out on social media about this?" Sarah motioned to the downed man.

The teen lowered his hand slightly and asked as if he hadn't quite understood. "What?"

"Just figured if you were going to make a recording. Hoping it would go viral. And you'd get lots of followers on Instagram or YouTube or wherever the hell you plan to post it. Maybe you'd like to tell the truth."

"What truth? I see cops. I see a man sprawled on the street. Doesn't take a genius to figure out what happened."

"Well, Mister 'It doesn't take a genius'. Since you have the situation all figured out, why don't you come downtown and help us nail the person who was trigger-happy tonight?"

"What?" Confusion washed over the kid's face. "He been shot? Dead?"

"I can tell you he's been shot," Sarah said even though Burt was pulling on her arm, maybe trying to get her to stop from saying anymore. "But can't tell you if he's dead. That's up to the coroner to determine. But like I said. We'd be happy for any assistance in figuring out who attacked this guy. I'm sure you just want to help."

The young man lowered his phone completely and backed away. "Okay, lady. You made your point. Don't want no trouble. Didn't plan on getting involved with no crime when I came down here with my amigos. Just wanted to do a little peaceful marching."

"That's what I thought." Sarah gestured for the teen to move on. "Go on. Go find your buddies."

The young man didn't hesitate. He thrust his hands into the pockets of his hoodie and hustled away.

"Maybe not your smartest move," Burt said, "That could've gone badly."

Sarah nodded. "But maybe it kept another video of somebody suspected of being killed by a police officer off the Internet." She paused and sighed. "We don't even know what the hell happened here. And I sure as hell didn't want to let some punk kid create another sensation by having his recording go viral. Aren't you sick of all that?"

Burt didn't respond. He really didn't need to. Every cop in the nation who wasn't a racist was sick of all that. Sarah took a step closer to the downed man. "Any ID?"

"Waiting for Walt to pronounce before moving the body to look. And the few folks around who'd talk to a cop didn't know him."

The crowd started to thin even more as a black SUV came slowly down the street. Sarah recognized Walt's private car. Considering the hour, she wasn't surprised that he'd come from home.

Walt pulled as close to the scene as he could, scattering a

few of the people who'd stayed to watch. He got out and walked briskly over, donning a medical mask on the way. "What do you have?"

Sarah also wasn't surprised at the lack of pleasantries. Walt wasn't into all that anyway, and in the middle of the night? Well. She wasn't either. "Male victim. Guessing about forty years old. But you'll be able to tell us more about the vic after the post. Won't you, Walt." The last was delivered as a statement.

He chuckled. "Of course. You're learning."

She smiled, hoping he could see it in her eyes above her mask. How often had he told her to let him do his job before asking a bunch of questions he couldn't answer on the spot?

He leaned close to the body. "At least it isn't a kid this time."

Sarah nodded. "We take the small consolations when we can get them." Then she moved away to let Walt do his preliminary exam, walking over to Burt.

"You have a chance to talk to any of the bystanders?"

Burt shook his head. "Too busy trying to keep the people from trampling me and the vic. But I think the Uniforms got a couple of statements."

Walt stood and approached, holding out a wallet and a cell phone. "Found these in his trouser pockets. I've called my prelim in to make it official. Guy's dead. Like you didn't already know that. My team should be here any minute for transport."

Sarah nodded. "Thanks, Walt."

He walked over to talk to the two uniformed officers who were still securing the scene, and then gave a little wave before returning to his car to wait for his team. Normally he'd stay there with the rest of them, but she couldn't blame him for seeking the security of a vehicle. Even though the crowd had thinned, there was tension in the air along with the noxious fumes, and the social distancing protocols were still in place because of the pandemic. Not that they could always stay six feet apart, but they did the best they could to keep each other safe.

Sarah turned her attention to Burt who was looking through the wallet. "Guy's name is Fred Cummings," he said. "And you were close with the age. Forty-two."

"Okay. I'm going to check in with the Uniforms," Sarah said. "Back in a minute."

Burt nodded, still digging through the wallet.

Sarah didn't recognize either of the cops in uniform, and they both gave her a chilly nod. Not a huge surprise since one of their ranks had been suspended without pay pending the outcome of an investigation into the death of an unarmed Black man. All the men and women in blue remembered that Sarah had not lost her pay when she'd been involved in the shooting a few years ago that left a Black kid dead. She didn't blame the officers. No cop likes to be called before IA, or the Review Board, or lose their job because of the use of deadly force against anyone, let alone a person of color. But the case against Officer Smithfield wasn't as clear-cut as the case against her had been. The kid she'd shot had a gun. The boy Smithfield had shot had a cooking utensil. Huge difference.

"Got anything for me?" Sarah directed the question at both of the officers.

The response was slow to come, but finally the younger one, who had a nametag identifying him as Officer Jackson, lifted his gas mask and spoke. "It was pretty hectic. Only a couple of people were willing to talk."

"Anyone see the shooter?"

He shook his head. "One guy said he saw the vic go down. Thought he'd just stumbled and was going to help him get up. Then he saw the blood and the hole in the back of the guy's shirt."

"Did he know the vic?"

Another shake of his head. "Figured the guy was alone, though. Didn't see anyone else react."

Sarah took a quick glance around. "Is the witness still here?"

"Said he didn't want to hang around. Was afraid of the mood of the crowd." Jackson pulled out a cell phone. "I got his contact info. For follow-up."

Slipping her phone out of the back pocket of her jeans, Sarah copied the information into her contacts as he read it off. "Thanks. Anything else?"

"Nope."

The one-word response was delivered in a neutral tone, so Sarah merely nodded and turned to walk back to Burt. She told him what Jackson had said, then asked, "Did you get anything from onlookers?"

"Pretty much the same thing as the Uniforms got. But I checked our vic's name and address while you were over there." Burt waved toward where the two officers were still standing. "You'll never guess who he was married to."

Sarah gave him a look. "Really? A guessing game in the middle of the night, Burt?"

He smiled. "You're right. Not a good time. Our dead guy's wife is the attorney representing the officer who shot that kid a few weeks ago."

"Smithfield?"

"Yup."

"Holy shit."

"Yup."

"Wonder if the wife knew he was out here at the protest?"

"Good question. Should we go find out?"

Sarah knew that was a rhetorical question. Middle of the night or not, they had to make notification. And it would be interesting to get her reaction to where her husband had been tonight.

"Want me to drive?" Burt asked.

She shook her head. "We're better off in our own cars. Then we can both head straight home afterward. Maybe get an hour or so of shut-eye before our day starts."

"I'll let Walt know we're leaving."

"Okay." Sarah glanced over to make sure the uniformed officers were keeping the scene secure, then turned to walk to her car. On the way, she debated the best route to take to the address in Highland Park, thankful that the street was deserted here away from the crime scene. She rounded a corner and had to step quickly aside to avoid running into someone. Looking closer, she stopped short. "Angel?"

"Sarah? What are you doing here?"

"What are *you* doing here?"

It took a long moment before Angel answered. "I'm tired of being silent."

What the hell? "You're here protesting?"

Angel nodded, not breaking eye contact.

"But we're cops. You realize you're protesting against the cops."

"Only racist cops."

"Tell me. How do our fellow officers know the difference between who you support and who you don't?"

"The good ones know who they are."

Sarah couldn't argue against that. She'd heard plenty of

remarks in the locker rooms and hallways. The deeply racist cops rarely hid it. She just wished she'd been better about calling them out on it through the years. But honestly, until this latest shooting, and the death of George Floyd before that, she truly hadn't understood the depth of the racial problems. She thought she did. She'd certainly had enough conversations with Angel and LaVon about racism. But maybe she hadn't looked deeply enough at her white counterparts on the force. She sighed. "So, this is why McGregor couldn't get a hold of you tonight?"

"I silenced my phone. Aren't we both supposed to be off duty?"

"We were. But the night team got called to protect the federal building so we're it when it comes to a homicide."

"Someone was killed?"

"Yeah. One of the protesters."

"So, he was Black?"

Sarah looked at her partner for a beat. then slowly shook her head. "It doesn't matter what color he was, does it?"

It took so long for Angel to respond, Sarah wondered if she was ever going to answer, then Angel said, "You just don't get it."

Sarah shook her head again. "I don't have time for a debate. Or discussion. Or whatever you want to do right now." She skirted around Angel and walked quickly down the sidewalk, calling over her shoulder. "Got to tell a woman her husband is dead."

CHAPTER FIVE

Same Night

Sarah pulled to a stop in front of a house that could be considered a modest structure in this high-rent area of Dallas. Less than a minute later headlights flashed in her rear view and she glanced back to see Burt pulling in behind her. She got out of her car and pushed the "lock" tab on the fob. It was pleasantly quiet here, especially after the cacophony of stun grenades and bullhorns and car horns that dominated the protest site. The only sounds Sarah could discern were tree frogs talking to each other and the far-away bark of a dog.

Burt joined her on the sidewalk that led to a large covered porch, the roof of which rested on two large cedar posts. Sarah wondered if Fred, or his wife, was responsible for the flowers that lined the walkway and the immaculately clipped lawn, or if they had a gardener. That seemed to be a thing now. Even people of lesser means often had someone else do the yard work.

When they reached the porch, Burt reached out and punched the doorbell. Sarah could hear the distinct chime ring through the still night air, momentarily silencing the nearest frogs, then the sound of the doorbell faded, and the frogs took up their song again.

"They were quiet for a minute," Burt waved a hand in the general direction of the pine tree at the corner of the house where the offenders probably lived. "Do people actually like that stupid noise?"

Sarah laughed.

"We have them in the cypress tree in my back yard. Drove me nuts last night until I hollered out the window."

"Okay. First, I can't believe you actually opened a window in your house in the middle of the summer. Second, why not cut down the tree? Third, I need to know this because?"

Burt smiled and gestured toward the tree again. "Got the buggers to shut up, didn't I? They don't like me talking any more than I like them."

Sarah cocked her head. He was right. It was blessedly quiet.

They waited another minute in silence, then Sarah heard a faint shuffling on the other side of the door. It creaked open, a security chain still attached, and a sleepy-looking woman wearing a burgundy robe that looked soft and silky peered at them through the narrow opening. "Can I help you?"

Sarah nudged Burt forward, and he showed his badge. "Dallas PD, ma'am. I'm Detective Aaron Burtweiler. This is Detective Sarah Kingsly. May we come in?"

Sarah watched the woman's eyes widen in apprehension as she glanced from one officer to the other. "What is this about?"

"Please, Mrs. Cummings," Sarah said. "We need to come in."

"Is it …? Has something happened to Fred?" The safety chain remained firmly in place while a myriad of emotions washed across the woman's dark face; a face that was almost lost in the gloom of the entry.

"This really would go down better if we were all inside sitting down," Sarah said.

A sharp intake of breath was the only response to that, but a trembling hand reached up to unhook the safety chain. Burt gently pushed the door open then grabbed the woman's elbow as she started to collapse.

Just off the entryway was a room that looked like a formal living area. It had a large plush sofa, which is where Mrs. Cummings needed to be. "Please tell me. What happened?" she said as Burt half-carried her to the sofa. "I told him not to go. Did he get hurt?"

Sarah wished it was only that as she put on her mask and took a seat next to the woman. "I'm sorry. There was a shooting."

"Oh my God!" The words ran together without a pause. "A shooting? I don't understand. It was supposed to be a peaceful protest. Just marching and carrying signs. No guns."

Sarah remained quiet, giving the woman a few more minutes to process. Then Mrs. Cummings shot her a wide-eyed look of alarm. "Was Fred …? Is he …?"

"Your husband was shot in the back," Burt said. "Unfortunately, it was a mortal wound."

Mrs. Cummings took a deep breath, perhaps trying to get her brain around the words 'mortal wound,' and Sarah found Burt's way of relaying the bad news interesting. Maybe it gave a person time to absorb it in stages. Certainly could be better than just saying 'your loved one is dead.'

After a few moments of a strained silence, tears rolled

down ebony cheeks and soft words came out on the release of a breath. "Oh, my God."

Sarah reached out and touched her hand. "Is there anybody here with you?"

"Just my children." She grasped the front of her robe in a tight grip. "Oh, my God. What am I going to tell them?"

"Can I call somebody for you? A friend or relative?"

No. I'll … it'll be okay." She took a deep shuddering breath. "I'll call my mother."

"If you're up to it, we need to ask you some questions," Burt said.

The woman shook her head. "Can't it wait? I can't even think right now."

Burt hesitated, as if considering, then sighed. "Not for long." He took a card out of his wallet and put it on the coffee table in front of the sofa. "We'll be in touch tomorrow. Keep my card for when you want to ask questions."

"Before we go, we do need to know if your husband was with someone tonight." Sarah said.

That question seemed to startle the woman for a moment, and when she didn't answer, Sarah continued, "A friend he was going to meet? To march with?"

"Oh." Mrs. Cummings glanced down, then back up and shook her head. "He said he was going to be alone."

Burt stood and Sarah took his cue. "Okay," she said. "We'll be in touch."

The woman nodded, then rose and walked with them to the door. Once outside, Sarah heard the click of the lock.

"This investigation's going to be a nightmare," Burt said as they made their way back toward their cars.

"Yup." Sarah started to open her car door, then paused. "I hate to leave her alone like that."

"Yeah. Well, her choice."

"Since when did you get a new dose of cynicism?"

Burt leaned against the roof of his car. "Sorry. I've just had enough of people making bad choices."

"Oh?"

"Yeah." He hesitated a beat, then sighed. "My daughter. She's blowing off a scholarship to take a gap year."

What he said surprised Sarah on two counts. First, she'd expected Burt to just ignore her comment about cynicism. The way most cops she knew deflected anything coming at them that threatened to break down some barrier including herself. Then there was the fact that in all the years she'd worked in the same department as Burt, she'd never known he had a daughter. Or a wife, for that matter. But then she'd never asked, had she?

Burt made no move to get into his car, so Sarah offered, "Maybe that's not such a bad thing. Considering the pandemic and all."

"That's what my wife says. But what's Joselyn gonna do next year when there's no scholarship? This daddy doesn't fit the stereotypical Jew rolling in dough."

Sarah couldn't help but laugh. "I'd never mistake you for that. Your Columbo look is a dead giveaway."

"Wish Jocelyn had your vision." Burt slapped the roof of his car. "Heading home and maybe get some sleep. Later."

Sleep sounded like a swell idea, but Sarah arrived at her apartment to discover that Cat had a totally different agenda. The minute she stepped inside, he twined himself around her legs and loudly demanded to know why she'd left him alone for so long. And did she know that his food dish was empty? At least that's what she figured he was saying when he followed her into the kitchen and stood over his bowl, with a look like 'Well?'.

Sarah chuckled as she poured kibbles into the dish. Cat had certainly evolved from that scared, shy kitten who'd snuck into her apartment, and her heart, a few years ago. She paused a moment to calculate the passage of time. Almost five years now. Five years since her long-time partner John had been killed, and in the midst of her grief, she'd softened and let the stray orange tabby take up permanent residence. Since then, she'd come to understand why people had a cat for a companion. Low maintenance. Snuggly warm bodies curled in a lap on a cold evening. And quiet. Except for when it came to demanding food.

Another deep-throated meow was Cat's way of pointing out that the stream of kibbles had stopped too soon for his liking.

"Just chill," she said. "It's not like you're going to starve to death."

He gave her a look that suggested perhaps he might.

Sarah chuckled again, topped off his food, then headed to her bedroom. Morning roll call was looming way too soon.

As tired as she was, Sarah couldn't fall asleep. She couldn't get the image of Angel at the protest out of her head. What the hell kind of explosion was that going to cause at the station?

It would no doubt be ballistic.

CHAPTER SIX

Thursday, July 2 - Morning

Sarah parked in the lot to the east of the new Jack Evans headquarters and eased out of the car. In many ways, she missed the venerable old building where headquarters used to be housed, with the CAPERS unit on the fifth floor and the creaking elevators that took them there. Still, there were nice perks in the new building, like smooth elevators and lots of windows. All bullet proof, at a cost she didn't even want to imagine, but she was glad they had the protection.

That protection was vital now as a throng of protesters threatened to break the line of uniformed officers in full riot gear who were on the steps doing their best to hold them back. The closer Sarah got, the louder the din of shouts became and she stopped to consider whether she should go around to another door or try to push through. No telling was some hothead would do, and there were a lot of angry people here.

She turned when she sensed a presence beside her and was relieved to see it was Angel. Her partner paused to scan the milling crowd, then said, "Another wonderful day in the neighborhood."

Sarah didn't miss the undertone of sarcasm in her partner's voice. "It seems to be what people do when they're pissed."

"Hmm."

"Pretty scary," Sarah continued as if her partner hadn't offered that noncommittal response. "Much worse than the protests a few years ago when I was the focus of all the anger."

"Maybe that's because since then too many Black men have been shot in the back."

Sarah turned and gave Angel a long look. "That wasn't us here in this building. It was some dumbass cop from the Northeast Division."

Angel's eyes flashed with the same fire Sarah had seen the previous night. "Maybe we didn't pull the trigger. And maybe that was a righteous shooting. Maybe yours was even a righteous shooting—"

"Wait a goddamn minute. You going back to that? Really? What have we done the past few years if we haven't moved beyond all the doubts? All the questions?"

"Have we really?"

It was a challenge as much as a question, and it momentarily silenced Sarah. Then she threw out a challenge of her own. "I've sure as hell tried."

Angel didn't flinch, but when she spoke, her tone had softened. "Yeah? A few years of trying doesn't magically change things. No matter the gains, there's still the great divide."

"Only if you say so."

"No! Not just because I say so. Because of history." Angel's voice rose with every word while anger flashed in her eyes. "History that said it was okay to have Black boys hanging from trees. History that said it was okay for White men to own Black men and beat them and rape their wives. History that makes people think it's okay for a White cop to put a knee on an unarmed man's neck. And … hold it … until the man dies."

But her voice cracked and faltered over the last few words.

The enormity of that anger hit Sarah with the force of a tidal wave, and she fought to keep the tone of her response measured. "I had nothing to do with that."

Angel took a breath and let it out slowly, pressing her fingers against her lips as if wanting to hold words back. Then she took another breath and spoke. "Not you personally. No. But decades of white privilege and white supremacy created an environment where … Where too many people think it's just fine to kill another nigger."

Sarah sucked in a breath and just stared for a moment. "I've never heard you use that word before."

"I've never been this angry before."

They stood in a visual standoff for several beats, the atmosphere around them charged with emotions and unspoken words. Then Sarah sighed deeply and waved one hand toward the front doors that seemed miles away at this point. "We'll miss signing in."

Angel hesitated for another beat, then nodded and pushed her way through the crowd of angry protestors. Sarah followed, assaulted by the emotions emanating from the people who jostled around her. She noted how they let Angel through without touching her, but elbows and shoulders pushed rudely at Sarah. At a point halfway up, a heavy boot caught her in the ankle, and she had to clutch at the back of the shirt of the man in front of her to keep from going down.

A nearby uniformed officer gave her a questioning look, and she shook her head. She'd take it like a man, as the old cliché went.

Upstairs in the CAPERS (crimes against persons) department, Sarah locked her purse in the bottom drawer of her desk and shucked off her tan blazer. Except for days she had to testify in court, her basic uniform was always light-colored t-shirt, jeans or slacks, and a blazer in a color that wouldn't clash too badly with her shirt, which was a pale-yellow today.

She'd just settled in her desk chair and pulled off her shoe to check the damage to her ankle when her phone rang in the jacket pocket. It was a summons from McGregor. She glanced over to see if Angel had received the same directive, but her partner was studiously focused on her computer monitor. Avoidance or actual work? Sarah had no idea. And obviously, she was the only one called to this meeting.

Quickly, Sarah shoved her foot back into her sneaker, then made her way to McGregor's office. He'd been lucky, along with some other lieutenants, to get a bigger office in the new headquarters, and he'd quickly filled up the extra space with his usual piles of folders, books, and boxes of cold-case files, but he'd kept a clear path to the window. That's where Sarah saw him standing when she limped into the room.

"Hey, Lieu."

"What a shit storm," he said without turning from his view of the throng of protestors in front of the building.

"Same kind that rained all over me a few years ago." Sarah joined him at the window.

"This one might get a lot worse before it's over." Now he turned and walked back to his desk, motioning for her to take a seat in one of the visitor chairs that she didn't have to empty of a pile of folders. If he noticed her limp, he refrained from offering a comment. Which was fine with her. Better to stay focused on business.

"What do you have on the dead guy?"

Quickly, Sarah shared what she and Burt had learned the night before. Or more precisely, what they hadn't learned.

"Maybe someone offed him because they were pissed about the wife representing the cop?"

"Could be. But why not just go after the wife?"

McGregor leaned back in his office chair. "Good question. What about the wife? She have a motive?"

Sarah shrugged. "Early days yet. But I did get a sense that they didn't have the happiest of marriages."

"But would she risk her law license to kill him?"

"Good point." Sarah paused to consider another thought, then said, "But there'd be no risk if the killing couldn't be traced back to her."

McGregor nodded slowly, then sat forward. "So? We don't discount her at this point."

"I'd say not."

McGregor rubbed a beefy hand across the stubble on his cheek. Even in the mornings, he had stubble on his cheeks. "Okay. Going back to scenario number one. If the husband got killed because of the wife's job, is she in danger?"

"Maybe."

"She have protection?"

"Have to see if her firm set anything up. If not, maybe we should?"

McGregor nodded. "I'll verify with the upper brass to see what we can do."

"I'll get with Angel. Start checking other possibilities."

When McGregor didn't respond, it made Sarah wonder

again why her partner hadn't been included in this meeting. Granted, Angel hadn't been part of handling the call last night, but still... Had McGregor somehow found out about her being out with the protestors? Was he waiting for Sarah to say something? Did he know she knew? Was this a test?

Geesh! Sarah shook those questions aside. She didn't need that kind of uncertainty if she was going to stay focused on the case. And that's what she needed to do right now. Wait for the next move from her boss and otherwise keep her mouth shut about Angel. She took a breath. "Okay. Walt's doing the post this afternoon. But he doesn't think cause of death is going to change. Two gunshots to the back. Upper left. Figures the shooter knew what he, or she, was doing."

"Anything good from forensics?"

Sarah shook her head. "Roberts doubts he'll get anything from the shirt the vic was wearing, but we can hope."

"Did we at least get lucky and find shell casings?"

"Nope. But not a surprise there. So many people milling around, any casings could've been kicked to Fort Worth. But the Uniforms are still looking."

McGregor didn't acknowledge her meager attempt at humor. He gave her a long, hard look, then asked, "Where was your partner last night?"

Okay. Here it was, and still the question blindsided her. When he hadn't asked earlier, she thought they'd moved past it. She struggled to maintain eye contact. "Hell if I know. Is that why Burt was at the scene? Angel was out of contact?"

"Yup."

The lieutenant continued to stare, and Sarah was sure he'd recognized her lie. She thought she'd melt under the heat she could see in his eyes, but she kept her body and mind as still as possible. She didn't know why she was going to such lengths to protect Angel, but, well, she was in it now.

Finally, McGregor nodded. "Okay. Get to work."

"Yes, sir." Sarah stood and walked to the door, willing herself not to turn back and tell all. Also willing herself not to limp so he'd call her back and see her face.

"Take Burt to the follow-up with the wife this morning."

Sarah froze for a moment, then, without turning, repeated, "Yes, sir."

Out in the hall, she leaned against the wall to ease the weight off her ankle that was still throbbing and took a few deep breaths to still the race her heart was taking around her chest. *Crap! Does he already know about Angel? Why didn't I just tell him the truth?*

She couldn't hang here outside McGregor's door forever, and she sure as hell couldn't go back in there. And the worst part of all? She might have just jeopardized her career for someone who didn't care.

Now, how the hell was she going to explain the lieutenant's latest order to Angel if her partner asked?

Fuck it all anyway.

She took the chicken-shit way out for now, texting Burt on her way downstairs.

CHAPTER SEVEN

Thursday, July 2 - Morning

S arah met Burt in the parking lot where they picked up an unmarked car. Even at nine in the morning, the temperature was already climbing toward 90, and sweat trickled down the middle of her back. She took off her blazer before getting in the passenger seat of the black Chevy Impala from the police lot. Not in the mood to fight Dallas traffic, she was happy to let Burt drive. She was also happy for the blast of AC when he started the engine. The air wasn't much past tepid, working its way toward cool, but any air moving was always better than sitting in the interior of a car that had turned into an oven.

"So," Burt said after they'd fastened their seatbelts. "What's up with your partner? Not that I don't like working a case with you, but isn't this a little unusual?"

Sarah knew she had to be careful in her response. Even though she was sure she could trust him to not tell any of the higher-ups about what Angel was doing, she didn't want to talk about it. Didn't want to open the spillway and take a chance the whole mess would come pouring out. And really.

It wasn't her place to be telling anybody about what was going on with her partner.

"You know, even though some people think so, I'm not McGregor's pet, and he doesn't tell me everything that goes into the decisions he makes. I just say 'Yes, sir' like everybody else."

Burt chuckled.

"Maybe he sent us to the interview because we made that initial contact together last night."

"True that," Burt said.

Sarah glanced at him. "True that? Is that some weird Native speak you picked up from your partner?"

Simms, Burt's usual partner, who was half Apache, was known to take great liberties with the English language and in playful moods mock the way Indians spoke in the old Western movies.

Burt shook his head. "That one's actually thanks to my daughter. She's trying to bring me into the twenty-first century way of talking."

"What's wrong with the way you talk? Always seems just fine to me."

Burt signaled and made a right turn. "Once she got into high school, her favorite expression to me was, 'Oh, Daddy. You sound like some old fuddy-duddy.' That hasn't changed in the last four years."

Now it was Sarah's turn to laugh. "She does know what you do for a living, right? "

"Yeah, well, apparently my job doesn't impress her."

They drove for a few more blocks, then Burt pulled the car to a stop behind a Lincoln Town Car that was parked in front of the Cumming's house. No swarm of cars and people like Sarah had seen by homes of other bereaved families in recent years. She didn't know if that was good or bad. Was there any right way for family and friends to respond to a loss? She sure as hell didn't know.

"You want to take the lead?" Burt asked. "The wife might relate to you woman-to-woman."

"Apparently, you've forgotten the stories about me. Angel has a much softer approach in interviews."

"I've heard," Burt said with a smile, unfastening his seat belt. "But you can start off. Then I get to be Good Cop. I like to be Good Cop."

Sarah returned the smile then got out of the car and shrugged into her blazer. She'd rather leave it off, but professionalism and all that. In the light of day, she noted that the house was well cared for. No peeling paint on the trim and the bushes close to the house had nary a stray branch. She was no gardener, so she had no idea what those white and lavender flowers were that danced in the morning sunlight, but they had to be something that could survive the blasting heat of a Texas summer. She knew that much. When she'd first come to Texas from Tennessee, she'd brought some primroses in containers that her grandmother had given her. They grew well through the summer in that milder climate of her home state, but they didn't survive the first summer here, even in the shade. After that disaster, Sarah had decided to stop killing plants.

Burt held back just a bit to let Sarah ring the bell, and a few moments later the door was opened by a stately Black woman with beautiful straightened silver hair. She wore slim beige slacks and a striking red blouse that added a glow to her face that was the color of a fine, rich milk chocolate. She was obviously well cared for, pampered even, and her age was hard to judge.

The woman looked them over with one brow arched. "May I help you?"

Sarah put her mask on, then pulled her badge from the waistband of her jeans and held it up, introducing herself and Burt, who also masked up. "Is Mrs. Cummings available?"

"If you care to step in and wait here in the entry, I will see if she is ready to talk to you."

"And you are?" Sarah asked before the woman took more than a step away.

The woman seemed a bit taken back by Sarah's brashness, and Burt leaned in to push against her shoulder as if to say, "Dial it back before we lose our chance."

If the woman found Sarah's approach rude, nothing in her demeanor changed to give that away. "My apologies, Detective. I am Regina Scott. Mrs. Cummings' mother. Surely you will forgive me if I appear to be a little protective of my daughter."

"I understand," Sarah said. 'Nothing about what we have to do is pleasant to us, either. But to catch whoever killed Mr. Cummings we must move quickly."

Mrs. Scott gave a slight nod. "I understand. I will go check in with my daughter."

A few minutes later, the older woman came back and escorted them into the living room. "Please have a seat. My daughter will be down in a moment."

"Are the children here?" Sarah asked.

"No. Amelia's friend Joan came to get them earlier this morning."

"Do they know?"

Regina nodded. "But not the details. Maybe they do not need to know the details."

It was part statement and part question, but Sarah

sidestepped it, moving to the fireplace where photos were lined up on the mantel in a neat row. Family pictures. A smiling Fred and Amelia, with two small boys. "How old are they?"

"Seven and nine now. Malcolm and Trevon."

"Detectives." The voice came from the doorway to the room, and Sarah turned to see Mrs. Cummings. Today, the woman was dressed in a fashion similar to her mother, and looking just as stylish. Her blouse was pale blue, her slacks gray, and her shoes were also gray. Her hair was pulled back in a tight chignon, accenting sharp cheekbones that were lightly dusted with blush, and her eyelids were ever so artfully touched with silver and gray.

The "look" was a bit of a surprise so soon after the loss, but Sarah reminded herself that just like there was no accounting of how friends and family would respond; there was no one-size-fits-all reaction from the people experiencing the loss of someone they loved. Sarah knew that from her many years of dealing with bereaved families, a perk of this thankless part of her job. Still, she hadn't expected to see the widow all decked out like she was about to attend a meeting at the garden club.

"Mrs. Cummings," Sarah acknowledged. "We just have a few questions."

"Certainly." Amelia motioned toward the sofa where they'd sat the night before. "Have a seat."

Sarah settled on one of the soft cushions and Burt chose a chair across from them. "I will leave you to it," Regina said, moving across the plush carpeting with her footfalls creating hardly a sound.

"May I call you Amelia?" Sarah asked.

The woman nodded.

"We're sorry we have to do this. But, well, as an attorney you must know."

"Of course." Amelia's expression remained impassive.

"This is a delicate question, but we have to get it out of the way." Sarah glanced quickly at Burt as if to ask him to pick up the line of questioning if need be. He gave her a hint of a nod, before she turned back to Amelia. "Were there any problems between you and your husband?"

"Define 'problems.'"

Okay, so this is how she's going to play it. "As in he was fucking someone else? You were fucking someone else?"

The only reaction was a slight tightening of Amelia's jaw. The woman didn't shock easily. Must be all that courtroom experience.

"There is no need to be crass, Detective. But let me just put a few things out there. I've been too busy with my practice for fucking. Not even my husband. As for Fred? I haven't hired a PI to follow him. But I have my suspicions."

"Did that possibility make you angry?"

The hint of a smile touched her lips. "We are both well past angry, Detective. We've had a friendly relationship for some time. Emphasis on 'friend.' For the sake of the kids. And because neither of us like a major change."

Hmmm. Interesting. Most successful woman wouldn't stay more than a second in a strained relationship.

Into the slight pause, Amelia added, "I'm aware that men are prone to their dalliances, and women are better off not making a big issue of it. Families can stay together if the woman turns a blind eye and doesn't cause trouble."

Huh. A mindset from decades ago, and so utterly contrary to the type of person Sarah had pegged the attorney to be, it took her a moment to find some kind of appropriate response. Her first impulse was to blurt out something snarky, but that would only anger the woman, and it was too soon for Burt to start playing his role. She took a deep breath, released it, and then asked, "Any particularly angry husbands out there?"

"I wouldn't know. Fred may have been unfaithful, but he was discreet."

"So? You didn't check up on him? Read his emails and texts?"

"His phone and computer are private. As are mine. We respected the mutual privacy."

"Then you don't know the password to either?"

Amelia shook her head.

"Isn't that a little odd? I thought most couples shared their passwords."

Amelia smiled, a forced expression that wasn't pleasant. "You're so naïve, Detective. That isn't the way it works in the real world."

Naïve? Sarah snorted to hold back a sharp retort. If only this woman knew the real Sarah Kingsly. But this wasn't the time.

"Am I under suspicion here?"

Sarah shook her head. "Not at the moment. But you know the drill, Counselor. Husbands and wives are always looked at first. Looked at hard."

"Is that supposed to scare me?"

Before tempers could flare, Burt shifted forward and asked, "Have you thought about people who might have wanted to kill your husband? Is there anyone else we can look at?"

Sarah didn't miss the emphasis he put on the last two words and hid her smile behind her hand.

Amelia tore her gaze from Sarah to face Burt. "Nobody in particular. But in addition to women, Fred did like to dally with cards."

"Serious games?"

She shook her head. "More the five and dime type."

"Five and dime?"

"Five-dollar ante and ten to raise."

"You seem well versed in how the game is played," Sarah said, drawing Amelia's attention. "You play a lot?"

"No. But a few times a year the wives in the neighborhood get together for a poker night."

"We're going to need the names of the players your husband shared games with." Burt slid a small notebook across the coffee table to Amelia. "Is it possible he got in a little too deep with one of them?"

Amelia looked up quickly. "I don't know who he played with. He quit the neighborhood games some years ago. As for those of us who still play, we're friends. Not members of a gambling den."

"After family, friends are next on the suspect list," Sarah said, drawing another cold look from Amelia.

"It isn't necessary to continue to tell me things I already know, Detective."

Sarah bit back another snarky response that tried to escape. She did *not* want to antagonize this woman. At least not now. "Where did your husband work?"

Amelia visibly relaxed, letting her shoulders down and easing her clenched jaw. "Hanson Construction. Fred was a master carpenter. Did framing and finish work."

"Any problems on the job?"

"Not that I'm aware of."

"Please add that contact information." Sarah gestured to

the notebook on the table.

After Amelia finished writing, Burt asked, "What did Fred think about you representing Smithfield?"

Amelia sighed. "He wasn't happy. But a hefty retainer helped. Fred hasn't worked much this past year with the pandemic and the economic slowdown. Home building hasn't picked back up yet."

"Did he lose his job?"

Amelia shook her head. "The boss kept him on the payroll, at a reduced level. Fred was good at the work. The boss didn't want to lose him."

"What about co-workers? Anyone at Hanson's who resented that?"

Amelia shrugged. "One guy got all in Fred's face about it a month or so back."

"Name?" Sarah asked.

"Jeremy something. He thought the only reason Fred was kept on was affirmative action. Lots of white folks think we only get ahead because of that. Too many white folks."

Sarah felt the sting of those last words, but she chose to ignore the taunt. She was always telling Angel that reactions are what causes more trouble than words, so she was trying hard to follow her own advice. But Amelia wasn't making that very easy today.

Burt didn't miss the dart or Sarah's reaction, so he jumped in again. "What about extended family? Anything there we should know about?"

"What are you insinuating?"

Burt held up his hands in a placating gesture. "Nothing. Just asking."

Amelia took a few moments before she answered. "Okay. There's a cousin who has walked the wrong side of the law.

He was involved in some drug business some time ago."

"Name?"

"Darius. But Fred hasn't had anything to do with him for years."

"Still, family blood is strong," Sarah said. "Maybe Darius came to him for help and when he refused ... well ..."

Amelia shook her head. "How would he know where Fred was last night? He didn't decide to go until just a couple of hours before he left."

Sarah remembered and it was a good point. So much of this interview was sounding like a judicial debate. No wonder Smithfield chose this woman to defend him. She was good.

"Write down any contact information you have for Darius." Burt pointed to the notebook that was still on the coffee table.

Amelia picked up the pen and wrote on the notebook before sliding it back to Burt.

"Thank you," he said, standing. "We'll be in touch when we have anything to share."

Amelia rose and escorted them to the door.

After they got back into the car, Sarah fastened her seat belt, then said, "That was one weird interview."

"No shit."

"She hardly struck me as the bereaved widow," Sarah added. "She was pretty guarded in her answers."

"Unless she was just touting her agenda," Burt said. "The racial commentary couldn't be missed."

"Yeah. That was thrown at us like a bunch of darts."

"Still." Burt checked for traffic, then pulled away from the curb. "If she knew about all her husband's 'dalliances' as she put it, and didn't seem to care, I don't see a motive there for her."

"You're probably right. Angel keeps telling me I'm too quick to look at the spouse."

"You're not the only one."

"Yeah. I know. But Angel thinks I'm rabid about it."

"How is it with Angel?" Burt paused for a turn. "You still haven't told me why it's me with you this morning and not her."

"Better you don't ask."

"Okay. The question is rescinded."

CHAPTER EIGHT

Thursday, July 2 - Afternoon

Angel stood and stretched after spending two hours on the computer. Her neck and back ached, and she knew that was as much from stress as sitting too long. The world was unraveling like an old sweater from which someone had pulled the wrong loose string. The reason for her being here on desk duty, not out on the murder investigation with Sarah, was not lost on her. Had her partner told McGregor about seeing her last night? Sarah hadn't even come back to the squad room after the earlier meeting with McGregor, so Angel had been left to wonder and worry.

That state of affairs didn't change now as Sarah bustled in, all business and little eye contact. After her partner was settled at her desk, Angel asked, "Get anything helpful from the interview with the widow?"

To Sarah's look of surprise, Angel added, "McGregor told me where you went. He called while you were out. Also told me to assist you and Burt."

Sarah took a moment to respond, and Angel figured her partner was sorting out the information.

"Okay," Sarah said. "We got a couple of things to follow up on. One is a cousin who was into drugs."

"A serious suspect?"

Sarah shrugged and wrote something on a piece of paper. "Might be. Or might be a long shot. Still, can you see if there's anything in NCIC on him?"

"Sure." Angel took the paper that Sarah handed over, glanced at it and saw a name and address. "Okay. Anything else?"

"Yes. Can you call this witness from last night and get his official statement?" Sarah forwarded the information to Angel's phone. "Name's Hector."

"That all?"

"Unless you'd like to attend the post."

"Is that an order?" Angel wasn't sure if she threw that out to rattle her partner, or just to vent a little but she was glad when Sarah simply shook her head and booted up her computer.

A few minutes later, Sarah stood and grabbed her phone off the top of her desk. "Back in fifteen."

Angel watched her stride out. Where on earth was she going, and why?

Downstairs, Sarah stopped by the vending machines and grabbed a Snickers bar for a quick sugar fix. Granted, not the healthiest of snacks, but one that never failed to satisfy. After unwrapping the candy and taking a small bite, she called Burt.

"What?" he said.

"Did I wake you from an afternoon siesta?"

Burt said nothing. Apparently, he wasn't in a joking mood, and Sarah hadn't worked closely with him enough to know how far she could go with nonsense. "Are you okay with me taking Angel to interview that Jeremy guy?"

"You found him?"

"No. But I'm going to the construction company to see if we can get a lead there."

"What does McGregor say about it?"

"It?"

"Don't do this, Sarah. I've got a killer headache."

"Sorry." Sarah paused for another bite of her candy bar, before hunger gave *her* a killer headache. "I didn't ask McGregor."

"Why not?"

"Didn't want to risk a refusal. My partnership's at stake here, Burt."

He sighed, but didn't respond.

"What would you do if Simms was all jammed up?"

Another sigh, then Burt said, "Okay. But this is all on you."

"Isn't it always?" She'd posed that more as a statement than question, which was a good thing, because Burt didn't answer. Instead, she heard the distinct sound of the call being ended.

Still standing in the downstairs vending area, Sarah looked up Hanson Construction on her phone, making a note of the address. Then she finished her snack and tossed the candy wrapper.

Upstairs, she headed for her desk, pausing when Angel handed over a single page of printout. "Not much here on that cousin. Looks like he's been keeping on the right side of the law for a while."

"Could be. Or could be he's gone deep under the radar."

"I checked with Ryan. They haven't run across Darius in some time."

"Which still proves nothing."

"I know. I asked Ryan to keep a lookout for him."

"And Hector?"

"Said he never spotted the shooter. Just saw the vic go down."

"Pretty much what he told the Uniforms." Sarah grabbed her blazer. "I'm going to check on something. You coming?"

Angel couldn't hide her surprise. "What about …? I thought you were working this with Burt."

"He's good with it."

"And McGregor? His mandate that I 'assist?'"

"Time's a wastin', Girlfriend." Sarah emphasized the drawl and the last word as she rounded her desk and headed toward the exit.

Angel hesitated just a beat, before jumping up and grabbing her burgundy blazer. Maybe they could sort out this whole mess later. Or maybe not. They'd been trying to figure out a relationship for over four years now. Just when Angel thought they'd been making headway a few months ago, this whole police brutality storm blew in and pushed them back to early days of uncertainty and wariness. Angel could no longer look the other way just to keep some harmony with Sarah or any of her other fellow officers. And that put her in a world of hurt.

After they got in the unmarked police car and started out of the parking area, Sarah filled Angel in on the details of where they were going and why.

"You don't think we should maybe talk about last night first?"

"I didn't tell McGregor."

"That's not what I meant."

Sarah shot her a quick glance. "Isn't it?"

"I'm more interested in what you think about seeing me last night."

"I don't know what to think about this whole fucking mess. So, for now, I'll stay neutral. Just focus on the job."

"Okay. Fine." Sarah laid a little rubber as she turned a corner.

~*~

Hanson Construction was close to Love Field, and Angel recalled seeing one of their signs at the airport when she'd taken LaVon there the week before. Her brother had been catching a flight to L.A, to attend a law and ethics conference. He'd said that while he was there, he'd take a few days of downtime once the conference was over. Then he got stuck when flights were canceled due to a surge in COVID cases in California.

She glanced over at Sarah, wondering if she dared ask how things were going between her and LaVon. Did his downtime include a need to get away from her? Not that that would be a bad thing. For Angel's family, that is. Her father was still bristling over the fact that his kids were consorting with the enemy. He didn't express it in those words, but his meaning was clear no matter the words. She was with Ryan and LaVon was with Sarah, both from the "whitey camp." Not that either of them had purposely made the choice with the intent to bring pain to their father, even though he saw it that way.

Sarah pulled the car to a stop in front of a red-brick building boldly proclaiming Hanson Construction in large white letters on a black banner-type sign above the door. The July heat shimmered on the asphalt, letting people know it was going to be another hot one in the Lone Star State. The minute she switched off the engine, the temperature in the car soared, and Angel quickly opened her door.

"You think this Jeremy could be the guy?" Angel asked.

Sarah got out and closed the car door. "If only. It would be great to solve this one in less than a day."

"I hope they have their AC cranked up high."

"Let's go see."

"You taking the lead?"

"Of course. It's my case."

That stung a little, and Angel glanced down so Sarah wouldn't see the reaction. Angel knew her sensitivity level was way too high since the Smithfield shooting, but she wasn't alone. Lots of folks in the department were walking around like everyone else was covered in prickly little cactus stingers.

Nobody wanted to touch a cactus.

Inside, Sarah and Angel were greeted with a blast of cold air and an inquisitive look from a man behind a large cluttered desk. The wall behind him was covered with bulletin boards hosting an assortment of papers, some with architectural drawings, and pegboards holding an array of small tools. "Ladies?"

Sarah showed her badge and introduced herself. "This is my partner, Angel. Are you the owner?"

The man nodded, but didn't lose his guarded expression.

"We need to talk to you about an employee."

The man raised one bushy eyebrow. "Name?"

"Jeremy," Sarah said.

"That's it?"

"That's it," Sarah said. "Only thing we know is that he worked for you until a few months ago. And he wasn't happy that Fred Cummings was kept on."

"What's this about? Something happen to Fred? He didn't show up for work today."

"He was killed last night," Angel said.

"Shit," Hanson leaned back in his chair. "Was he the guy on the news?"

Angel nodded.

"Shit," Hansen said again. "He was a good guy."

"That's what everyone says," Sarah said. "But someone didn't think so."

Hansen sat up straight, the old office chair creaking a protest to the sudden movement. "That's got nothing to do with me."

"Maybe not. We'll have to see. Right now, we need a last name and contact information for Jeremy."

"I have three Jeremys working for me."

"We don't want the ones working for you," Sarah said. "Just the one not working for you anymore."

The man took a moment to sort that one out, then asked, "You think he killed Fred?"

"We'll know the answer to that after we talk to him."

Hanson looked like he wanted to ask another question, then sighed and swiveled to open a drawer in a battered metal filing cabinet to the right of his desk. "Just a sec."

~*~

Jeremy Cantu was a big bear of a man, and he wasn't any more welcoming than his former boss when the detectives knocked on the faded wooden screen door of his aged frame house just off Greenville Avenue near Gaston and introduced themselves. He didn't open the outside door, letting them stand in the blazing heat of the sun to peer at him through a dusty screen. "Whata' ya want?"

"Just a few questions about a former work associate," Angel said.

"Well, listen to all them fancy words. You some kinda uppity nigger?"

Angel wrenched the door open, the force of her anger pushing Cantu back. "Don't you ever—"

Before she could finish, Sarah grabbed her arm and pulled her back, while Cantu screamed, "Get that bitch out'a my face."

Angel struggled to get free, but Sarah pushed her out onto the porch. "Stay there." Her tone left no room for disagreement. Then Sarah went back in, striding right up to Cantu until they were almost nose to nose. "That wasn't a bitch in your face. This is a bitch in your face. You insult my partner, you insult me. And we can both kick your ass. Got it?"

Cantu gulped, then nodded. Amazing how easy it was to take down a big bully sometimes.

If only it could be this easy all the time.

Realizing that she'd let her protective mask slip, Sarah

pulled it over her mouth and nose while stepping back. "Now," she said, lasering him with a glare. "You'll get a mask and invite us in like a civilized person. And answer our questions. Got it?"

While Cantu rummaged through stacks of paper and old magazines on a coffee table that stood in front of a blue sofa that had grey stuffing escaping through holes in the seat cushions, Sarah prayed that the man didn't have the damn COVID virus. Even though it was uppermost in her mind on most days, there were times she forgot. Like now. When anger trumped logic and reasoning. Well, she'd just have to wait and see. Just like everyone else who might get exposed. This whole pandemic was like a viral crapshoot. You could roll a lucky number, or snake eyes, at any time.

Cantu looked up. "Can't find no mask."

Sarah took a few steps back. "Just stay there."

Angel stood just inside the room, staying close to the front door, and Sarah thought that was the best place for her partner.

Standing was good. It maintained authority.

"Okay," Sarah said. "I'll be brief. Where were you last night?"

Cantu seemed to consider throwing out a wisecrack as a smirk crossed his face, but the expression quickly disappeared into a shrug. "Around."

"Around where?

"Me and a buddy went to some strip clubs." The sneer resurfaced. "Gotta problem with that?"

Sarah ignored the jab and pulled her notebook from the pocket of her blazer. "Name and contact info for your buddy."

"You never told me what this is about."

"You're the one who shut that path down," Angel said

from across the room. There was enough ice in her tone to freeze Alaska.

He waved a dismissive hand. "Okay. Okay. I shouldn'a said what I did."

Sarah realized that was probably as close to an apology as they were going to get, but her only acknowledgement was to soften her tone when she repeated the request for the name of his alibi. After providing the information, Cantu asked, "Who are you investigating?"

"A man you used to work with," Sarah said. "Fred Cummings. He was killed Wednesday night."

"Oh, Jeez!" Cantu wiped a hand across his face. "Oh, man."

His shock and surprise seemed genuine, but the reaction didn't fit what Cummings' wife had said about Cantu being angry about being let go while Fred was kept on the job. But Sarah would hang on to that bit of information for the moment. "You were close?"

"Nah. Not like buddies or anything. Ran with different groups. But nobody deserves to go like that."

"Like what?"

"I'm not a moron. I know what homicide means." He paused a beat then asked, "So what's it got to do with me?"

"We heard you were pretty angry about the job situation. Him getting to stay on after you were let go."

Cantu rubbed a hand through his greasy hair. "You think I offed the guy over that?"

Sarah didn't answer, just held his gaze.

"Okay. I was pissed. But it was a momentary thing. You get mad, you get over it. End of story."

This new and improved, softer version of Cantu was easier to deal with, but Sarah couldn't forget the volatile man who'd insulted and threatened her partner. Had he really gotten over the perceived injustice? Or had he gotten even?

"Do you own a gun, Mr. Cantu?"

He shook his head vehemently. "Never owned one in my life."

"Not even for hunting?"

"Hell, I'm a blowhard, but I don't cotton to killing critters."

Sarah held his gaze for a long moment. They could easily check to see if he was lying about owning a gun. And beyond that, there wasn't anything else to clarify at the moment. "We'll be back if your alibi doesn't check out," Sarah said as she turned to go.

Not a surprise that Cantu didn't stand to escort them out.

Back in the car, Sarah made a quick phone call to Cantu's buddy who confirmed the alibi. If any other suspicions arose around Cantu, they could always go interview the guy in person. Push a little to see if he'd change the story. But for now, the alibi seemed solid enough, especially since there hadn't been enough time since their exit for Cantu to call his friend to set up a lie.

Sarah didn't start the engine right away, and Angel turned to her after fastening her seat belt. "We just going to sit here and roast?"

"I don't like that guy."

"Was it something he said?"

The hint of mirth in Angel's voice brought a slight smile. "You get that a lot? The N word?"

"Not like it used to be." Angel shrugged. "But it's always there, you know. Just simmering under the surface. I can see it in so many eyes when people meet me."

"Christ." Sarah shook her head slowly. "I had no idea."

"Yeah. Well. We don't talk about it much anymore, do we."

Not a question. A statement, and Sarah gave her partner a sharp look. "I didn't think we had to anymore. Thought we had all that racism shit done with."

"Maybe it was done with for you. But it's never done with for us."

Before Sarah could respond, her phone pinged with a message, and Angel's phone was close behind.

Sarah read the message first. "McGregor wants us. Meeting at the station. Maybe something popped."

"We can hope."

"Hope like hell he didn't find out about this." Sarah gestured between herself and Angel.

"You really didn't clear it with him?"

"Nope."

"Oh, God!"

CHAPTER NINE

Same Afternoon

Walking into the conference room, Sarah was glad to note that McGregor stood alone near the head of the table. The other brass wasn't there, and neither was Price, which was the biggest relief. Actual policing business took a second seat to publicity needs when he sat in on these briefings. As far as she was concerned, the PR guy didn't care a bit about how hard the job was. It was all about how the investigations looked on the evening news. He wanted it all clean and sparkling and positive, but sometimes investigations just looked like shit. That's just the way it was. There was nothing pretty about murder and drugs and all the depravity mankind inflicted on one another.

Geesh. Where'd that all come from?

Sarah shook her head and took a seat across from Burt, giving a quick nod to Ryan and McGregor. Angel pulled out the chair next to her.

Chief Dorsett walked in, trailed by a short, rather plump Asian woman. Everyone in the room stood.

"Sit everybody." Dorsett waved a hand. "Bringing a new

member to the team." She turned to the other woman. "Detective Chang."

"Just so you know, people," Chang said in perfect English with only a slight hint of accent and a slight hint of a smile. "I'm Chinese. Not Korean. Not Vietnamese. So don't confuse me with those others. My name is Wei Chang. Pronounced 'way' so that's easy enough. Right? You can get my attention, just holler 'hey way.'"

Sarah liked the sardonic sense of humor and didn't even mind the blue and purple streaks in the young woman's long black hair that was tied back in a ponytail at the nape of her neck. The young woman wore distressed jeans and a silver tee-shirt, the front blazoned with a large green dragon. Some of the others, Dorsett and McGregor in particular, seemed to have a hard time giving Wei more than quick glances and Sarah covered a smile with her hand, knowing how much this image scraped against their three-piece suit approach to professional attire when not in uniform.

"Detective Chang is an expert on social media, smartphones, and computers," Chief Dorsett said. "She'll be assisting all investigations that require her expertise. And lately those numbers of cases are growing more and more."

Dorsett turned to Wei and gave a nod. "Briefly tell the others about your expertise."

"Okey-dokey." Sarah didn't miss the slight flinch on the Chief's face, but the older woman smothered any other reaction. Sarah swallowed the urge to laugh as Wei continued, "I do Facebook, Twitter, Reddit, Instagram, and Goodreads. Not many criminals hang out on Goodreads. I just like books. I also do WhatsApp. And I can get really deep into the Dark Web when necessary."

Sarah leaned closer to Angel and whispered "WhatsApp?

I haven't heard of half of this shit." Angel put a finger to her lips in the proverbial 'be quiet' gesture.

McGregor stood and walked over to shake Wei's hand. "Welcome aboard. I'm Lieutenant McGregor. When Dorsett goes back to her cushy office upstairs, I'm in charge of this motley crew."

"Does LT have a first name?" Chang asked.

There was a brief hesitation during which McGregor's face hardened, then quickly relaxed. "Yes. But you can call me Lieu or McGregor."

"Yes, sir."

"That will do, too."

For the first time since she'd entered the room, Wei lost a bit of the sparkle of her humor and cast her gaze to the floor.

Sarah knew why McGregor had bristled at the use of LT. Maybe she'd tell the new girl sometime.

Maybe.

After Dorsett took her leave, McGregor went back to his chair at the head of the table and sat down. Sarah motioned to Wei to take the empty seat on the other side of her. None of the other detectives had bothered to make room. Were they just too surprised at having an Asian woman join the team, or simply that inconsiderate? Sarah opted to believe the former.

McGregor shuffled some papers on the table in front of him, then glanced at Sarah, "Where're we at with this Cummings shooting?"

"Interviewed the ex-employee the wife told us about," she said. "He has a pretty solid alibi."

"Pretty solid?" McGregor turned to Burt and Sarah sucked in a breath. Would Burt give it away? She planned to tell McGregor about taking Angel with her, but not now.

Barely missing a beat, Burt spoke. "I was slammed

prepping for the upcoming court date on that rape case Simms and I caught a few months back. Asked Sarah to take Angel along for that interview."

McGregor looked pointedly from one to the other. He didn't say a word for so long, Sarah had to physically keep herself from squirming. Finally, McGregor ran his fingers through his graying hair, and sighed. "You people are going to be the death of me yet."

Sarah breathed a little easier, but didn't respond. She'd known McGregor long enough to recognize when to speak and when to keep her mouth shut. This was a keep-your-mouth-shut moment.

"That bit of info about Angel going to the interview doesn't leave this room," McGregor said, his tone leaving no space for argument. "Kingsly and Johnson, you're walking one very high tightrope here."

Angel leaned forward as if to speak, only to be stopped by McGregor's raised hand and pointed finger. "You. You're so high on that fucking tightrope, you could fall and break a few bones. You don't want that. I don't want that. And I'm damn sure your partner doesn't want that. You were told to keep a low profile. That means in house. Not out on the case where reporters can find you. Are we clear?"

"Yes, sir."

McGregor gave a slight nod, then turned back to the papers on the table, finally pulling out a sheet. "Okay, Ryan. What can you tell us about the Darius character? Was the vic connected?"

"Only as cousins," Ryan said. "I checked with my CIs and nobody put the two together in the past year or so."

"And before that?"

"Apparently Cummings helped Darius out of a jam three

years ago. Some product went missing on Darius's watch and Cummings stepped up with some cash to cover."

"That's pretty impressive stepping up," Sarah said. "Could they still be close and just under the radar?"

Ryan shrugged. "Anything's possible."

"So. If he got crosswise with some drug boss, there's still the question of how anybody would've known Cummings was out there that night," Burt said. "The wife seemed to think it was a spur of the moment decision to join the protest."

"What if he was being tailed for something not related to drugs?" Sarah said. "His wife indicated that he did some gambling. Also played around."

"That's a stretch," McGregor said.

"What about the wife?" Ryan looked at Burt. "What was your take on her?"

"She seemed genuinely distraught when we talked to her." He looked at Sarah who gave a nod of affirmation. "And she didn't hold back on the problems in the marriage."

"She was actually pretty matter of fact," Sarah said. "That doesn't mean we're taking her off the suspect list. Just not putting her number one."

"Anything from the cell phone?"

Sarah shook her head. "The wife doesn't know the password. We haven't been able to get in."

"Can you handle that, Detective Chang?"

She brightened. "Yes, sir."

McGregor gave a slight nod. "Okay. Unless something comes from the phone records, looks like all we have is a maybe on the druggie cousin. Also, the gambling angle. Check that out and dig deeper into the vic's background. And his wife."

"On it, boss," Sarah said.

McGregor gave her a look between a smirk and a smile. Sometimes her humor hit him crossways.

"That's it, folks," McGregor said. "It's late. Go home and come back fresh in the morning."

Sarah hung back as the others filed out. McGregor stopped shuffling the papers on the conference table and looked at her. "What?"

"The way you are about Angel. You know?"

McGregor took so long to answer, Sarah thought maybe he wouldn't. Then he nodded.

"How'd you find out?"

"Does it matter?"

"Probably not." She waited a beat, wondering if he was going to ask her about it, but he just resumed stuffing papers into that folder. "What are you going to do? Besides keeping her on desk duty for now?"

"Haven't decided."

"Can we look the other way?"

"Really? You really ask me that?" McGregor slammed the folder closed and glared at her. "We're in a tight place here, Sarah. Don't make this any harder for me."

"What are we supposed to do if we start splintering on the inside? Doesn't that play into the hands of all those people that would like to see us just go away?"

"I don't know the answer to that, Sarah. Jesus! None of us knows the answer to that. And I don't know what Chief Dorsett is going to have to say about it either. I don't even know if I want to tell her."

Sarah couldn't remember the last time she'd seen McGregor so distressed. Unlike his anger that could build until he looked like the pressure would blow the top of his head off, today was different. His face sagged, and even his whole body seemed to have lost its inner support, like a ragdoll that lost its stuffing. And his eyes had lost their normal sharp intensity. "I'm sorry, Lieu. This is hard for all of us. But it's going to come out eventually, isn't it? At some point other cops are going to see her. It's going to be reported to other department heads. And there's already dissension between the uniformed officers and us."

"That's the first I've heard of it."

"You know us cops. Taciturn to the extreme." She offered a brief smile that he tried to match and failed. "But let me tell you about the crime scene last night. If things had been any icier between the Uniforms and me and Burt we could've have been in Siberia."

McGregor sighed and grabbed the folder. "Christ! I should have retired last year. Then I wouldn't have to be in the middle of this."

"Too late. We are in the middle of this mess. So, buckle up and hang on to the aw-shit bar."

Ready to head home after clocking out, Angel hurried to the parking lot where she'd left her car that morning. She reached for the door handle, but hesitated when Ryan jogged up. "You busy tonight?"

She gave him a searching look, then shook her head.

"Want to grab a bite?"

"I'm not feeling very sociable."

"You don't have to be social. Just hungry." That was delivered with the smile that always melted her.

When she still didn't respond, he said, "I'll talk. You eat.

Or we both eat and not talk. What do you say?"

Normally, she'd play along with the banter. Remind him that if she answered, she'd be talking. But that just felt so wrong today. Everything felt so wrong since that kid was shot. "I'm sorry. Another time?"

Ryan's smile slowly faded. "You okay?"

"What do you think?"

She didn't mean to stab him with her words, but that anger that was bubbling inside her all the time now surged out of her control. She took a breath and let it out slowly. "This is why it's best we don't get a bite to eat as if everything is normal. Nothing is normal."

"You think I don't know that?"

Angel didn't answer.

"You think I don't care?"

Angel touched his cheek. "I know you care. It's just …"

"Just what?"

"I … I need to be with my people."

Ryan's eyes widened in shock. "Thought I was one of your people."

"You don't understand."

"Try me."

Angel sighed and leaned against the fender of her car. "I can't come to work every day and pretend the world is okay. Especially the world of police and Black people. As much as you care. As much as Sarah cares. You don't *know* like I do."

"Hey. I hate what happened in Minnesota, and what Smithfield did here, as much as you do."

"Then why aren't you out there protesting?"

"What? You want me to risk my job?"

Angel didn't respond.

"Oh, my God. No. Tell me you aren't …" He let the

sentence fade and still Angel said nothing. "Who knows?"

Angel took a tissue from her purse and wiped the moisture from her forehead. It was more than the heat and humidity making her sweat. She knew that. "Sarah."

"Not McGregor?"

"Maybe. I don't know."

"Sarah wouldn't tell him?"

"No."

"How can you be sure?"

Anger flared for a moment. "She wouldn't. She's my partner."

Silence followed, and Angel appreciated the late evening breeze that blew through the parking lot, scattering empty drink cups and papers along the concrete and cooling the air. The sun was starting to fade into dusk, splashing the sky with streaks of orange and gold and pink. She turned and reached to open her car door.

"Is this your way of ending us?" Ryan asked.

"I don't think so."

"Not exactly the answer I was hoping for, but I'll take it. What *do* you mean?"

Angel turned and faced him. "Maybe nothing. Things are just confusing right now with all the protests and the realization that White people can still kill Black people with impunity."

"I don't condone that."

"What about your family? Your friends?"

"What about them?"

"Do they agree with you or do they excuse the cops who are trigger happy?"

"We don't really talk about it."

"Well, see. That's the big difference between you and me.

Us Black folks, that's all we talk about. That's all that's been talked about for decades as White people have lynched Black people or beaten Black people to death. My ancestors huddled in fear that it could happen to them, or somebody they loved, next. And some of us still huddle in fear."

Angel fought back the tears that threatened to erupt. Not wanting to appear weak but also not wanting to put more of a guilt trip on Ryan then she already had. She took a deep breath and grabbed the door handle again. She needed to get inside the car. End this painful conversation.

To Ryan's credit he didn't say anything, and he didn't try to pull her into an embrace; he simply reached out and lightly touched her hand. That was almost her undoing but she clenched her teeth held her emotions in check.

"I'm truly sorry for all that." Ryan spoke quietly and Angel stood rigid, not opening the car door, but also not knowing how to respond to his words that revealed so much.

After a long moment of silence during which the only sounds to be heard was the rattle of empty soda cans being pushed along by the wind, Ryan spoke again. "Are you going there tonight? To protest?"

The questions surprised her, and she glanced over her shoulder. "I don't think so."

"When ... Well ... when you do ... Be careful."

The kindness in the timbre of his voice almost shattered her thin hold on control. She looked away for a long moment, then glanced back at him and nodded. She couldn't speak. She didn't trust her voice.

He gave her a quick chin nod, then stepped back.

Angel wrenched open the door and got into the car, backing out with a squeal of rubber; her emotions in a turmoil.

What did she want from Ryan? At the moment, she really

didn't know. Part of her had hoped that Ryan would offer to go with her to the protests. She knew she had no right to expect that, or to ask that of him. But if he truly cared about the injustices, wouldn't he want to show that he cared? "Walk the walk," as therapists are always saying.

Wouldn't Sarah?

Angel sighed and eased off the gas pedal before she had to explain herself to a patrol officer. There were no easy answers to any of the questions spinning like bingo balls in her head. But it wasn't her head that was causing the most stress. She didn't know if there would ever come a time when her efforts to balance race and relationships would stop feeling like tearing her heart in two.

Sarah had just settled on the sofa with a bowl of macaroni and cheese for supper and a rerun of Blue Bloods streaming on Netflix when her phone buzzed with an incoming call. She picked up and checked the caller ID and at first, she didn't recognize the number. Then it registered. Jolene. It was her cousin Jolene from Tennessee. They hadn't spoken since last year and her gut told her that her cousin wasn't just calling to chat, so she answered with a tentative, "Hello."

"Sorry to have to make this call, Sarah. But I have bad news."

"No need to apologize, Jolene. We're kin after all. What is it?"

"It's my daddy." She spoke in a soft, wavering voice, then she hiccupped and said, "That damn COVID done took him."

"Oh, Jolene. I'm so sorry." Sarah took a moment to absorb

the news, then asked, "How's your mother handling it? And your brothers?"

"We're all damn mad, that's for sure."

Sarah wondered just what they were damn mad about. That he was gone? That he didn't get vaccinated? Jolene had told her last year that Uncle Homer wasn't going to get the shot when it came out. Had Jolene? "When did it happen?"

"He got sick about a month ago. Spent the last two weeks in the hospital." Jolene chocked on another sob, then took a breath to continue. "He was so stubborn. He didn't want to go at first. But Mama made him. He was struggling so hard to breathe."

Another burst of crying halted the words, and Sarah waited it out. Then she asked, "Any arrangements made yet?"

"Will you come?" The question was asked on a soft whisper, and for a moment Sarah was taken back to her childhood when she and her cousin were close. Such a long time ago. And lots of shit thrown around the family since then. Which created a major problem.

Sarah wasn't sure she even wanted to go. That was a horrible thing to think, but there was no way around it. That branch of her mother's family was living way off the grid. Had been for too many years, and there was no way that Sarah could ever be comfortable there, not even for the one person she still cared about.

"Please?"

Oh, God! Okay, maybe she owed her cousin something. Maybe her grandmother would want her to be a better person than some of the aunts and uncles that Grandma had sometimes wished had never been birthed. The ones who'd gotten so off track, they were like train cars colliding with what was right. But even without acceptance of the lives they were living, Grandma never stopped loving those children. The ones she'd carried and the ones brought into the family by marriage. She just didn't always like them. Something Sarah shared with her in spades.

"Send me details, and I'll see what I can do," Sarah said. "But I can't promise what with travel restrictions and demands here on the job."

"I understand," Jolene said. "I'll let you know. And I guess we'll see you … or not."

"I really am sorry you lost your daddy," Sarah said. "Truly. And you tell your mama and your brothers that I said so."

"Okay," Jolene's voice broke on that single word and Sarah simply disconnected.

She held the phone against her chest and thought about her Uncle Homer. He'd been a kind, gentle man when she was a kid running wild with Jolene in the woods around the family homestead, pretending they were warriors protecting their home. That all came to a screeching halt by the time they were teenagers. The security Sarah always found in that home went away shortly after Uncle Homer lost his job, and the drinking started up like he was a man who was never going to see another glass of whiskey again. His soft heart had turned to stone, and there was so much anger and fear living in Jolene's house, Sarah no longer wanted to go there. She was more than a little afraid of him, and she hated seeing the disintegration of a man and his family.

After Sarah came to Dallas, her grandmother called one day to say that Homer had moved the family deeper into the mountains and was living off the land. "You wouldn't know him anymore," Grandma had said. "He's meaner than that ol' rabid fox that got the chickens last year."

"He was well on his way before I ever left."

"Sure was. An' I never thought he could get any worse. But damn if he didn't."

Sarah had been a little afraid to ask, but she did care about her cousin. "How's Jolene?"

"Doing okay. Considering. Stays with me a lot to be out of the house. But the brothers live on some kinda compound with their daddy. All of 'em are into that neo-Nazi stuff. Drive around with Confederate flags flappin' on the back of their trucks."

"I'm sorry to hear that, Grandma. But thanks for letting me know. You take care of Jolene."

"Do my best."

A year or so later, her grandmother had called to let Sarah know that Jolene married a man who worked with her brother, Jacob, and they'd moved to the compound with the rest of the family.

While Sarah hadn't thought about this part of her family since last year, maybe she should try to go to the service. For Jolene. And to put flowers on her grandmother's grave.

CHAPTER TEN

Friday, July 3 - Morning

Sarah glanced up to see Ryan striding toward her desk. He wore his usual 'uniform' of chinos, a white Polo shirt, and sneakers that had seen better days. He also sported a wide smile. "What's up?" she asked.

"Russell from Vice put me onto someone who can fill us in on the gambling scene in Dallas. Guy who runs a revolving card game." Ryan glanced over at Angel who was seated at the next desk. "Want to come along?"

She shook her head. "I'm grounded."

"Thought maybe you could sneak out."

Another shake of her head. "Can't risk it. But anything else I can help with?"

Sarah could see the disappointment on Ryan's face, but he quickly covered with a grin that was as fake as a counterfeit twenty. "You got it. Check on forensics and then see if Walt finished the post?"

Angel nodded and looked away.

Sarah picked up a hint of tension between her partner and Ryan as he turned away from Angel and faced her again. Was it more than the disappointment of not working together? Of course, there was a lot of shit going on with Angel, and Ryan may have gotten a glimpse of said shit. Sarah wondered what he thought of it, if he did know, but this was not the time to broach that sensitive subject.

"Got a meet-up with this guy in an hour," Ryan said to Sarah. "You in?"

"Absolutely." She stood, put on her shoulder harness with her weapon, grabbed some plastic evidence bags and latex gloves out of a desk drawer, then shrugged into her gray blazer. Today's t-shirt was navy blue. After taking a photo of Fred Cummings off her desk, she followed Ryan without looking back at Angel. She didn't want to see a mirror image of Ryan's disappointment.

"Where're we headed?" Sarah asked as Ryan drove the unmarked police car north on Central Expressway.

"Richardson. Little diner called Ronnie's."

"A diner? Really?"

Ryan nodded. "Maybe the last one left in the whole state."

A memory of bacon and eggs and pancakes oozing with syrup made Sarah's mouth water. The breakfasts she'd had with her grandmother at a small place in Bluff City, Tennessee where she'd grown up sure beat the granola bar she'd had this morning with her coffee at Hussein's convenience store.

Ryan exited Central Expressway at Arapaho and went west for about a mile, slowing at a small building that looked like it had been converted from a fast-food place. The sign proclaimed, "Ronnie's Diner."

"Well, I'll be." Sarah slipped out of the car and admired the old-fashioned sign.

Ryan joined her at the door to the restaurant and stalled her with a hand on her shoulder. "Russell told me this place is usually busy despite the pandemic. But today … Well, you'll see."

Inside, the place was conspicuously empty, except for a man at the counter not far from the door; two more men sat ram-rod straight in a booth about midway down. The man in the last booth had his arm slung casually across the back of the low banquette bench.

"That's Moe at the far end," Ryan said in a low whisper. "You okay without a mask? Might go better without since he isn't wearing one."

Sarah looked closely at the wizened elderly man who looked like the gnome her Aunt Pauline had in her garden back home; chubby, round face, bushy eyebrows and a little goatee, sporting a bright red jacket. "Don't let appearances fool you," Ryan whispered, as if he'd been privy to her reaction to seeing the little man. "He's a savvy guy. Runs almost everything illegal in the area, and doesn't go anywhere without protection."

Taking another look at the other men who pretended to be ignoring her and Ryan, Sarah realized that they were definitely dealing with a man who was into a lot more than just organizing a few casual card games.

The little man called out, "Manuel. Check 'em."

The tall, muscular man at the counter abruptly stood and strode over to Ryan and Sarah. He easily found their weapons, including the little Berretta in Ryan's boot. "Get 'em back when you leave," the man said in a soft, smooth voice.

It was clear that challenging that directive would not be wise. Manuel had a large Glock strapped to his belt, and his arms were bigger than Sarah's thighs. He was not a man to be messed with.

Acknowledging with a slight nod, Sarah and Ryan passed

the big man and walked to the last booth, sliding in across from Moe, who wasted no time with pleasantries. "You got five minutes."

Sarah showed the man the picture of Fred Cummings. "Was this guy one of your regulars?"

That was met with a slight shrug. "Regular at what?"

Ryan leaned closer. "Come on, Moe. If you aren't going to give us any info, why meet at all?"

Another shrug.

Sarah leaned back into the cracked vinyl of the booth. "Maybe I'll just sit here and have a late breakfast while you're deciding whether you want to talk or not. She waved the waitress over and ordered bacon, eggs, toast, and hash browns.

After the waitress walked away, Moe finally found his voice. "You gonna eat all that?"

Sarah offered the slightest of smiles.

Ryan slid the photo of the dead man closer to Moe. "As much fun as it is to watch you and Sarah play that game, I have things to do today. So. Just answer the question, and we can all move on."

"Okay." Moe pushed the photo away with the tip of his index finger on one hand, as if it might be contaminated with some deadly germ. "He came to the games. Sometimes. Not every week. Maybe once, twice a month."

"Did he tend to win?" Sarah asked

Moe shook his head. "It's better for the bank when players lose."

"The bank?"

"Yeah. After players lose the money they brought, sometimes they need to borrow."

"And you loan it to them." Not a question, as Sarah

already knew he probably did. She just wanted to see what he'd say in response.

"For a fee." He smiled, but his eyes remained hard and cold.

A realization dawned on Sarah. That's one way Moe lined his bank account. If he even had a bank account like most people who weren't involved in criminal activity.

"Then this guy lost every time?"

Moe shook his head. "He was pretty good. Sometimes he'd win."

"How often?"

"Not a lot."

"How often is 'not a lot'?" Ryan asked, his voice carrying a little harder edge than Sarah's.

Moe turned those cold eyes to Ryan. "I don't keep records. Certainly, you understand why."

"Yes, I do," Ryan said. "And we're not here to bust your balls. Just need information. Can you remember if any of those wins were recent? In the last month or so."

Moe took a swallow of his coffee, then set the mug down on the table with a clunk. "Nothing I tell you can be connected to me. Capice?"

Sarah had to swallow the urge to chuckle at the little man talking big. Afraid laughter would escape if she opened her mouth, she merely nodded.

"You got it," Ryan said.

"Okay. He won big a couple of times recently."

"Who lost against him?" Sarah asked.

"I can't be telling you that." Moe smiled, another cold, malevolent expression that chased away any desire to push too hard. It was easy to see how this diminutive man could instill respect, and maybe even a little bit of fear, into the players who came to his table. "My clients would be most unhappy indeed."

"Your clients would be more upset if vice should pay a visit to your little establishment," Ryan said.

"You said you wouldn't do anything like that," Moe said.

"That was when we thought you were cooperating." Ryan leaned back in the bench seat and waited.

"The game moves around." Moe glared. "We can stay ahead of you guys from vice."

"Don't be so sure of that." Ryan tapped the table lightly with two fingers. "If Russell tracked you down to set up this meeting, he could find one of your games."

Moe seemed to consider this, glancing from Ryan to Sarah who had just started to dig into the order the waitress had brought. Finally, Moe sighed. "Okay. One of the guys who had a couple of big losses was Sam Getty."

"We need more than just a name," Sarah said through a mouthful of hash browns.

"This can't come back on me." Moe reached over and grabbed a piece of the bacon from her plate and started slowly chewing. If the move was meant to intimidate, Sarah didn't find it particularly scary. More amusing than threatening. She smiled at him and took the other piece.

"It won't," Ryan said.

"Okay." Moe snagged a triangle of toast from Sarah's plate. Another try at intimidation? It looked like they were playing some odd game of chess with the food. Whatever was going on, helping himself to her food had her slightly off balance, and maybe that was the little man's intent. Sarah ate the rest of the hash browns, then took the last piece of toast. If he wanted the remnants of egg still on her plate, he was welcome to it. She pushed the plate closer to the middle of the table, but he ignored it, chewing the last of the toast before speaking again. "Getty owns Tri-County Medical Supplies." He brushed crumbs off his hands. "You can probably find him at one of his stores."

"Phone number?" Ryan asked.

"Don't know."

"Then how do you contact him about the revolving card game?"

Since the food was gone, there was nothing for Moe to use as a stalling tactic. "You do call your clients. Right?" Sarah said.

He sighed and pulled out a smart phone and started scrolling. Finally, he stopped to call out a number.

"Thanks." Sarah stood and dropped a couple of bills on the table. "That'll cover my part of the breakfast. You can pay the rest since you ate half of it."

Beside her, Ryan sucked in a breath as Moe sat rock still, his smile frozen on his face. It chilled the whole room, and Sarah waited, rooted to the spot. Had she gone over some line that would get them both shot? Then Moe gave her a slight nod and a genuine smile before waving to his bodyguard. "Let 'em go."

Manuel lumbered over and escorted them out the door. At the entrance, he handed over their weapons. "Have a nice day."

"Have a nice day?" Ryan sputtered. "We weren't in there shopping." He whirled on Sarah. "And what was that stunt you pulled? We could've been killed."

Yeah. What was that stunt? It had been a while since Sarah had been so reckless on the job or otherwise. Angel had tended to be a good influence, pulling Sarah back from whatever precipice she was perched on. But things were so wrong now. Between them as partners. In the department. In the city. Her emotions were running way past high.

Finally, Sarah said, "Got us some respect, didn't it?"

Ryan shook his head and walked toward the car, pulling out his cell phone before getting in. "Gonna call Angel. See if she can get some info on this Getty character."

Sarah nodded, then slid into the passenger seat. After a minute or two, Ryan got in beside her and fired up the engine for some AC. "She'll get back to us in five," he said.

"Okay." Sarah fastened her seatbelt to be ready to roll. "Sorry about my stunt."

"Yeah. Yeah."

"Really. I am. I shouldn't have put you in danger."

"It's over. Just curb the impulse if it comes again."

Sarah dipped her chin in acknowledgement. Then when the silence had stretched a few more minutes she asked, "Curious. How'd your buddy in Vice manage to get this meet with Moe?"

Ryan rested his elbow on the window ledge and leaned into his hand. "They've known each other since they were kids. Some kind of family friendship thing."

"So, they're pals."

"Maybe once, but not anymore. After Russell joined the force, he pulled away when he realized what Moe was getting into."

"Has he ever attempted to arrest him?"

Ryan shook his head. "Not sure why, and I didn't ask. If they have an agreement, I don't want to know."

A couple of seconds later, Ryan's phone buzzed with a call. He listened for a few seconds, then said, "Thanks."

"Angel?"

"Yes. Getty's main store is in Carrolton."

"We could write a travel piece on visiting all the Dallas suburbs. If we were writers, that is."

Ryan chuckled, then put the car in gear. "Angel also said he's a registered gun owner. A .38 Smith & Wesson. Roberts told her that the slug that Walt dug out of the body probably came from a small caliber weapon like that."

"Could it be we solve a case in two days?"

Ryan pulled into traffic and headed toward Plano Parkway. "In your dreams, Sarah. In your dreams."

CHAPTER ELEVEN

Same Morning

I t took twenty minutes to get to the store that was on Parker Road just off the expressway.

"Looks kinda small for the main store," Sarah said when Ryan pulled into a parking lot in front that only had six spaces for customer vehicles.

"Maybe he warehouses most of the inventory."

"Could be."

They went inside, and Sarah glanced at the wheelchairs, walkers, and oxygen tanks on one side of the large room. Before she could check out any of the other merchandise, a tall, thin man walked up to them, offering a hand and a wide grin she could see despite his mask. "Afternoon, folks. What can Getty Medical do for you today?"

Sarah guessed this was the man himself, all false cheer and officiousness like some business owners can be.

"You can start by telling us how upset you were that you lost over two grand to Fred Cummings a few weeks ago." Sarah accompanied that with a flash of her shield.

The color drained from Getty's face, and he quickly

looked around the store, taking note of where another couple stood by the shower chairs, talking with an employee. "How do you know about that?" he asked in a low whisper.

"We're detectives. We investigate. And we're here to ask the questions. Not to answer them. Perhaps you'd like to invite us to your office, where we can talk about this in private?"

"Certainly. Certainly." Getty led the way to a door at the rear of the showroom.

The office was small but neat, and, thankfully, there were two extra chairs; standard folding chairs with gray fabric seats. Sarah and Ryan waited until Getty settled behind his cluttered desk before they sat.

"We're not going to mess you up about the card games," Sarah said. "We're here about Cummings' murder."

"What?"

The reaction seemed to reflect genuine surprise as he slumped back in his chair.

"Don't you keep up with the news?"

"You talking about the guy who was shot a couple of days ago? That was Fred?"

Sarah nodded. "And we need to know where you were Wednesday night."

"You think I killed him?"

"Just answer the question."

"Okay. Okay." Getty swiped a hand across his nearly bald head. "I was home."

"Can anyone verify that?"

"Wife was gone. Visiting her sister in Oklahoma."

"Any other family at home?"

He shook his head. "Kids are grown and gone."

"Not looking too good for you so far." Ryan leaned

forward in the chair. "How angry were you about losing to Fred?"

Getty shrugged.

"I'd think two grand is worth more than a shrug."

"How do you know that?" Getty asked, a hard edge in his voice. "Who told you?"

Without missing a beat Sarah said, "We found a list of losers in Fred's belongings. Guess the guy liked to gloat."

"Bastard."

"Yeah. Well, he's a dead bastard," Sarah said. "Any idea of who else might be angry enough about losing to Fred to take him out?"

Getty took a moment to consider then said, "We don't share names outside of the games. Sort of like AA, you know."

Sarah slammed her fist on the desk. "This is a murder investigation. Not a fucking recovery program."

Getty was so startled; he pushed his chair back on its rollers, clunking against the wall. "Chill. Okay. Give me a minute."

"She has a short fuse," Ryan said, his tone pleasant and measured. "So, you might want to consider cooperating before she really gets mad."

"Okay. Okay. There's this guy, Brent. He lost big, and he was really pissed. Was screaming at Fred and had to be restrained."

"Thank you, Mr. Getty," Sarah said, using the same pleasant inflection Ryan had. "That wasn't so hard, was it? Now we just need a last name and contact information."

"Robinson. Brent Robinson. Don't have his number, but he's the GM at Archer Sports in Frisco."

"Just one more question," Ryan said. "Where do you keep your gun?"

"Gun?"

Ryan didn't even bother with a response, just waited the guy out. In those few moments, Getty seemed to regain some of his bluster.

"It's at home. In a lockbox."

"Not here at the store? For protection?"

Now Getty leaned forward, elbows on the desk threatening to dislodge a pile of papers. "It's my business where I keep my gun. Okay?"

"Sure. But the deal is." Ryan kept his voice even, not rising to the confrontational bait. "The bullet that killed Cummings came from a Smith & Wesson. Quite a coincidence that you have one."

"Hey, man." Getty held up a hand, palm out. "It's my constitutional right to have a gun. Certainly, as officers of the law you know about the Second Amendment."

"Of course we do, Mr. Getty." Sarah opened her jacket to reveal the butt of her weapon. "I even support my right under the Second Amendment."

Since she was getting so tired of every Tom, Dick, and Jack having a gun, leaving police officers to wonder which one of them was a stable sensible gun owner and which one might be off crucial meds, she considered adding that her right was perhaps a little more legitimate than his. But this was not the time to try to educate an asshole.

Nothing was said for a moment or two as Getty glowered. Sarah waited for a few beats, letting him know that his glower meant shit to her, then she said, "We need your weapon for testing."

"I didn't shoot Fred."

"Here's another thing," Ryan said. "Even though you seem like such a nice guy, we can't take your word for it. Need a ballistics test. And for that, we need your weapon."

Getty sighed. "Now?"

Sarah nodded.

"Okay." Another deep sigh. "Let me tell Jeremy that I'm leaving."

After Getty took care of that notification, they put him in the back of the unmarked car and followed his directions to his residence, just a few miles up Parker. He led the officers inside a modest brick ranch-style house to a bedroom in the back. Bed neatly made, Sarah noted. Briefly, she wondered if the wife had returned, or was Getty just not like so many men who didn't think the effort of making a bed was worth it when they were just going to get into it later.

Getty pushed clothes aside in the walk-in closet to reveal a gray metal gun safe. "What's the combination?" Ryan asked, stepping forward.

"I'll get it." Getty reached out, but Ryan stopped him with a firm hand on his arm.

"This is the way it works. You tell me the combination, and I open the safe." Ryan didn't let go of Getty's arm.

After a moment, Getty wiped the perspiration off his face with his hand and rattled off the combination. Ryan snapped on latex gloves then twirled the dial to open the safe. Inside was a single gun, a Smith and Wesson. Ryan picked it up and dropped it into the evidence bag that Sarah held open for him.

"Will I get my weapon back?" Getty asked.

"Depends on the results of the tests." Ryan said.

"It's clean, I'm telling you."

Sarah turned. She'd had about as much of this guy as she could stand. One minute a simpering bitch, the next a blustering asshole. She didn't like either version, but they still had to take him back to his store.

Ryan pulled to a stop in front of the store, and Sarah got out to open the rear passenger door for Getty. "We'll be in touch." she said, already turned to get back in the car.

Once buckled up again, she asked, "What next? Ballistics or continue our tour of the suburbs?"

"I'll see if Hanks is available. If this is the gun, we can skip Frisco." Ryan activated his phone and called in, listened for a moment, then disconnected. "Got his voicemail message. Out for lunch, but will be back in half an hour. Why don't we grab something then head that way?"

"I'm still full from breakfast with Moe," Sarah said. "But go to someplace with strong coffee and I'm in."

Timothy Hanks was a small man. Everything about him was small; height, weight, hands, feet, and tiny eyes in a round face. But his intelligence, as well as his experience as an expert ballistic forensic scientist, was huge. Sarah was glad he worked for the DPD, even if it was only part time.

"You do know I have other cases," he said after Sarah told him why she and Ryan were standing in the middle of his lab.

She nodded. "But one little look-see, and you can either help us clear a major case or clear a suspect in the major case."

He waited a long minute, then sighed. "Let me see the gun."

Ryan put on latex gloves, took the weapon out of the evidence bag and handed it to Hanks who already had gloves on. "It's loaded. We checked."

"Duly noted." Hanks hefted the gun. "Nice little weapon. Lightweight. Good balance."

"That's what makes it so popular," Sarah said.

Hanks opened the cylinder and checked the load. Three bullets. "Roberts already sent over the bullet that killed your guy. I'll fire this baby and compare."

"When can we get results?" Ryan asked.

"As soon as I have any." Hanks deadpanned that comment, then smiled. "End of the day suit you?"

"Sure."

As they walked out, Sarah asked, "Shall we go to Frisco?"

"Let's check in with Angel. See if she has anything else from Roberts on trace at the scene."

"You really don't want to go to Frisco, do you?"

Ryan shook his head. "Too damn far. And the traffic. Went there once with Simms to see the Stars complex. Vowed I'd never go back."

"Well, look at you, all intimidated by a few cars."

Ryan shot her a look that said he wasn't finding this amusing.

"Okay, I'll drive."

"Forensics report first." His tone had a slight edge of impatience.

"Your taco not agreeing with you?"

He shrugged. "Just want this day to be over. This case to be over. This civil unrest to be over."

"Don't we all."

Angel was elbow deep in papers spread across her desk when Ryan and Sarah approached. She gave Ryan a brief, hesitant smile and nodded to her partner. "Good timing," she said.

"Just got a preliminary report from Walt. He did the post this afternoon."

"Results?" Sarah pulled a chair over and sat beside Angel's desk.

"Cause of death as expected. The bullet clipped his aorta, so he bled out internally."

"So, it wasn't quick," Sarah said.

"No."

"Anything else?" Ryan asked.

"Full tox screen isn't in yet. But preliminary tests didn't show any illegal substances." Angel referred to one of the papers. "Stomach contents included wine, undigested beef and potatoes, and greens from a salad."

"Any sign of other trauma?" Sarah asked.

"Just slight contusions consistent with the body hitting the concrete."

"What about forensics?" Ryan asked. "Anything from Roberts?"

"Nothing of much help. But residue on the back of Cummings' shirt shows he was shot at close range from behind."

"Did they find anything else on the clothes? Something to indicate the shooter touched him so we can get DNA?" Ryan hitched one hip on the corner of Sarah's desk, across from Angel's.

Angel shook her head. "Roberts said there was so much trace on the victim's clothes, it'll take time to sort it all out. Not a surprise since the crowd was so tight, despite the virus running rampant. People jostling each other as they surged toward the Federal Building. She stopped abruptly, realizing she might have said too much, too openly. Words that could make anyone who heard them wonder how she knew about the jostling crowd. Words that could be used against her. Those who had her back never would, but there were still some who didn't want her there. A woman. A Black woman. Despite all public appearances, this was still a White man's domain.

CHAPTER TWELVE

Friday, July 3 - Afternoon

After a grueling drive north from Dallas to Frisco, Sarah vowed she'd never go there again. This would be her first and last time.

"Told ya," Ryan said as they got out of the car in front of the sporting goods store.

Sarah ignored him, stretching a bit to get the kinks out. Then they walked toward the store that was set back from the road all by itself on a plot of land that could turn into a strip mall if someone had the interest and the money to do so. Archer Sports was huge and a bit overwhelming, reminding Sarah of why she avoided most big-box stores. Not only was it hell finding what she needed in those great behemoths, she could fall dead in one of the aisles and maybe not be found for days. The little independent sporting goods store in Dallas where she got her running shoes and jogging shorts suited her just fine. It was owned and run by a nice man from Pakistan, Habib, who was always there with a smile and great customer service. "You want to buy. Okay. Not want to buy. Okay, too. Nice to see you." His approach to salesmanship never failed to amuse her.

After they walked in and wandered down an aisle filled with bicycles that were all much fancier than the one Sarah had ridden as a child, and pricier, they spotted a young man wearing a mask, tan slacks, and a blue shirt with the store logo proudly displayed. Ryan waved him over. "We need to see the manager."

"I'm one of the assistant managers," the man said. "May I help you?"

Sarah pulled her jacket open to show him her badge. "We need to see the head guy. Brent Robinson. Your GM."

"Uh. Okay, I guess."

"You guess?"

"Uh. Right." The man, really not much older than a teen, was clearly rattled, and Sarah almost felt sorry for him. Almost being the operative word. She was tired. She was cranky. And she was fresh out of whatever patience she might have had at the start of this day.

Before she could say anything confrontational, Ryan stepped forward. "Take us to your boss. Please."

"Sure. Uh, okay. This way."

The kid led them to the back of the store and stopped in front of a door marked 'Office.' He knocked, a light tentative sound, but one that was obviously heard because a gruff voice called out from inside, "I said nobody should bother me."

The young man leaned close to the door. "Sorry, boss. But I got two police officers here who want to talk to you."

"What about?"

"I don't know. They didn't say."

Silence for a beat, and just when Sarah thought she might need to kick the damn door in, the voice called out, "Okay. Bring 'em in."

The young man opened the door wide enough for Ryan and Sarah to step through. A big, burly man sat behind a cluttered desk that took up most of the space in the small room, and there were no chairs other than the one he occupied. Boxes, stacked head-high, lined one wall, the other held a narrow table with a coffee maker, a stack of Styrofoam cups, packets of sugar, and a can of powdered cream.

"Nice place you got here," Sarah said, not even trying to hide the sarcasm.

Robinson had barely glanced at the detectives when they came in. Now he looked directly at Sarah. "You interrupted my work to comment on my decor?"

"No. Mind if I sit?" Not waiting for an answer, she positioned three of the larger boxes in front of the desk and sat. "This should be okay. I don't weigh much."

Behind her, she heard a slight snicker from Ryan. At least he was now out of his funk.

Robinson stared at her for a long moment. "You nuts, lady?"

Sarah shook her head. "Just exhausted. And you can call me Detective Kingsly. This here's Detective O'Donnell."

"Whatta you want from me?"

"Need to know where you were last Wednesday night," Ryan said from his perch holding up the wall by the door.

"Until you tell me why, I don't have to tell you shit."

"We don't want to hear any shit. Bull or cow," Sarah said. "But you can talk to my partner in a more pleasant tone of voice."

Robinson twirled a pencil in his fat fingers, obviously taking his time to decide whether to cooperate or not. Then he said, "I think that's the night me and the missus went to the movies."

"In the middle of a goddam pandemic you went to see a movie?"

He shrugged. "We're tired of staying home all the time."

Sarah shook her head. Maybe the pandemic should just take all the assholes off the face of the earth. Then she shook that thought away. Her granny would tan her hide if she knew the ugly thoughts Sarah was entertaining.

"Okay." Sarah shifted to get more comfortable on the boxes that had started to slant ever so slightly. "We know about the card games."

"Whoa—"

She held up a hand. "That horse has already left the barn, Brent. No stopping it now. So, we need to know how angry you were about losing a big chunk of change to Fred Cummings at the last game?"

He considered for a moment, then said, "How would you feel if you lost four grand?"

"I'd be pissed," Ryan said.

"You got it," Robinson said "I was pissed."

"Pissed enough to off the guy?" Ryan asked.

For a moment the man lost a bit of his composure, and then the bravado came back. "What the hell are you saying? He's dead? And you think I had something to do with it?"

"Did you?" Sarah asked.

"Did I what?"

"Have something to do with it?"

Robinson pushed away from his desk so hard and fast, his chair slammed into the wall behind him. Sarah stood, ready to make a move if the man posed a threat.

"Take it easy." She opened her jacket for easy access to her weapon and held up one hand, palm out.

In response, Robinson opened both arms in a placating

gesture, but when he spoke there was no hint of appeasement in the tone of his voice. "Listen up, detectives. I'm only going to say this once. You're right. I didn't like losing all that money to Fred. Yes, I was angry. No, I didn't kill him. Now, if you have any more questions, call my attorney."

Slowly the man lowered his hands and scribbled information on a piece of paper and handed it across to Sarah, who took it, giving him her own cold glare before slowly turning to join Ryan.

"Thanks for your cooperation," Ryan said after he opened the door.

Robinson gestured to the boxes by his desk. "You gonna put those back?"

Sarah shook her head. "Call a stocker."

CHAPTER THIRTEEN

Friday, July 3 - Late Afternoon

Sarah grabbed a Kit Kat from the downstairs vending machines before going to her desk. There were a lot of snacks that were healthier, but the department didn't stock the machines for nutritional value. Candy bars lived longer in a glass and metal home than did a salad.

She was still munching when she got to her desk. Ryan was seated across from Angel, but Sarah directed the question to her partner. "Got anything?"

"Hanks sent over the ballistic report. The gun you gave him isn't the murder weapon."

"Damn, I was so hoping," Sarah said.

"Story of our lives," Ryan said. "Bursts of hope crushed by facts."

Angel nodded, shuffling papers back into a folder.

"Anything else?" Sarah asked.

Before her partner could answer, Chang bustled in, her bright ebony eyes and wide smile radiating excitement.

"You have news, I gather," Sarah said.

Chang nodded. "I got into the phone."

Sarah grinned. "Pull up a seat and tell us what you found."

Chang took an empty chair from a nearby desk and dragged it over, brushing aside Ryan's move to help. "I got this. I may be little, but I'm strong."

Ryan touched his forehead as if tipping a hat. "Yes, ma'am."

Chang offered him a smile, then positioned the chair at the corner of Sarah's desk. Once seated, Chang opened a folder she had tucked under one arm, pulling out three sheets of paper, handing copies all around. "This is a list of the calls Mr. Cummings made in the past month. I can go back further if needed. But notice here a number he called a lot."

Chang tapped a highlighted line on the sheet resting on Sarah's desk.

"Did you check it out?" Sarah asked.

"What? And do your job?"

"Pardon me?" Sarah didn't mean to sound harsh, but the day had been long and much too frustrating.

"Sorry." Despite the word of apology, Chang didn't seem to take offense at Sarah's tone. Her perpetual smile didn't break.

Sarah shook her head and sighed. "No. I'm sorry. I should've picked up on your joke."

Chang waved slim fingers in a dismissive gesture. "All fine."

"What do you have on the number?" Angel asked.

"Looks like Mr. Cummings might have had a lady friend."

"Not a surprise." Sarah rotated her neck to ease some stiffness. "The wife pretty much told us he had."

"Name and address is on the bottom of your papers."

Chang smiled in delight. "Who needs to get a haircut?"

Sarah ran her finger down the page until she came to the information. Then she understood Chang's question. Fred Cummings was calling Wanda Lopez, the owner of The Beauty and the Beast Salon and Spa in North Dallas.

"I've got it up here on my computer." Angel turned her monitor so the others could see the screen. "It's open until seven today."

Sarah checked her watch, then glanced at Angel. "Want to schedule a bit of pampering?"

"What about?" Angel gestured in the direction of McGregor's office.

"It's the end of our shift. We leave separately and go in our own cars. Who's to know?"

Ryan cleared his throat. "I'm still here, ladies."

Chang raised her hand, another mischievous smile tugging at her lips. "Me, too."

"You could come with us," Sarah said.

They both shook their heads, Ryan with much more emphasis than Chang. The young woman pulled a finger across her lips as if zipping them. "No hear. No see. No tell."

Sarah laughed. With each interaction, she was liking Chang more and more.

"Make sure Wanda is still there," Sarah said, pointing to the phone number on the website.

Angel picked up her cell and dialed. When the call was answered, she said, "Hi Melody. My name's Charice, and I'm needing a new 'do. All my friends just rave about Wanda. About how she can make me into a new person. But, well, you must know how hard it is to make a drastic change." Angel paused to listen, and Sarah couldn't hold back a grin. She'd never heard Angel go into full acting mode before.

"I knew you'd understand, Melody." Angel looked to Sarah and offered a smile back. "And before I change my mind about this, I was hoping to be able to come by to chat with Wanda. A woman doesn't want to cut off all her dreads without some expert input. Is she there by any chance?" Angel paused again for a response, then finished. "Oh, that's wonderful. I can be there before closing. I won't take up much time at all. Just a quick chat."

Sarah laughed as Angel hung up. "I'll nominate you for an Oscar."

"You'll have my vote," Chang said.

Chang was turning to leave when Sarah held up a hand. "Can you run a background check on a Sam Getty and Brent Robinson? See if there's anything hinky in their past?"

"Okey-dokey."

Ryan gave a brief salute and followed Chang out while Sarah went back to her desk. A few minutes later, Angel turned off her computer, slid some files in the bottom drawer of her desk, then stood and grabbed her purse.

Sarah stayed at her desk for another fifteen minutes, then made her own exit.

In the rush-hour traffic, it took forty-five minutes to get to The Beauty and the Beast Salon on Preston Road just north of the George Bush Tollway. No artery heading south from downtown was optimum during rush hour, but Sarah figured Preston was a notch better than taking Central Expressway, which could be more aptly called a parking lot between four and seven each evening. A year and a half into the pandemic and people were tired of the lockdowns. Work and social life had slowly started up again.

Sarah pulled to a stop a few spaces from Angel's car and got out of her Taurus. Angel quickly joined her and they strode up to the door of the salon.

The cool interior of the shop was refreshing after the heat of summer that still lingered even this late in the day. Each time she had to make that dash across concrete she knew would burn her feet if she were barefoot was a reminder of why she preferred the cooler winter months, short as they were, in Texas.

Angel followed her into a spacious open entry area that had a display of scented candles for sale to the right. The cloying aroma made Sarah put on her mask and take a step to the other side of the room where a receptionist sat behind a counter above a glass case holding a variety of lotions, shampoos, and other beauty items. The young girl had long, straight auburn hair and a face so well made up the makeup wasn't immediately apparent, but at a closer look, Sarah could see the light touches of color above and below dark, sparkling eyes.

The woman, who had a nametag announcing that she was Melody, flashed a smile that was evident despite her mask. "Hello, ladies. Do you have an appointment?"

Angel took a step closer to the counter. "We don't. But we need to speak with Wanda."

The air of welcomeness slowly faded. "She's busy in her office. Is there anything I can help you with?"

Sarah showed the girl her badge. "This is police business. And that business is with her."

A frown of alarm crossed Melody's face, then she regained her composure and quickly stood. "Yes, ma'am. I'll tell her you're here."

Moments later, Melody came back, followed closely by a middle-aged woman with a slender figure, curly hair pulled back from her face with a paisley headband. At first glance it wasn't immediately clear what her ethnic background was, other than the fact that it wasn't Caucasian. Could be Mexican or some other Hispanic heritage coloring her face a light sienna. A puzzled frown creased her brow. "What can I help you with, officers?"

Angel glanced at the receptionist, as well as a woman getting a haircut at a station nearby. "It might be best if we talk in your office, Ms. Lopez."

Alarm flashed in Wanda's dark brown eyes for a moment, then she offered a hint of smile that was obviously forced. Nothing moved on her face except her lips. "Certainly. Right this way."

Sarah gave a nod to Angel to let her know she could take the lead, then fell in step slightly behind her partner. They entered a room big enough for a medium-sized desk, two short filing cabinets with bottles of beauty items filling the surfaces, and a single chair behind the desk. There were a couple of rolling stools, like the ones most often seen in doctors' offices, stacked on atop the other in a corner to the right of the desk. Wanda quickly unstacked them and rolled them forward. "Sorry I don't have any chairs."

"This will work." Angel hooked one of the stools with her foot and pulled it over.

"I'm okay standing," Sarah said.

Wanda nodded and sat in her office chair. She didn't even ask the question again. The one she'd greeted them with in the reception area. It was almost as if she knew.

"We need to talk about Fred Cummings," Angel said.

"I wondered how long it would take."

"How long for what?"

"To find out about me. Us." Wanda put a ruby-red fingernail against the corner of one eye, as if pressing back a tear.

"You were close?"

Wanda waited a beat as a few tears breached the dam; her efforts to hold back her grief failing. "I couldn't believe the news when I saw it on television."

"Why didn't you come forward?"

She wiped the dampness from her cheek and held up her left hand, a wide gold band flashing in the light. "My husband. He doesn't know. And I need to keep it that way."

"That might not be possible," Sarah offered from her vantage point.

"If he finds out, it could be bad for me."

"Dangerous?" Angel asked.

Wanda nodded. "Francisco … he's … not a nice man."

Sarah knew what the woman meant. She'd seen too many not-nice-men in her career and the women they brutalized. "We'll do our best to—"

A loud pounding on the office door interrupted her "Miss Wanda. You got to come see the news. There's a riot and a cop just got shot."

"What the—" Before Sarah could finish, her phone erupted with the screech of an alarm, much like the ones for Amber alerts. But this one was a Blue Alert. From the department. A second later the same screech sounded from Angel's phone.

Sarah looked at Wanda. "We gotta go." She dropped a business card on the desk. "We'll be back in touch. But call me if you need help before that."

~*~

The surgery waiting area was packed. Officers in blue paced the corridor just outside the entrance. Nobody spoke as Sarah passed them. They didn't have to. The message rang clearly in the silence. She nodded a silent greeting to Doug and then hurried into the large room, spotting McGregor off to the left with Burt and Simms. There was no sign of Angel or Ryan. When the crowd shifted, she saw Lieutenant Webb.

In a far corner, a television was fastened to the wall and an image of the Channel Eight reporter, Bianca Gomez, standing in front of the storefront that had broken windows. Someone had muted the sound so it appeared that she was pantomiming the news. During the frantic drive from the salon, Sarah had listened to reports on a radio news station but information had been sketchy. The reporter had simply said that a police officer had been in the process of clearing looters from an appliance store and had been shot. Name being withheld … blah blah blah. She'd switched off the radio and concentrated on getting to Presbyterian Hospital in one piece.

Sarah strode quickly to McGregor. Trepidation made her hesitate, but the question had to be asked. "Who?"

McGregor leveled his gaze at her. "Ryan."

"Oh, no." She hesitated again. The next questions were harder still. "Is he …? How bad?"

"Caught one in the gut. Tore him up big time. The docs are trying to put his insides back together."

"Fuck."

McGregor pulled a handkerchief out of his pocket and mopped the moisture from his face. "I'll allow you that one."

Sarah shuddered. She didn't know what else to say. What could she? They were both in their own private hell with painful memories of other days. Other hospitals. Other officers injured or killed. She put her hands deep in the pockets of her jeans and turned away. Partly to hide the tears that threatened, but partly to avoid the anguish she saw on McGregor's face.

Looking at the television, she watched the silent news for a few moments before turning back to her boss. "What the hell was he doing out there?"

McGregor gave a slight nod toward Webb. "He said Ryan was going to meet with a CI on a drug case. Apparently when the violence and looting started, it gained momentum. People took to the streets smashing windows to grab whatever. Ryan was just in the wrong place at the wrong time."

Another painful silence stretched between them, then Sarah asked, "What are his chances?"

McGregor shrugged. "Docs wouldn't venture a guess."

Sarah just stared at him for a moment. "Double fuck."

"I'll give you those, too."

"I don't have to drop money in your swear jar?"

He shook his head and gave her a weak smile.

Weak smile? Weak joke? Anything to release some of the tension that swirled around the room like smoke from a fire, feeding into everyone's anxiety.

Angel burst into the room. Snarls of heavy traffic had delayed her, and she'd been frantic on the drive to the hospital. She hadn't even bothered trying to listen to news reports. Her mind had taken her back to a warehouse with men down. One of them Chad. She didn't want to go there. She didn't want to remember, but her mind had other plans. Who was it this time?

Once she spotted McGregor, she went straight to him, her eyes asking what her lips couldn't.

"It's Ryan," he said, his blue mask almost smothering the words.

At first, Angel didn't comprehend. She didn't want to comprehend. Emotions churned, threatening to overflow, and she clamped her teeth tight to hold them in, looking at McGregor, but not seeing him. Hoping she hadn't heard him right. Those stupid medical masks distorted so much. Still, his eyes had told it all.

There was a light touch on her arm, and she turned slightly to see Sarah. Angel twisted away, not sure if she wanted any support from her partner. She felt so disconnected from Sarah. From the department. From everyone in this room. There were no other black faces among the people gathered here. Angel had no idea why that mattered so much. This wasn't her only time to be in a crowd where nobody else looked like her, but lately things had started mattering that hadn't for a long, long time.

"Angel. Come and sit down."

Relinquishing resistance, Angel let Sarah pull her to an empty chair where she sat rigid, not saying a word; only half aware that her partner had removed the "do-not-sit here" sign for social distancing and sat next to her. Sarah didn't speak, either. She just rested a hand on Angel's arm.

A woman with short-cropped silver hair in a ring of curls around a plump face marched into the room, her medical mask flapping because it wasn't secure over one ear. She was trying to get it in place as she hurried. The woman's entrance broke the trance that Angel had been in. She turned to Sarah and whispered, "You know who that is?"

"No. You?"

"Maybe Ryan's mother."

"You never met her?"

Angel shook her head and watched as the woman stood very still for a moment, bright blue eyes above her mask flicking from face to face, before she moved toward McGregor. *Funny, I didn't even know Ryan had a mother.* Then the absurdity of that thought hit Angel. Of course, everybody has a mother. People aren't dropped to the Earth in pods from some other planet. The fact that Ryan hadn't spoken about his mother could be because the conversations Angel had with Ryan had seldom gone in the direction of parents. She preferred not to talk about hers with him, so he'd obviously taken a step back from the topic with her.

The whispered exchange between the woman and McGregor lasted a few more minutes, culminating in the Lieu giving her shoulder a quick squeeze. Neither of them looked comfortable with the gesture, both standing awkwardly for another few seconds. Then the woman straightened and moved her mask to wipe a tear from a cheek already lined with smears of makeup. She looked around the room, then turned and walked toward Angel and Sarah.

For a moment Angel panicked, wondering if the woman was just coming because there was an empty seat in this row. Or was she purposely heading toward Angel? Did McGregor tell the woman about her relationship with Ryan? Could that possibly be bothering her?

"May I?" The woman pointed to the empty seat one over on the other side of Angel.

Angel nodded, and the woman eased down with a sigh before facing Angel. "Lieutenant McGregor told me who you are." A pause, then, "I'm Marie O'Donnell. Ryan's mother."

Nerves jangling, Angel didn't know what to say, so she elected to say nothing. If Marie found that rude, she gave no indication.

"Ryan told us about you. Me and my husband." She glanced off for a beat, then faced Angel again. "I would've preferred our first meeting to have been over dinner. But ..." The rest was lost in a shrug.

There was a real warmth in Marie's words that eased the frozen part of Angel's core. That place that had turned to ice the moment she first heard about the shooting. In some ways it was good to have that cold dark center warm up a bit. But she was afraid to let it defrost entirely. That icicle deep inside was the only thing holding her upright.

Still afraid to speak. To move. To do anything that would cause her to break. Angel gave Marie a wan smile that she hoped the woman could sense despite the mask.

"We don't have to talk." Marie reached over to pat Angel on the knee. "We can just sit here and wait together."

Those words did come dangerously close to destroying Angel's composure. She clenched her teeth tight to keep words, emotions, from spilling out and turned her face away; just concentrating on breathing the way Randy taught her at the dojo. In: one two three four five. Out: one two three four five.

All pretense of relaxing disappeared when a woman in scrubs walked briskly into the room. Streaks of red on her shirt and pants were not a planned decoration, and they were a clear indication that this was a surgeon. The doctor looked around at the assembled crowd. "O'Donnell family?"

Angel started to step forward but held back when Marie stood. "I'm his mother."

"I'm Dr. Elizabeth Fielder. May we speak in private?"

McGregor moved a little closer. "We're family, too."

"Ah …" The doctor glanced again at the cluster of anxious people in the room, then looked to Marie, who gave a slight nod.

Then, as if to reinforce her permission, Marie said, "Family takes many forms."

"There are rules."

"I know," Marie said. "If I have to sign something, I will."

The surgeon took one more look around the small group, then turned back to Marie. "No need. Your son is out of surgery. We removed the bullets. Two of them. One in the spleen, taking out part of his liver while it bounced around in there. The other tearing up his colon. All has been repaired. He's in ICU and still in critical condition."

"He made it through. Thank God," Angel murmured even though it had been a long time since she'd thanked God for anything.

"What are his chances?" McGregor asked the question since Marie seemed too stunned to speak.

"No predictions at the moment," Dr. Fielder said. "It's so often used it could be a cliché. But the next twenty-four hours are crucial."

Nobody spoke. It was as if words couldn't be found.

The doctor glanced around again. "Sorry folks, but only one person can go in right now. And only for five minutes."

Marie turned to Angel, a question in her eyes that Angel hadn't expected. Really? She would let Angel go first? After just a brief consideration, Angel shook her head. "You go," she said. "I've got work to do."

Without a word to anyone, not even Sarah or McGregor, Angel rushed out of the room. She didn't wait for an elevator, instead racing down the stairs and through the lobby.

Outside, she tore off her mask and found a secluded corner of the hospital complex. There she leaned against the wall, letting her emotions tumble out in a flood of tears and a stream of cussing that would have made her partner proud. Then, after giving herself fifteen minutes to cry and rage, she found a tissue in her pocket, one of the many she'd grabbed in the hospital waiting room, and mopped her face. She took another minute to focus again on breathing deeply and rhythmically until she was calm enough to drive.

She hadn't been lying when she'd said she had work to do.

She was going to find the bastard who'd shot Ryan.

CHAPTER FOURTEEN

Saturday, July 4 - Morning

Quite often, Angel had this holiday off and she'd be with her family, having the traditional Fourth of July celebration that went far beyond burgers and dogs on the grill. There'd be the ribs her father had smoked overnight, along with greens, corn on the cob, and watermelon. Then her mother would bring out the desserts, including her infamous coconut cream pie. After they were sufficiently stuffed, they'd all pile into the old station wagon, just like when she and LaVon were kids, and drive to Fair Park to watch the fireworks.

Today, however, was anything but traditional. No fireworks at the park and concerns about gatherings, even with family, had skewered a lot of holiday plans. *Damn pandemic!*

Last night, after managing to drive home from the hospital despite the swirling emotions and tears that came and went like the periodic gully washers that would spring up unexpectedly and flood the streets, Angel had started thinking about what dregs of humanity might have been connected with that band of looters.

And who might know some of those dregs.

There was no doubt that it would be people on the fringes, with perhaps one foot in regular society and the other dipping into nefarious activities. Folks who were firmly in the camp of the law-abiding citizens would join peaceful protests, and even scream until their lungs were about to burst, but most of them held back from crossing the line into breaking the law. But other folks weren't so reticent.

Those considerations took Angel down a path to her young adult days. The days when her high school boyfriend, Bobby, had been involved with drugs. It had started simple. Just a toe into the deep water. Just smoking weed now and then, but sadly for her, and for him, that experimenting had evolved into hardcore drug use. After it became clear that he was headed for serious trouble, she'd begged him multiple times to go to rehab, but he'd refused. Finally, she'd given him an ultimatum.

He'd made the wrong choice.

Tyrell, one of their mutual high school acquaintances, had also gotten caught up in the drug scene even though he'd not gone as far down as Bobby had. Tyrell had avoided becoming a broken-down addict, but for a while had flashed the money and fancy clothes of a fairly successful dealer and everyone knew he'd moved up to being a mid-level distributor. That was before the Dallas gang unit had cleaned up his neighborhood, and he got out of the gang. He'd been one of the lucky ones who was able to walk away instead of having to be carried away.

Angel hadn't stayed in close contact with Tyrell after she'd levered her boyfriend out of her life. But she'd seen Tyrell at the funeral of Stacy, a mutual friend who'd been killed in a robbery at a jewelry store a few years after college graduation. At the funeral, Tyrell had accused Angel of being an Oreo because she'd recently joined the police force, something many folks in Stacy's neighborhood found traitorous. When Tyrell spoke up so rudely during what was supposed to be a solemn occasion, Angel had instinctively slapped him, and that was the last she had seen of him.

What is old Tyrell doing now?

Last night Angel had opened her laptop and started a search for Tyrell Henderson, surprised when she found him pretty quickly on Facebook. Didn't he worry about the former gang leaders finding him? Or maybe there was a whole new set of gangsters in charge who didn't even know his name. Still. Pretty ballsy to be on social media in her opinion.

There wasn't an address listed on his profile, just a notation that he lived in Dallas, and Angel figured that his parents probably still lived in the old home on Cole Street. And maybe Tyrell would gather with his folks for the holiday the way they'd all done as kids. She could've gone to the station last night to do a more in-depth search for him and his family, but after she'd gotten home, she'd downed a few too many glasses of wine to get behind the wheel of a car again.

So here she was now, parked a few doors down from the white frame house she remembered from the time she'd come here as a belligerent sixteen-year-old trying to convince Tyrell to stop selling drugs to her boyfriend. *Oh, how naive I was back then.*

Despite the restrictions of the pandemic, there were quite a few cars parked in front of the house, and Angel had to go down half of the block to find a space to pull in. She stepped into the summer heat that immediately brought perspiration to her face. She'd dressed in shorts and a loose tee, figuring that was better than looking all professional and cop-like, but hot air, barely moving in a light breeze, still assaulted her. She was glad she didn't have to walk much further.

Instead of going to the front door like a polite visitor would, Angel opted for following the uneven walkway to the gate leading to the backyard. She put on a mask, lifted the hatch of the gate made from cyclone fencing, and walked around the corner of the house to the spacious backyard. Three picnic tables were set up. One loaded with food. One loaded with adults visiting, playing cards or dominos, and drinking beer, some wearing masks, others not. At the third table, she saw kids land briefly for a sip of soda or water before flitting away to continue games of run and chase.

One of the men glanced up as Angel came further into the yard. He leaned forward and spoke to the man across from him, who turned in Angel's direction. She immediately recognized Tyrell, who hadn't changed much in the years since they last seen each other. Same close-cropped hair with designs sculpted in. Thin, angular face. Small diamonds in each earlobe and a quizzical frown.

He obviously didn't have the same instant recognition. He stood and walked toward her with a pleasant but impersonal expression. "Hello. Are you—" Then it must have registered. "Angel? What the fuck? What are you doing here? You're the last person I expected to see today."

"Yeah. I know our friendship has been strained."

"Strained? That's one word you could use."

"We need to talk. I was hoping we could meet for coffee or for a drink."

"You do know I'm married, right?"

She gave a slight shake of her head. "It's not a date. But you can bring your wife along if you'd like. Does she know about your sordid past?"

Tyrell didn't say anything, and Angel could almost feel the chill surround him.

"I know all about it. I knew back then, and I still have access to your records."

"I was a minor. Records are sealed."

Angel smiled. "I'm still with the cops."

"Is this some kind of a blackmail attempt?"

"Not at all, Tyrell." Angel softened her tone and her stance. "Please. I just need your help."

He chuckled. "That's a good one."

Angel sighed. "Listen. Could we just cut through all this crap?"

He didn't respond and Angel sighed again, then said, "You hear about that officer who was shot?"

Tyrell nodded but remained silent.

"The looting that was going on. A lot of it could be gang members out there. I've seen the videos. You could help identify them."

Tyrell glanced toward the table, some of the folks clearly interested in what was going on. "Okay. Okay. But not here. Not now."

"Fine. Give me your number." She opened her phone and entered the information as he gave it to her.

Before Angel could turn to leave, a plump woman she recognized as Tyrell's mother approached them with a wary smile. "Tyrell, who is …" The question trailed off as the smile widened. "Angel. What a nice surprise."

"She was just leaving, Ma."

"Nonsense. Stay and eat with us. Unless you need to get back to your family?"

It was tempting to say yes. To stay. To be normal for a

little while. But nothing was normal right now. There was no way she could be pleasant. Smile and engage in small talk. No way she could relax and join a joyous celebration of a special holiday. Especially not with Tyrell shooting daggers at her.

"Thanks for the invite, Mrs. Henderson," Angel said, hoping the pleasant tone of her response didn't sound too forced. "But I really do need to go."

"Of course. But you come back sometime, you hear?"

Angel knew the woman meant it. It wasn't just a polite ending of the conversation that some people used. The Henderson home had always been wide open when they were all in school together. Her and Stacy and Bobby and Tyrell. They'd crash there and have bread buttered and grilled in the waffle iron, along with sodas. Mrs. Henderson always made sure there were plenty of sodas on hand.

But that was all before Bobby and Tyrell got mixed up with drugs.

Angel smiled at Mrs. Henderson. "Thanks. Maybe I will."

Back at her house, Angel stripped out of her sweaty clothes, ready to take her second shower of the day, but before she stepped into the bathroom, her phone pinged, signaling a text. She glanced at the screen to see the message was from LaVon: *Where are you?*

at home

Are you coming? He was probably at their parents' home already. There was a scaled-down version of the holiday gathering planned.

no

Why not?
just can't. I'll explain later.

Angel waited to see if LaVon would text again, but her phone remained silent. Apparently, he accepted her lack of reasons and decided to just leave it.

After a quick shower Angel dressed in clothes more appropriate for the hospital and headed in that direction.

A few officers in uniform stood like guards outside the entrance to the ICU waiting area. Angel gave them a nod and hurried past. The waiting area was almost empty, per the directive that most of the people leave after the first crisis yesterday. Lieutenant Webb sat in the far corner, and Marie was in a seat in the middle of the room. Angel sat down next to Marie. The normal polite pleasantries didn't seem to be in order, so Angel simply asked, "How is he?"

"No change yet." The other woman gave a slight shake of her head. "There's some concern because Ryan hasn't roused from the anesthetic. But the doctor said that happens sometimes after the body's been through so much trauma. Like it doesn't want to become aware of the pain. And I want to believe her …"

Marie didn't finish her thought, and Angel took her hand in a gentle squeeze. They sat there for a while in silence. There wasn't really anything that could be said that could ease the concern for either one of them. Then a soft alarm sounded on Mrs. O'Donnell's phone. "I have it set to let me know when it's time to go see him," she said after silencing the noise.

Angel removed her hand that had been clutching the

older woman's. "Okay. Go ahead."

Maria shook her head. "No. You go."

Angel drew in a breath. "Really?"

"Yes. Really."

"Thank you," Angel whispered as she stood.

Shock washed over Angel after she stepped into the ICU room and saw Ryan looking like a deflated life-sized doll sprawled on the bed. His normally ruddy face was almost as white as the sheet pulled up to his waist, and his chest moved so imperceptibly under the hospital gown, he might not have been breathing at all. That thought scared the shit out of her, and she moved quickly but quietly to the bed. She took his hand in hers, the one that wasn't taped up with tubes that were sending fluids into his body. It was so cold it was like picking up ice. She recognized the cannula in his nose, having learned what that was when her mother was so terribly sick in the hospital several years ago. That tube was giving Ryan's body much-needed oxygen; not just for breathing but also for healing. She squeezed his hand, then flinched when an alarm started screaming from the monitor by his bed. Before the realization of what was happening hit, a nurse ran into the room. Then a voice cried out from overhead speakers. "Code Blue! Code Blue! ICU. Room 214."

Almost immediately, a horde of medical staff raced into the room, pushing a cart that had a squeaking wheel ahead of them. Angel didn't know why that sound registered amidst all the excited exchanges between nurses and techs and the doctor, but it did. *Why didn't someone oil that damn wheel?*

Then she felt a large hand grasp her arm as she was pulled out of the room. She heard that same someone speak, a low male voice, "You need to let us work, ma'am."

She was deposited in the hall and the nurse —Angel

assumed he was a nurse, rushed back into the ICU room.

She stood rooted to the gray tile. Silent. Helpless. Terrified.

On one level it looked like pandemonium in the room, but Angel was aware that it was well-practiced pandemonium. Something this team was trained for. Practiced. They knew how to get a patient to breathe again. Regulate a heartbeat. Do whatever was necessary to pull Ryan out of the crisis. They *would* pull Ryan out of this crisis.

A tsunami of helplessness threatened to drop Angel to the floor, and she backed up to lean against the wall and steady herself. Then she heard rapid footsteps approaching, and she turned to see Marie, a stricken look on the woman's face. "Oh, my God." Marie's voice was distorted with panic. "I heard ... that ... the announcement. I wasn't sure ... was it his ..."

Angel put an arm around the woman as much to steady herself as Marie. "It's going to be okay." That was the only thing Angel could think of to say, even though she was having a hard time believing it.

After twenty more minutes that felt like hours, the noise and commotion in the room started to ease. Staff members exited, once more pushing the cart ahead of them. Even though they were walking more slowly, the wheel still squeaked. For a moment, Angel had the wild thought that she should tell them how well WD40 works on stiff wheels.

Absurd thought in the midst of the frightening moments.

Ryan's primary nurse stayed to put a clean, smooth top sheet over Ryan, and she folded it lightly across his upper chest.

After checking a few things and speaking quietly to the nurse, the doctor stepped out and approached Marie and Angel. "He's okay for now." Dr Fielder gestured for the women to pull up their masks.

Angel complied, forgetting that she'd pulled it down in the commotion. But when the alarm started shrieking, she hadn't been able to breathe. She'd needed air.

When the women had their masks in place, Dr. Fielder continued. "I'll be honest. Mr. O'Donnell is still not out of the woods. But he's strong. He made it through this crisis, so I am guardedly optimistic for what's ahead. But, a note of caution. Anything could happen, and I'm not definitely saying that he's going to pull through."

That was the most that the doctor had said to either of them since day one, and Angel was a little surprised. She remembered the doctors always speaking in short sentences. Clipped tones. Not revealing much when her mother was so seriously ill. This level of openness and empathy was refreshing.

Angel only wished she could find it hopeful.

CHAPTER FIFTEEN

Monday, July 6 - Morning

Sarah always preferred to drive when going to an interview, either her own car alone or one from the station with someone riding shotgun. For the past few years, Angel hadn't objected to being the passenger. Today, sitting in that seat while Burt drove down Central Expressway felt wrong. So did doing the job without Angel. So did doing the job while Ryan was still in the hospital, fighting to live.

"You want to take the lead with this douchebag?" Burt asked, not taking his eyes from the road.

Sarah rearranged her thoughts. "Sure. I like hammering a douchebag."

The douchebag in question was Wanda's husband Francisco Lopez, and Sarah and Burt were on their way to talk to him at his construction business on the south side of Dallas. During the background check on him, they'd discovered he owned a Smith & Wesson .38 pistol. And, if he knew about his wife messing around, well ... Sarah had a good feeling about him as a possible for the murder of Cummings. What she didn't have a good feeling about was Ryan. Made it hard to stay focused as much as she tried. She sighed. "This feels almost traitorous."

"What?"

"Going out like this with Ryan so critical." She shrugged. "Acting like everything's normal when it isn't."

Burt didn't say anything, and Sarah sighed again, then looked out the side window at all the buildings flying by in a blur of grays and whites and sepia. "I keep thinking we should be at the hospital. Offering support to his mother. And Angel. God, she must be having an awful time of it."

"I know." Burt checked his side view mirror and signaled for a lane change. They were on Central Expressway, making pretty good time toward Lopez Construction.

When Burt pulled into the drive leading toward the office of the construction company, he picked up the conversational thread as if fifteen minutes or so hadn't elapsed. "I'm not going to use the old standard 'this is what Ryan and Angel would want us to do.' That might be true, but it's also a crap platitude that does nothing to make us feel any better. But bottom line? We've got a job to do."

"Another crap platitude."

"Yeah, but true." He gave her a minute, then asked, "Are you ready?"

"Sure. Let's go see if we can catch a bad guy."

After Burt pulled in front of the building that looked like it could house offices, Sarah got out and stretched, looking over at a larger metal building with a large dock. Bay doors were open above the dock, and two men were carrying long planks of lumber out and loading them onto a heavy-duty pickup truck.

The detectives walked over and Sarah called out, "Mr. Lopez?"

One of the men removed a ball cap that had seen better days and wiped a hand across the sweat on his face. "Who's asking?"

"Dallas PD," Burt said. "Can you come down here?"

The man jumped, landing easily on the dirt in front of the dock. He was tall and heavy, most of that weight in muscle. "What's this about?"

Sarah nodded to the office building. "Could we talk inside where the sun isn't roasting us?"

"I got work to do." Lopez jerked his thumb toward the other man who was still on the dock, leaning against the doorframe. "He doesn't work well alone."

"Then he won't work with you down here," Burt said, keeping his tone moderate. "We only need a few minutes."

Lopez seemed more willing to comply with Burt's request. "Be back in five," he said to the man on the dock. "Don't disappear." Then he turned and led the way to the office.

Stepping in, Sarah took note of the cluttered desk, the lack of any seating other than the metal chair behind the desk, and the refreshing coolness of the interior. She and Burt put on their masks, but Lopez didn't. He also didn't go to the chair. He leaned a hip on the corner of the desk, folded his arms across his chest, and waited.

"Do you know Fred Cummings?" Sarah asked.

"You mean the guy who was bonking my wife? That's what I know about him."

"How angry were you that he was, as you put it, 'bonking your wife'?"

That question was met with a cold stare.

"Cummings was killed last Tuesday." Burt seemed to throw that out as a casual comment, but Sarah noted a flicker at the corner of Lopez's eye and a tightening of his jaw.

Silence again for a long, tense moment, then Lopez said, "Is there a reason you're jacking me up about this?"

Sarah gave him her most ingratiating smile. "Well, Mr. Lopez. We've been told that it doesn't take much to stir your anger. Maybe get riled up enough to kill someone if you thought the reason was good enough."

Lopez didn't respond, just pulled his arms more firmly across his body. Sarah didn't know if the body language meant he was holding something in or it was a protective measure.

"If you have an alibi for last Tuesday night," Burt said. "we'll be happy to go hassle somebody else."

"Let's see." Lopez loosened one arm and scratched his head as if he could shake information loose by that gesture. "I had a few brewskis with my compadres. Then I went home. Had a few brewskis with my wife. And just for the record we went to bed together. I did her. Then we both went to sleep."

"Did her?" Sarah blurted.

"Yeah. You know." Lopez moved his hips in a humping motion.

"You son of a bitch." Sarah made a move toward Lopez, ready to deck the bastard, but Burt grabbed her arm in a firm grip to hold her back.

"Leave it, Sarah." Burt said, his voice leaving no room for argument.

Sarah took a deep breath to still her pounding heart and bit her lip until she tasted blood. God, how she wanted to beat this guy to a pulp, but as pleasurable as it would be to take her frustration out on an asshole, that would not further their cause here.

"Mr. Lopez," Burt said in that same conciliatory tone he'd

used before. "My apologies for my partner. We're all pretty strung out about the police officer who was shot. I'm sure you're aware and can understand."

The man gave a brief nod. "Okay. Just keep that *punta* under control."

Punta? *Really? Does this guy have no sense at all of what it means to insult a police officer?* It was all Sarah could do to resist decking Lopez and dragging his ass to jail, and again Burt must've sensed her anger building. He put a restraining hand on her shoulder and quickly asked Lopez, "Do you own a pistol?"

After a moment's hesitation, Lopez said, "I did. Don't have it anymore."

"What happened to it?" Burt asked.

"Stolen." The response came in a quick rush.

"From here?"

"No. Out of my truck."

"Did someone break into your truck?"

Lopez shook his head. "Couple'a weeks ago, I left it unlocked when I ran into Lowe's."

"Not a wise move," Burt said.

"Didn't mean to. Just one of those things."

"When did you notice the gun was gone?"

"That same day. Was going to bring it in here to lock it up. But it was gone."

There was something about the way Lopez was answering these last few questions that raised a little red flag for Sarah. He was so smooth and quick to respond, yet his demeanor was anything but smooth. His eyes shifted nervously from her to Burt, as if trying to assess whether they were buying his story. And a thin sheen of perspiration had popped out along his hairline. Clearly, he was not as comfortable as he was trying to sound.

Sarah was now calm enough to speak in a civil tone. "Did you report it?"

Lopez shook his head.

"Why not?"

A shrug this time. "Work was busy. Forgot about the gun."

Sarah sighed deeply. "You should still report it."

"Why?" Now his voice was tinged with a touch of humor and he'd relaxed his defiant stance. "You officers know. Right?"

"There are protocols, Mr. Lopez," Burt put in before Sarah could erupt again. "Just call it in and file an official report. You do have the serial number, right? Conscientious gun owner that you are."

Lopez obviously missed the sarcasm in Burt's tone. "How can I give the serial number if I don't have the gun?"

Burt gave a slight shake of his head. "We need names and contact info for your drinking buddies."

"Only got one phone number."

"That'll do." Burt pointed to a pad of sticky notes on the desk. "Write it down. Full name of your friend."

Lopez scribbled on the paper, then handed it over to Burt. "You done with me now?"

Burt nodded. "We'll be in touch if we have more questions."

Outside, Sarah watched Lopez swagger back to the loading dock. "He's not one of my favorite people."

"You made that abundantly clear in there." Burt offered a little chuckle.

"Yeah. But you got to admit he's a real dick."

"He is that."

After they got in the car and Burt was pulling away from the business, he asked, "What did you think of his story about the gun?"

Sarah laughed. "It was great. He could write fiction."

Burt nodded. "It's a shame we don't have the gun for a ballistics test. Or the serial number to trace it."

"Yeah. If he's our guy, we'll just have to come at him with a new angle. He seems to be a pressure cooker kind of guy. If the alibi doesn't pan out, we can bring him in for a formal interview. Maybe push until he blows and confesses."

Now Burt laughed. "Good strategy, but I'm not sure I'd want to be in the same room when you crank up the steam."

"Oh, come on, Burt. It'll be fun."

They were quiet for a few minutes while Burt maneuvered his way into traffic on Central Expressway. Then he asked, "If he wasn't with his wife after leaving the bar, you think she'd lie for him?"

"Don't know." She thought for a moment. "She does hate him. I could see that last night. But I also saw fear. Those emotions push people in different directions."

"It's almost lunch time," Burt said. "You want to stop for a burger someplace and then call the alibi witness?"

"Sure. I'll message Chang. See if she can dig up any info on Lopez's friend."

"Got a preference on lunch? Simms always makes me go to Micky Ds."

"Oh, please no. Let's go to Keller's. It's got the best burger I've tasted in a while."

Sarah was mopping the last of the catsup from the paper with the last fry that had come with her basket when her phone buzzed with a message. She wiped grease and tomato off her fingers and opened the text. It was from Chang:

Here's the skinny on your guy. He's a roustabout. Works for Shell on the Gulf. Off right now because of an injury, but not in hospital. One arrest for drunk driving & resisting. Back in 01. Nothing since. Lives at the Coronado Apartments in Lakewood. 7414 E Grand Ave.

Sarah quickly typed back a "thanks," then looked over at Burt. "Got an address for Ted Milan. Over in Lakewood. Want to call first or just show up? He should be home. He's off work with some kind of injury."

"Let me just wash up first."

A smile tugged at Sarah's lips. Maybe Burt's daughter was right about him being a dinosaur. He was just old school gentleman enough to avoid saying he had to go take a piss. Speaking of which. She stood and bussed their table and when Burt came back, she said, "My turn. Meet you out at the car."

Ted Milan was a burly man with a face turned to leather, a testament to the years spent working outdoors in sun and wind. He had come to the door on crutches, his injury apparent by the boot cast on his left leg.

"Help you?" he asked. "I'm guessing you're not from the physical therapy place."

Sarah shook her head and introduced herself and Burt, finishing by saying they just had a couple of questions. She nodded to the crutches and his injured leg. "Would you be more comfortable inside?"

He shrugged as much as the crutches would allow. "Is it going to take long? I am expecting someone for therapy."

"We'll be brief. But it would be nice to step out of this

blazing afternoon sun."

"Okay. Whatever." Ted backed up a couple of paces. "Come on in."

They waited until Ted closed the door, then turned to lead them into a sparsely furnished living room that had a La-Z-Boy recliner facing a large screen television and a sofa, separated from the chair by a table that held a bottle of water plus a couple of vials of pills. Magazines were stacked on a bottom shelf. Ted sank into the chair and dropped the crutches on the floor next to him. "Okay officers, what's this about?"

"Are you friends with Francisco Lopez?" Sarah asked, sitting on the edge of the sofa to face him.

"Sort of. More like drinking buddies if we happen to meet up at the same club."

"Did you happen to meet up with him last Wednesday? First of July?"

"Is he in some kind of trouble?"

"We're just trying to clarify some things in a case we're working."

"Does it have anything to do with that dude who was shot that night that you're asking me about?"

Sarah gave him a level gaze. "We're not authorized to give out details about an ongoing investigation."

Ted actually laughed at that. "Nice one, lady." He paused for a few moments then said, "Okay. Yes. I did see Lopez at The Old Crow. We had a few drinks. Talked a bit about the sorry baseball season. As in the lack of a baseball season. My injury and me being off work."

"How long were the two of you swapping stories?" Burt asked.

Ted shrugged. "Don't think either one of us paid attention

to the time. We were just palling around, you know? Drinking and talking."

"So, you can't say for sure what time he left the bar." Burt posed that as a statement, not a question.

"Well … Actually, it might have been around ten. I think the news popped up on the TV in the bar right about the time he was leaving."

"Your doc okay with you drinking while taking these?" Burt walked over and picked up the bottle of pills.

"I don't tell him. But if you gotta know, I don't take the pills if I'm going to the bar."

"Drive yourself?"

"Yeah. Right foot works just fine." Ted wiggled his ankle as if to prove his point.

Burt put the pills back down. "You be careful out there. Would hate to have to pull you out of a wreck."

That comment seemed to dampen Ted's friendly mood. He crossed his arms over his chest. "We done here?"

"That's all we need for now." Sarah stood. "If we have any more questions we'll be in touch."

Ted started to get up and Sarah motioned for him to stay seated. "Don't bother. You want us to lock the door?"

"No. Somebody from physical therapy is supposed to be here anytime. Save me the trouble of getting back up again."

"What happened?" Burt nodded to the cast.

"Slipped on an oil slick." Milan gave self-deprecating chuckle. "Would you believe it? A goddamn oil slick on an oil rig."

"Guess it's good you can laugh about it," Burt said.

"Better than crying. Real men don't cry."

"Don't count on it," Burt said.

Sarah snapped her seatbelt in place as Burt cranked the

engine and turned the AC to high. "Well, one half of the alibi pans out. We'll have to see what the wife has to say."

"You want to go check that out now?"

Sarah shook her head. "Need to type up the reports on these interviews. Then I'll call Wanda to see when her husband came home that night."

CHAPTER SIXTEEN

Monday, July 6 - Late afternoon

S arah didn't see Angel at her desk and wondered briefly where she might be. She hadn't seen her partner since yesterday, but maybe it was good that Angel was having some time away. Remembering how awful it was when John died, Sarah had no delusions about what her partner might be going through with Ryan hovering somewhere between life and death.

She shrugged out of her jacket and sat at her desk, then opened her phone to call the beauty shop. The girl who answered said that Wanda had left for the day and gone home. Since she sure didn't want to cause any trouble for Wanda at her house, Sarah decided that verifying that end of the husband's alibi could wait until morning. So, after writing up reports from the day's interviews and emailing them to McGregor, Sarah decided to head out a little early herself. She could swing by the hospital to check on Ryan.

Half expecting to see Angel in the ICU waiting room, Sarah was surprised that the only person there was Ryan's mother. She went over and sat down next to Marie. "How's he doing?"

"No change." Marie shook her head. "He still hasn't regained consciousness."

There wasn't anything that Sarah could say to that. This wasn't the time for platitudes or false hope, so she just patted Marie's arm and sat there in silence. A few minutes later, she felt the vibration of her phone in her jacket pocket and stood up. "Sorry, I've got to take a call. I'll be back in a few minutes."

Marie nodded and Sarah went out to the hallway. The call was from LaVon. "Hey, girl. You up for some company tonight?"

"I take it you're not still stuck in L.A.?"

"Very shrewd detecting, Detective."

Sarah chuckled. LaVon had been stranded in California for two weeks following the cancellation of a law conference where he'd been on the slate of speakers. Since air travel had virtually come to a screeching halt in the year of the pandemic, she realized it was somewhat of a miracle that he'd been able to get on a plane. "A flight must have come up quickly. Yesterday it sounded like you were stuck there forever."

"My mama always says I'm one lucky dude."

"Your mother does not say dude."

"Okay. You caught me out. So how about tonight?"

The offer was tempting. Very tempting, but Sarah hesitated. "I'm here at the hospital and Ryan's mother is all alone. I think I'll stay with her for a while."

"There's always later."

Later would be perfect. "My place about eight?"

Sarah stayed at the hospital for another hour, declining the offer from Marie that she could see Ryan for the next five-minute visit opportunity. Sarah didn't need to see another colleague fighting for his life. She'd wait and see Ryan when he woke up. When he could talk about what happened. "I hate to leave you alone," she said after a while, "but I need to get home."

"It's okay," Marie said. "My husband is here. He just went to the hotel for a rest after the long drive here. He'll come back in a little while and bring some dinner."

Snuggled against LaVon on the sofa, Sarah should've felt relaxed. Earlier, they'd had dinner, Chinese take-out that LaVon had brought, and dessert afterward in her bedroom. Now they had popcorn for actual dessert and were watching "The Good Fight" on TV. It was one of his favorites. He often said how much he wished he could get away with half the shit that Diane Lockhart pulled, and Sarah reminded him that it was fiction. Lots of shit can happen in fiction that wouldn't happen in real life.

For the next fifteen minutes Sarah let the sound and images wash over her, without much really registering. Then she leaned forward and picked up the remote to mute the television.

"What the …?"

"Sorry. I just can't focus on the show."

"What's wrong with it?"

"Nothing. I really like the chutzpah that Diane has but I can't hold on to the story tonight."

"Chutzpah? That's a new word for you."

"It means the same thing as 'she's got balls.' Just a little more polite."

LaVon chuckled and reached for a handful of popcorn. "So, what's got you so unfocused tonight?"

"A lot." Sarah took a few kernels of popcorn. "Mostly, Ryan's condition. But I'm also worried about Angel. She's pulled away. Barely speaks to me."

"She's dealing. Silence is her way of handling tough stuff."

"Is that your way, too?" Sarah let the question stand there for a moment, then said. "You haven't said anything about her and Ryan. Or what she's going through."

"What's to be said? I hope he's going to be okay. That's what everybody hopes. But her stuff is her stuff."

Sarah took a moment to think about what he'd just said. It sounded so cold in one way. But then maybe it was just his logical way of compartmentalizing things in his life. And they were both adults. She grabbed more popcorn, chewed, then said, "How are your folks reacting? I'm sure they know about her and Ryan."

LaVon nodded. "Surprisingly, they're in Angel's corner. At least for now."

"Huh. That's a surprise."

There was another long pause, and LaVon fingered the remote on the cushion between them. Then Sarah said, "I wish Angel would let *me* in her corner. Between that kid getting shot. The protests. COVID. And now Ryan, she's royally pissed at the moment and taking it out on me."

When LaVon didn't respond right away, Sarah twisted to look up at him. "Hey I didn't mean that as a slam to Angel. You know that, right?"

"I know. It's a horrible time for everyone."

"Care to share your thoughts on all the horrible stuff?"

LaVon wiped his hands on a napkin. "Where do you want

me to start?"

"Wherever you want."

"Okay. But only if you're sure. We've never talked about this before."

Sarah realized he was right. They'd always avoided topics that might be sensitive for either of them. "I think we should."

"Okay." LaVon twisted the napkin for a moment, then dropped it in his lap. "I'll start with last May and what happened to George Floyd. My take is that police officer should rot in hell."

"The judicial system doesn't put people in hell."

"True. But I wish we could."

There was a vehemence in his voice, Sarah had never heard before, and she almost didn't ask the next question, but she knew she had to. "What about what's happened here closer to home?"

"Smithfield's a rookie cop. What was that? His second or third time out on the street?"

"That excuse him?"

"No. But what he did is different from what Chauvin did to George Floyd. That was so deliberate. So obviously hate-filled."

There wasn't anything Sarah could say in contradiction. LaVon was right. The killing of George Floyd was so heinous, she hadn't been able to watch more than two minutes of the video that went on for seven more minutes. She'd never seen a person being killed in such a purposeful way before, and there was no way on God's green earth to excuse that police officer. Or the ones standing around letting it happen. The whole thing disgusted her, and for a little while had even made her consider turning in her badge. She hated being associated with nasty, racist cops like Chauvin. Not that there were many in Dallas PD who were as awful as him, but even a few can be a scourge on any department.

Smithfield being living proof of that.

His training officer was Paul Degazio. A cop who'd come up through the ranks the hard way and had a family legacy of policing in the Deep South that went way back. It was more than a rumor that Degazio was a racist, and who knows what garbage he'd been feeding the rookie.

But all that aside. What mattered to her right now was how this might affect her relationship with this man sitting beside her on the sofa.

He nudged her. "Hey. Where'd you go off to?"

Stalling until she had enough courage to ask the question that was burning to be asked, Sarah ate a few kernels of popcorn and washed it down with the beer that was on the table in front of them. Then, without looking at him she took a deep breath and asked, "Where does this White officer fit in your overall view of police and systemic racism?"

She heard him take a quick intake of breath, but she still kept her eyes averted.

"Whoa, girl," he said. "You don't ask an easy question."

Now Sarah did glance over, trying to read the expression on his face. "But I really need to know. If things are going to be more than temporary between us, it's really important."

LaVon reached out and lightly rubbed his thumb across the top of Sarah's hand that was resting on her leg. He took so long to answer that she started to worry, involuntarily twisting the fabric of her shorts. He stilled the nervous movement of her fingers with his large hand.

"Okay," he finally said. "The easy answer is I don't think you're a racist. Otherwise, you wouldn't be trying so hard to make things right between you and Angel. And you certainly wouldn't be bonking a very dark Black man."

"Bonking?" Sarah asked with a slight chuckle. "That's not a word I expected to hear from the mouth of a well-respected attorney."

LaVon smiled. "I've always kind of liked that word. So much more polite than 'fucking.'"

Sarah pushed his knee with hers. "Okay, Counselor. That was a nice deflect but what else is there beyond the fact that you don't think I'm a racist?"

Before he could answer, a notice of breaking news flashed across the television screen catching Sarah's attention. "Hold that thought," she said, picking up the remote and unmuting the sound.

The image on the screen switched from Diane Lockhart kicking ass in the courtroom to Bianca Gomez of Channel Eight News. In that breathless tone that reporters had started using, she told viewers that there'd been another shooting downtown.

At the same time, Sarah's phone vibrated on the coffee table, and she reached out to grab it. "Shit!"

"What?"

Sarah held up a finger and took the call, not in the least surprised that it was McGregor. "Get downtown now," he said. "Burt's already on his way."

Briefly, she considered asking why not Angel, then thought better of it. Once more, just saying 'yes sir' was the wisest choice.

"Gotta go," she said to LaVon after ending the call.

"Not surprised. Go ahead. I'll clean up here."

"Thanks." Sarah leaned into him for a quick kiss, then hurried to her bedroom to change clothes and grab her gun. She had a feeling she was going to need it.

BRUTAL SEASON

~*~

The scene was chaotic, much like what Sarah had found the other night, with people milling around and uniformed officers doing their best to keep them back from the body. Burt was already there, standing next to the body of a young, Black woman sprawled on the pavement. When Sarah got closer, she saw that blood had pooled around the body and half of the woman's chest was a mangled mess.

"Jesus," Sarah said, leaning down to get a better look, using her phone's flashlight. "Somebody definitely wanted her dead."

"Or it could be random. Not specific."

Sarah stood and looked at Burt. "What makes you say that?"

"Witnesses say there was a guy walking around with a big gun. Spewing hate and racial slurs. Kinda like that guy in Wisconsin last year. Shot those folks during a protest."

Sarah nodded. Burt had a point. "What kind of big gun?"

"Military style. Maybe an AK47."

"This guy," Burt pointed to a tall, thin Black man wearing jeans and a tee-shirt advertising Trinity Hall standing a few yards away. "He noticed the guy with the gun. Said he looked like trouble."

"Well, he sure was trouble." Sarah gestured toward the man. "He got a name?"

"Henry Lucas."

"What's the skinny on him?"

"Student at Baylor. Came up here for the demonstration. He got some pictures of the gun-toting guy."

"That might make our job easier."

"Not necessarily. Nobody actually saw the shooter. And it might not have been the man sporting the assault weapon."

"On the other hand, it might be." Sarah gave Burt a smile, then walked over to Henry. She introduced herself and asked him how long he'd followed the guy with the gun.

"I saw him early on when folks were just starting to gather. Right away I noticed he didn't belong. Not that there aren't some White folks marching with us. Not dissing the White folks."

"That's okay. No offense taken. Other than the gun, what drew your attention to the guy?"

"An attitude. For sure he wasn't here to help get our message across. He bullied up to a couple of young teens and told them to get off the streets. Said all these marches and protests weren't right. That what we're doing isn't right. And he had this hat. Said White Lives Matter on the brim."

Oh great. Sarah sighed. "My partner said you have some pictures. Can I see them?"

"I'll pull them up." Henry activated his phone. "But the images aren't that good." He gave a self-deprecating shrug. "To be honest, I was scared to get too close to him."

"Don't blame you." Sarah reached out for the phone.

Henry pulled back. "If you don't mind. I'd rather hang on to it."

That seemed like an odd stance to take, but then Sarah thought about the mistrust of police that was sweeping through the Black community. It was understandable that Henry was cautious. She nodded. "Okay."

He shifted so Sarah could see his screen. "I have four shots of him."

Henry scrolled through the images of a White man of average height and build. The man wore a camouflage jacket despite the heat of a July night, and he had a ball cap with the brim pulled low. She couldn't read the inscription, but trusted Henry's word. And she had to agree with his assessment of the quality of the photos. They weren't great shots. But the techs in the IT department had all kinds of magic in their computers.

"Would you be willing to come down to the station and let our tech people download the images?"

Again, a hesitation and wariness. "I'm not comfortable with anybody else handling my phone."

Something about his increased reluctance to let go of his phone raised a niggle of alarm. "You have something to hide?"

"No, ma'am. But it's my private property. Police have no business looking at private things without a warrant."

Stated respectfully, yet with conviction, and when Sarah thought about it, she realized it was perfectly reasonable. This young man knew his rights, and nothing about him said criminal or gang member. With the advent of a smartphone in almost everyone's hands, the DPD had briefed everyone a few years back on this exact situation. Pictures and phones and rights and privacy. But damn. She rubbed her fingers across the perspiration beading on her forehead. "Here's the deal, Henry. These pictures can help us identify this man and determine if he shot this woman. I understand your hesitancy but I'm in a bind here."

Henry shifted from one foot to the other and Sarah waited him out. She didn't want to push and have him back off completely. Then he finally spoke. "What if I text you the images?"

Sarah thought about that for a moment. Would that break the chain of evidence? But then, this might not be evidence of the crime. Just pictures of a guy walking around with a gun, who might, or might not, have been the shooter. "Did you actually see this guy fire the shot that hit the woman?"

Henry shook his head. "I was ready to leave and had started walking away. Then I heard the sound of gunfire. Once you hear it, you never forget. People started yelling, and I came back. To see if I could help. I was a medic in Iraq."

"You had military training, yet you were scared of this guy with the gun?"

"Yes, ma'am. When he was strutting around. All puffed up like he was looking for trouble. As a kid, I learned to avoid the kind of trouble he was after. Then in the service I learned to stay away from trouble unless ordered to engage. That's why I stayed a good distance away to get those pictures."

Sarah's assessment of Henry as a stand-up guy rose another notch. "Okay. Send me the photos." She gave him her number and waited while he completed the transmission.

After hearing the ping of a notification, she opened her phone and checked the message. Four images were attached.

"Got 'em. Thanks." She looked up at Henry. "We need your contact information."

Henry nodded toward Burt. "He's got it. Can I go now? Early class tomorrow."

"Sure."

Sarah walked back to Burt. "Hate to think this is a pattern that we haven't seen the end of."

"Hope not."

The crowd had thinned during the time Sarah had talked to Henry, leaving only a few stragglers on the corner. A woman had her cell phone out, pointed toward them. Sarah gestured in the woman's direction. "She think we're going to assault the body?"

Burt snickered. "Who knows? Smartphones are great. Some of the time. Then they aren't so great."

Sarah nodded and stepped back when Walt headed their way. With a wry grin he said, "You gotta quit doing this to me, Kingsly."

Sarah gave a weary chuckle. They all wished they didn't have to call each other out to see another dead body. "If I could."

Walt checked for any sign of life, something that had to be done despite the big hole in the woman's chest that pretty much said she was dead. Then he rolled the body, revealing a small tan purse that was just big enough to hold a few essentials hidden underneath. The outside of the purse was streaked with the woman's blood, showing up in the semi-darkness as splashes of mahogany stain. Sarah pulled latex gloves from her back pocket and snapped them on. Then she picked up the purse and looked inside, rifling through a few credit cards until she found a driver's license.

"Phyllis Abrams," Sarah said. "Thirty years old. Address is 2704 Melrose. Richardson."

Burt wrote the details in his notebook. "Anything else?"

"Credit cards. But only three. One for gas. One for JCPenney. And one for Staples."

Walt held up a large plastic evidence bag, and Sarah dropped the purse inside.

"Any idea of what kind of weapon was used?" Sarah asked Walt.

Instead of his usual joke about not asking questions at the scene, he just shook his head.

"Could it have been an assault weapon?" Burt asked.

"Possibly. The bullets do mess up a person big time." Walt stood. "But it could've been a semi-automatic handgun with a big load. I'll know more when I look inside."

Sarah swallowed hard. That wasn't a post she was looking forward to attending. Maybe she could foist that off on Angel, if her partner was still able to work cases and not just sit at a desk and file reports. "When do you think you'll get to her?" Sarah nodded toward the dead woman.

Walt shrugged. "Won't know until I see what's waiting for me when I get in tomorrow morning. I'll text you."

"Thanks."

"Anything else going to forensics?" Walt held up the evidence bag with the purse.

"Not now," Sarah said. "Uniforms are still looking for shell casings. Looks like the shooter cleaned up so we're not counting on finding any."

"Okay. My team will take her in. We'll send the trace on over to Roberts when we do her."

As much as Sarah enjoyed the banter she traded with Roberts, she was glad that Walt was taking the purse in. One less thing for her and Burt to take care of. They still had so many loose strings from the first shooting, she welcomed whatever help they got.

Sarah turned, having more than enough of the blood and body parts on the pavement. "Let's go talk to the parents," she said to Burt.

"Okay. I'll let Grantham know we're leaving. He's with the guys looking for brass."

"Want to meet at the house?"

Burt nodded and Sarah walked the two blocks to her car, hoping she wouldn't run into Angel again.

She didn't.

CHAPTER SEVENTEEN

Monday, July 6 - Night

The door was opened by a thin man with a full head of silver hair that was in stark contrast to the mahogany color of his skin. Sarah couldn't recall ever seeing hair so white before. It virtually glistened in the beams from the porch light. "Mr. Abrams?"

The man nodded, something in his demeanor suggesting that he realized a late-night visit by two official-looking people didn't mean good news.

Sarah introduced herself and Burt, then asked, "Is your wife home?"

That question sealed the deal for Abrams. His face slowly crumpled. "Please don't let it be Phyllis," he whispered as he moved aside so the detectives could step in.

The small entry led to a living room, modest in size, but it appeared to have comfortable furniture; a sofa with white crocheted doilies on the arms, as well as a recliner, also sporting coverings on the arms. A small wooden rocker with a quilted cushion stood in one corner, reminding Sarah of one that had been in her grandmother's living room.

On the drive into that Richardson area that abuts North Dallas, Sarah had noted some homes in dire need of paint and repairs, as well as yards overgrown with weeds, but this house was tidy on the outside, as well as inside. It spoke well of the occupants.

"Who is it, Jerry?" A light-complected woman came into the room, pulling a robe tight around her thick waist and ample bosom. She took one look at the detectives and cried out, "Oh, no. Oh, no."

The man rushed to her and guided her to the sofa. Sarah pulled the nearby rocker close to them, while Burt remained standing in the doorway.

"Mr. and Mrs. Abrams, I'm so sorry …"

A loud keening chased her words away. Mr. Abrams rocked in rhythm with the words, "Not Phyllis. Not Phyllis. Please God, not Phyllis."

Mrs. Abrams patted his knee in the same rhythm and Sarah wondered when the woman's grief might explode. But it didn't. It just slipped out of her, one tear at a time, until there was a veritable river flowing over plump cheeks.

Sarah gave them both a few minutes, then pulled out her phone where she had a close up of the dead woman's face. This couple did not need to see the rest of their daughter. She held out her phone, picture turned down. "When you're ready." She paused. "Tell us if this is your daughter."

Mr. Abrams nodded, and Sarah turned the picture toward him. "Yes." His voice was so soft she had to strain to hear. Then he swiveled to pull his wife into his arms.

After another long painful moment, he asked in that same soft voice. "What happened?"

"She was killed. At the protests tonight." Sarah hoped he wouldn't ask for more details. No way did she want to tell him about the ugly, gaping hole in his daughter's chest.

"Like that man the other day?"

"We don't know yet," Burt said without leaving the doorway. "It's too early in the investigation to know if they're connected."

"They both be Black." Mrs. Abrams spoke with more strength in her voice than her husband. "It's connected."

Antagonism seemed to stiffen her spine even more, and Sarah could feel the heat building in the small room. Whatever she said next could either cool things down, or ignite more flames. Before she could put the right words together, Burt pulled a ladder-back chair from the kitchen close to the sofa and sat facing the distraught couple. "If I may be so bold," he said. "Are you folks churchgoers?"

Sarah turned to him in surprise, and he lifted one hand slightly. A silent command for her to wait.

"You want us to pray our daughter back alive?" the woman asked, shock and anger making the words cut the silence like knives.

"No, ma'am. But with your permission. I'd like to share something with you." He paused and finally Mr. Abrams gave a short nod. "This is part of a prayer my partner taught me. I think the message fits. *Remember*: *If the Creator put it there, it is in the right place. The soul would have no rainbow if the eyes had no tears.*"

Nobody spoke for several moments, then Mrs. Abrams asked, "Why you tell us that?"

"So you won't see us as the enemy. And to ease your troubled hearts just a little."

Fresh tears streamed out of the woman's eyes, and then her shoulders sagged, as if her inner tension was being released in the river down her cheeks. "That don't bring our

Phyllis back," she murmured.

"No, ma'am. It won't. That wasn't my intention."

Sarah waited to let the mood shift even more, then said. "We are so sorry for your loss. And even though this is such a painful moment, are you able to answer a few questions?"

The woman nodded.

Sarah turned to the husband. "What do you do for a living, Mr. Abrams?"

"Jerry. Call me Jerry. My wife, Anna. We clean the office buildings."

"Any trouble at work that could have fallen on your daughter?"

He shook his head.

"Did your daughter work with you?"

"No." The word was almost as forceful as a slap, and Sarah turned quickly to Anna who appeared to have a bit of the antagonism back. "She go to school. College."

At first, Sarah had thought the woman's manner of speaking was lack of education, but now she realized that English wasn't this woman's first language. There was a hint of an accent that Sarah couldn't place. Haiti? Jamaica?

"We want ..." Jerry stumbled over the word. "Wanted better for her. She works ..." again the stumble, "worked at Starbucks during the day. At night go to SMU to study law."

Sarah exchanged a quick glance with Burt as the small thread of connection was made.

The significance of the glance was not lost on Anna. "What?"

"It may be nothing," Sarah said.

Anna seemed poised to say something else, then just let out a deep sigh.

"When can we see our girl?" Jerry asked.

"If you want to go tonight, officers can take you to make the formal identification," Burt said. "But it's late. That can wait until morning."

The couple looked at each other, silent messages passing back and forth. Sarah remembered seeing how that happened with one of her aunts in Tennessee. Aunt Pauline who was her mother's sister. Pauline, like Grandma, was one of the sane ones in the family, and she'd stayed married to Rupert for as long as he'd lived. Some people who lived together that many years seemed to have a way of speaking without words. Others went through years of being together unable to effectively take part in any form of communication.

"We will go tonight."

"Okay," Burt said. "We'll get a patrol car over."

"Need to ..." Anna gestured at her robe without finishing the sentence.

"Of course," Sarah said. "We'll wait outside. Make the arrangements."

On the front walk, Sarah gave Burt time to call for the patrol officers, and when he was finished, she gave him a half-amused look. "You surprised the hell out of me in there."

"What do you mean?"

"You know exactly what I mean. I didn't know you were into religion."

Burt grinned. "I'm not. Just been hanging with Simms for too many years. Some of his Native spirit stuff rubs off on me. Gotta say, I kinda dig the prayers."

"Dig it?" Sarah laughed. "I haven't heard that since I was a kid."

"See. My daughter's right. I am a dinosaur."

"Does Simms mind you referring to him as Native? The proper term now is Indigenous."

"Yeah, well, proper can go where the sun don't shine. Simms and I are tight. He doesn't care what I call him, and the feeling's mutual."

Sarah smiled inwardly. Crusty old Burt. But she was glad that his partnership with Simms was so 'tight.' She sure wished the hell she could say the same about hers with Angel.

It was nearing midnight by the time they finished up at the Abrams' house and Sarah headed home. She held on to a slight hope that LaVon might still be there, but he'd probably gone to his own place earlier. He had to be in the office first thing in the morning. As she drove, she wondered again if their relationship was going to go any further than it had. Great company. Great sex. Add an abundance of laughs and tender moments, and that made a good foundation on which to build a future. More than she'd had with any other man in her life up to this point.

But ...

But they had this huge barrier comprised of race, color, and culture. Since they'd moved beyond the occasional coffee or riding lesson to serious dating a few months ago, she'd only been to his parent's house with him once for dinner. His mother had been very polite and cordial, in that stiff way of someone not happy with the social situation, but putting on the good-hostess face. Father shooting daggers at her across the table, not even pretending on the good-host front.

Anxious to leave that night, she couldn't wait for dessert to be over, although truth be told, she would have loved another piece of Mrs. Johnson's lemon meringue pie. But one more dagger or stilted comment would have pushed her over the good-visitor cliff. On the way back to her apartment, she'd told LaVon she wasn't eager to go back.

"Give them time," he'd said. "They'll come around."

Sarah gave a slight shake of her head. "I don't know. But I wonder about the change in your mother. A few years ago, she was championing me to your father. Said I was a good partner for Angel."

LaVon let out a soft chuckle. "Professional partner was one thing. This ..." he gestured between them. "This is something totally out of her comfort zone."

"I didn't think she was bigoted."

"We all are in our own way, aren't we?"

Even as his question popped into Sarah's mind again, now several months later, it wasn't one that had a single, simple answer. Instead, it was a question that was more effective as a reminder to carefully consider words and actions.

As for her own family. She really had nobody of great importance back in Tennessee to care one way or another if she was dating a Black man. Well, her Uncle Homer would've had some strong opinions, but she didn't know what her cousin Jolene would think. Still Sarah doubted she'd ever take LaVon to her hometown anyway. Too many rednecks there for his, or her, comfort, which was one of the reasons she'd been eager to leave once she no longer had a reason to stay.

If her grandmother were still alive, she'd support Sarah all the way. That thought brought a sudden wash of tears that surprised her. It had been over ten years since her grandmother had died, and these occasional hits of grief always caught her off guard. The blows weren't as strong as they'd been the first few years after she'd lost the most important person in her life besides John, her former partner, but they were accompanied by a sharp pang in the region of her heart.

Of course, the events of the past few years didn't help matters. Losing her previous partner and almost losing her job had loosened the scab that had formed a couple of years after her grandmother had died. Grandma Ruthie had taken a troubled pre-teen child into her home and into her heart after Sarah's father ran off and her mother killed herself with drugs. Grandma was poor, so life was hard, but the old woman was soft and sweet. She was also very wise, and Sarah was ever so grateful to have had the years with her that formed the woman she had become.

Sighing, Sarah pulled into her parking space at the apartment complex and got out of her car. After locking it, she headed toward her unit. Her hunch was right about LaVon leaving. Nobody greeted her except Cat who wound his orange body around her legs, emitting a throaty meow as if he hadn't eaten in weeks.

She poured chows into his bowl and stroked him a bit to get him to settle and eat. Wouldn't it be great if she could solve these cases as easily as she could satisfy Cat?

CHAPTER EIGHTEEN

Tuesday, July 7 - Morning

As usual, McGregor's office was almost buried under piles of papers and reports. It hadn't taken long for the brand-new office to resemble the old, which could have been a home for a hoarder. Sarah gestured to the clutter. "Thought the new plan was to go paperless."

He just glared. "What do you have?"

Okay. No time for humor. That wasn't a good sign. Sarah could always tell when the pressure from higher up was killing him. She just hoped he'd manage to stay away from the bottle. He had almost two years sober now. Would be a such a shame to destroy that.

Sarah didn't have to ask what case his question was referring to. The media coverage about last night was intense, which was probably driving the pressure from the brass. So, she quickly briefed him on what happened at the scene as well as the interview with the parents. "One detail the press doesn't know yet is that the girl was a law student at SMU where Amelia Cummings is a professor. Won't be a secret long, though."

"Another mess for us to get mired in." McGregor put an elbow on the desk and rested his chin in his open palm. "What do you have from forensics?"

"Not much of any use. They did their usual clearing of the scene. But Roberts doesn't think any of it will connect with the killer."

"Could it be the same shooter?"

"On the surface it doesn't look like it. But we'll check to see if there is a connection between her and Mrs. Cummings. She isn't the only law professor."

There was a knock on the door and Chang poked her head in. "Got some good news, boss."

McGregor waved her in.

Chang looked around for a place to sit, offering a smile to Sarah who was seated in the only chair not covered in manila folders.

McGregor made a small gesture for her to get to it. "The news?"

"Yes. Okay. I ran the photo Sarah sent through NICS and got a match. The man in the photo is Eric Gunther. He lives in Arkansas in a small town near Texarkana." Chang paused to look at the screen of her tablet. "The town is Rondo, in Lee County."

"I take it he has a record, which is how you got this so fast," Sarah said.

"You betcha." Chang grinned and read from her tablet. "One arrest ten years ago for assaulting the owner of a convenience store in Texarkana. On the Arkansas side. Served five of a seven-year sentence."

"Is that the only one?" Sarah asked.

"Nope. As a senior in high school, he fought with a Black student. Hurt the other kid pretty bad, according to the report.

But the parents didn't press charges, so our friend got off."

"Report say why the parents didn't press charges?" McGregor asked.

"No. But I was curious, so I did a little Google sleuthing. Appears Eric's family tree had a few apples of the KKK variety." Chang smiled as if delighted with her reporting. "Perhaps that was a reason enough for the other family to be reluctant."

"Okay," McGregor said. "Did your sleuthing happen to turn up a current address and phone number?"

"Already e-mailed to Sarah, along with info on the Lee Country sheriff. Unless he's a member of the KKK, too, he might want to give an assist. But a heads-up. The number for Gunther isn't in service."

"A burner?" Sarah asked.

"Probably. Check to see if you got my message."

Sarah opened her phone and checked e-mail. There it was. She glanced at Chang. "It's here."

"Also ran the checks on those two names you gave me the other day," Chang said. "Getty and Robinson. Nothing criminal in their history."

"I'd almost forgotten about that," Sarah said. "Thanks for that info."

Chang nodded, then waited. Finally, McGregor, who'd apparently zoned out for a moment said, "Uh, right. Sorry. Good work, Chang."

The young detective smiled again, nodded, then left. Sarah waited a beat then asked, "You okay, Lieu?"

"Yeah. Why?"

"A few minutes ago. You drifted off somewhere. Poor Chang didn't seem to know whether to leave or wait for some other directive from you."

"Had to take a moment to set priorities."

"And?"

"Go get this bastard. Then maybe we can wrap this case up. The sooner we get him and his gun, the sooner we can either nail him or eliminate him for the killing last night."

"Overtime not a problem?"

"Nope. Dorsett opened the bank."

Sarah returned to her desk and pulled up the e-mail from Chang that included the name and phone number for the Lee County Sheriff. Before she called, she googled Lee Country Sheriff Department and saw it was small, only the sheriff and one deputy. The office was in Mariana, another small town eleven miles from Rondo. Since Sheriff Sam Goodman was African American, Sarah guessed he had no KKK family members.

She dialed the number provided and the call was answered by a woman with a sweet southern drawl who said she'd be happy to transfer the call. A moment later, a man who sounded more like a professor at a college in the North than a Southern lawman came on the line. "Detective Kingsly, how may I be of assistance?"

A bit surprised at the unexpected, Sarah paused just a beat before answering. "Thanks for taking my call."

"Of course."

When he didn't say more, Sarah quickly told him about Eric Gunther and why she was interested in him. She finished by asking if the sheriff was familiar with Gunther.

That question was answered first with a short laugh, then Goodman said, "As much as I'd like to deny any knowledge, I know a considerable amount about him. He's been a thorn in the county's side for years."

"How long have you been sheriff there?"

"Twenty-two years."

"Then you know about the assault when he was in school?"

Sarah heard a deep sigh before an answer. "I encouraged the family to press charges. Poor boy Gunther hit had a broken jaw. Several broken ribs. And maybe some other fractures that weren't found at the time. He never played football again."

Even though she already knew, Sarah wanted the sheriff's take on why the family resisted his advice. So, she asked.

Goodman chuckled. "Surely that's a rhetorical question, Detective."

It was her turn to chuckle, then she said, "It would just be helpful to know how openly racist he might be."

"There's no 'might' about it. While the Klan no longer wears the robes and gathers deep in the dark web, it is very much alive and well."

"I need to come to interview Gunther. Do you know if he's back in your area?"

"Not at the moment. But I can send my deputy by to check Gunther's place."

"Can that happen today?"

"God willing and the creek don't rise, as the people here like to say."

Now the man sounded like a country lawman, and Sarah smiled as she signed off.

After verifying with Roberts that so far there was nothing helpful from the crime scene, and probably wouldn't be,

Sarah decided to pay a visit to Mrs. Cummings. She texted Burt to see if he could come along, getting a quick response that he was following a lead in the burglary case with Simms.

Okay. She'd go by herself.

The same elegant woman answered the door when Sarah knocked. Her composure slipped just a bit when she saw who it was. "Do you have information for us, Detective?"

"No. I'm sorry there's been no progress on the case. But I would like to talk to your daughter about something that might be related."

The woman opened the door and motioned Sarah to step in, leading her to the same sitting room as last time. "I'll see if she can speak to you."

As the woman walked away, Sarah wondered why some people thought that a response to a request from a police officer was open to debate.

A few moments later, Mrs. Cummings entered the room, looking every bit as well put together as before. Nary a hint of grief anywhere.

"How are you, Mrs. Cummings?" Sarah asked.

"How do you expect me to be?"

Okay. That set the tone. "My apologies. I won't take up much of your time. We need to know how well you know the students in the class you teach at SMU."

"Well enough, I suppose. But it's a very large class."

"What about a young woman named Phyllis Abrams?"

When Amelia didn't respond right away, Sarah opened her phone and showed her the picture of the young woman.

"Oh dear. Was she the woman killed last night?"

Oddly enough Amelia seemed to show more concern for the death of the girl then she had for her husband, but Sarah was at least happy to see a sliver of humanity in the woman.

"Do you recall her at all?"

Adele nodded. "She was very bright and determined. Came to my office several times for advice."

"Is it possible your husband knew her?"

"In the biblical sense?"

Sarah smiled to show the woman that the question hadn't rattled her, if that had been Amelia's intent. "I was suggesting socially, but, sure. Was Phyllis one of your husband's dalliances?"

"I wouldn't know, Detective. She never told me, and he certainly wouldn't have divulged that information. Fred didn't attend many of the social gatherings I had here for my students, but he did make an appearance at the last Christmas party."

"Did he meet Phyllis then?"

"Probably. He never could pass up a pretty face."

Sarah hesitated just a beat before speaking again, weighing the wisdom of asking the next question. But what the hell. It will either reveal something helpful to the investigation or get her thrown out on her ass. "Just when did your marriage start falling apart, Mrs. Cummings?"

"That's none of your business."

There was ice in that response, but Sarah pushed on. "Anything about your husband is our business. You never know what little details might lead us toward the person who decided to put a bullet in his back one hot July night."

Amelia took so long to answer, Sarah was beginning to think she wouldn't. Then she asked, "Have you ever been married, Detective?"

Sarah shook her head.

"Then you don't know how it all starts out so perfectly. So romantic. You're so much in love, in lust, that you can't keep your hands off each other. You're each other's best friend. At least you think you are. Then the kids start to come. And there are complications. You can no longer enjoy the carnal company of each other. And the one with the most needs? Well, he satisfies those needs elsewhere."

Wow. Sarah didn't know what to say. First of all, this was the first side of real humanity she'd seen Amelia in all of the interviews. Secondly 'carnal company' was terminology she'd never heard before, but she sure as hell was going to remember it.

"So? Fred went elsewhere?"

Amelia sighed. "I'll spare you the whole sordid history. But yes." She sat up straighter. "And eventually I did the same."

"Are you seeing anyone now?"

"No."

"How long has it been?"

Amelia's eyes lost their softness. "How could that possibly matter?"

Sarah didn't answer. She also didn't break eye contact. Finally, Amelia sighed again and spoke softly. "Jamel wouldn't hurt Fred."

"Full name and phone number," Sarah said.

"One moment." Amelia rose and went to a side table, opened a drawer and took out a piece of paper. She wrote on the paper, then handed it over to Sarah. "I'll repeat. He wouldn't hurt Fred."

"How can you be sure?"

"He knew that would hurt me. And he'd never do that."

"When was the last time you saw Jamel?"

"Almost three years ago. He was a para-legal in the law firm. We broke it off when we both came to our senses. Our relationship could ruin us both."

"Is he still with the firm?"

"No. He moved over to Jenkins and Gilchrest when a better offer came along."

"Another woman?"

"A better salary."

"So why not get back together when fraternization was no longer an issue?"

"Another woman did come along. She's now his wife."

Sarah stood and put the paper in her jeans pocket. "Thank you, Mrs. Cummings. I'll be in touch if there is anything else."

Amelia escorted her to the front door where she hesitated a moment. "Please don't think too badly of me for, well, anything."

Outside Sarah stood by her car for a moment. What an odd conversation this had been. Normally she left an interview with a clear sense of the person, but Amelia was an enigma. One moment living up to her reputation as a ball-crushing attorney and the next softening to someone Sarah could possibly like as a friend.

Weird.

Back at her desk a half hour later, Sarah called the number Adele had given her for Jamel. The call went straight to voicemail. She decided to try the law firm. After following a couple of prompts in the voicemail system, she was put through to Jamel Robinson's office, where a secretary answered. After identifying herself, Sarah asked to speak to Mr. Robinson.

"I'm sorry, Mr. Robinson is not in today. May I take a message?"

"When do you expect him back?"

"That's hard to say."

"You can't say or you won't say?"

"What is this in regards to?"

"A murder investigation."

"Oh. I see. Well, Mr. Robinson may be out for the next week. He's in West Texas. A family emergency."

"Can you tell me how long he's been gone?"

"Let's see." Sarah could hear the rustle of papers as if the woman was checking a paper calendar or desk planner. Apparently, some people still used them. "He left the last weekend in June. Started his three-week family emergency leave then."

"Okay. Thanks." Sarah hung up. The only good thing to come from that, was she could scratch another name off a list of possible suspects.

She sighed, stood and stretched, then headed to the breakroom for coffee. She was just pouring a cup when her phone rang. She set the mug down and answered.

"Sherriff Goodman here. We've established your man is in my fair state."

"Thanks." Sarah added a dollop of cream to the sludge that passed for coffee. "I'll come out this afternoon."

"If you'd like assistance, meet me at my office and I'll provide escort."

"That would be great. I'll call later with an ETA."

"Sure thing."

McGregor walked into the breakroom and headed for the coffeepot.

Hey," Sarah said. "I was just about to call you. Got a lead on that Gunther guy in Arkansas. Talked to the sheriff about going out there with him this afternoon."

"Okay. Take Burt."

Sarah had a feeling it wouldn't be wise to ask why not

take Angel. She drained the last of her coffee, rinsed the mug and put it back, then walked out. "Wish us luck," she said to McGregor as she passed him.

He raised his glass in mock salute.

CHAPTER NINETEEN

Tuesday, July 7 - Late Morning

Angel drove aimlessly for a while after leaving the station. She didn't want to go home alone. She didn't want to go back to the hospital. That was too damn depressing. And she didn't want to go to her parents' house. It would be okay to talk to her mother, but if her father was home, well, she wasn't in the mood for his anger toward her. Or the snarky comments meant to stir more rancor and unrest. The city didn't need any more of that. She didn't need any more of that.

Without giving it a whole lot of thought, Angel ended up in front of the dojo. She parked and turned off the engine and sat there for a few moments debating about whether she should go in or not. The summer heat increasing to an intolerable level in the car made the decision for her, so she got out, grabbed her gear from the trunk, and went inside. In the locker room, she changed into her dobok and walked out into the main room. There were only a few people practicing some patterns, so Angel angled to the far left where there was open space. She stopped at the edge of the dark green mat to prepare herself for the workout, mentally repeating the five tenets at the core of the Tae Kwon Do philosophy: courtesy, integrity, perseverance, self-control, and indomitable spirit. The intent was to center the participant and ensure they were ready for the exercise. The tenets were also supposed to follow them out of the dojo. Most of the time, Angel found that they did. This whole process of working physically and mentally usually had her calm and focused for at least a week afterward, but today she wasn't so sure about the self-control part. That was tenuous. She'd have to see where control was at the end of her workout.

Practicing her patterns was the antidote she needed, and after a half an hour of fluid movements and kicks and punches that made up the forms she'd mastered for her black belt, the tension in her muscles eased. She spent another half an hour in some less strenuous Tai Chi movements, incorporating a little bit of yoga before finishing and spending a few moments just standing with her eyes closed, focusing on her breathing.

In that moment of quiet, she thought about Ryan and how critical his situation was, and just like that, her calm started to fade. *Damn it. He couldn't die.*

She shook that dismal thought aside and headed to the locker room and the showers. After washing the sweat from her body, Angel stood a moment under the hot spray until her emotions settled again. Then she quickly dressed and hurried out. She didn't even want to talk to Randy today. Normally she looked forward to conversations with the master at the dojo but she wasn't ready to be emotionally vulnerable right now.

Outside she paused in the shade of a sweeping elm tree and opened her phone, searching her contacts until she found Tyrell's number. She dialed it, and he answered on the third ring. "Hey, Tyrell. Let's meet up for lunch."

"Really, Angel? You call me at my job."

"I don't even know where you work. Hard to tell when calling a private number."

"You're not going to like it."

"Like what?"

"Where I am."

Angel moved to her car, got in and cranked up the air. "I don't care where you work. Just give me a half hour."

"When?"

"Now."

"I can't just walk out."

"Where the hell do you work?"

He took so long to answer, Angel wondered if he'd hung up. Then he said, "The law firm of Cummings and Barnett."

At first it didn't register. Then the realization hit. That was the firm representing Smithfield. The lawyer whose husband was shot last week. Her stomach lurched. "If you're kidding, that's a sick joke."

"No joke."

"You're an attorney?" Angel asked, mentally trying to figure out how a guy with his sordid background ended up at a law firm.

"Paralegal."

Angel absorbed that information, but pushed away the myriad of questions it raised. The only important thing was to get Tyrell's help.

"The office is downtown, right? On San Jacinto?"

"Yes."

"There's a Starbucks down the street from it. Meet me there in thirty minutes."

"I told you I can't just walk out."

"Yes, you can. You work for a big shot law firm. Meet

me."

Angel hung up and turned her car back toward downtown. She had no idea if he would meet her or not, but when she stepped onto the patio of the coffeeshop, there he was at a table in the far corner. He wore a suit and tie and a very anxious expression. The table was bare, and so was his face. It was too damn hot for masks.

She stuffed hers back into her purse and hurried over. "Thanks for coming. You want something?"

He shook his head. "You've got ten minutes."

The edge in his voice told her this was nonnegotiable, so she sat down. There was no time for pleasantries, or for coffee, or asking how the hell Tyrell ended up a paralegal, so she asked, "Have you thought about what I said the other day? About the looting and who might have taken part?"

"I haven't been involved with that scene for years."

"Maybe not. But you know people. People who are still involved. And people who might be all riled up to go on a rampage and end up shooting a cop."

Tyrell glanced away, and Angel didn't know if it was to think about a response, or to think about walking out. "Come on, man. You owe me."

His head shot around. "What?"

"You forgot how I saved your ass in high school."

He glared. "Low blow, Angel."

"Yeah. But I'm willing to do what I have to."

Neither spoke for a moment, and Angel briefly recalled the night they were at the park. She trying to get her boyfriend to go home. Keep him from buying more drugs. And Tyrell ready to supply whatever Bobby wanted. When the cops drove slowly up the street, then stopped, Angel had stayed to talk to the officers while Tyrell and Bobby raced off. She'd managed to convince the cops the two guys were just debating about who was going to take her to prom. Maybe the convincing was in the absurdity of her lie.

Across from her now, Tyrell sighed. "Okay. My friend Darnell has a nephew who was tight with Jamel Frederickson. The nephew's a real hot head. Right after George Floyd, he went ballistic. Said every White cop should die."

"You think he meant it, or just sounding off?"

Tyrell shrugged.

"Does this kid have a name?"

"Yeah. But I'm not sure I want to give it to you."

"I'm a police officer investigating an attempted murder." Angel put as much steel in her voice as she could. "Forget that we're two friends chatting. Got it?"

For a moment it looked like Tyrell wanted to laugh, but the inclination dissolved the longer she held her gaze on him.

"Okay, his name is James."

"Last name?"

"Franklin. But everyone knows him by James."

"Everyone?"

Tyrell gave a slight shake of his head. "Coy doesn't play well with you."

"Wasn't trying for coy. Geesh, Tyrell. I just need to know more about this guy."

"Okay." Tyrell tapped a finger on the table. "He's got friends where he hangs out. Those friends back him up in whatever goes down around the hood."

"How dangerous are those friends?"

"Just don't get crossways with him."

Angel took a moment to absorb that bit of advice, then asked, "How well do you know this James? How old is he?"

"Seen him around is all. Darnell had some parties back

before this pandemic hit. James was there sometimes." Tyrell paused a beat then added. "He's not a kid. Probably early twenties."

Angel leaned forward and said softly, "I need to meet the guy. Set something up."

"You know I can't do that, Angel. I'm out of that life, and I can't risk my future."

"And just what future does my friend Ryan have?"

The force of the emotions behind those words stunned Tyrell into a momentary silence, then he finally said, "I can't be anywhere near him."

"Fine. Just tell me where he hangs out."

"Hamilton Park."

"That area was cleaned up a couple of years ago. How come he went back?"

"I don't know. Ask him when you see him."

"That mean you'll set something up?"

Tyrell nodded. "Can't promise anything. But I'll pull in a couple of IOUs."

"Okay." Angel leaned back in her chair. "Thank you. Call me when you have a meeting set."

"Then we're done, right?"

"Hate for that to happen. Friendships run deep."

"Maybe so. But there's a limit."

With that, Tyrell stood and walked toward the street. No looking back or hesitancy in his steps. Angel wondered what it must be like to work for the law firm representing Smithfield. Anymore, she wasn't sure how she felt about being a police officer. The gap between her and her colleagues, especially those of the Caucasian background, was getting wider and wider.

How could Tyrell do it?

CHAPTER TWENTY

Tuesday, July 7 - Afternoon

Burt cut the usual three-hour drive to Texarkana to just under two and a half. Then another thirty minutes to where they met Sheriff Goodman. In person, he looked very much like the intellectual that his voice had portrayed, but his firm handshake and iron gaze indicated he was no softie. "Our guy still at his place?" Sarah asked after introductions had been made.

Goodman nodded. "Had my deputy stay on site."

"Thanks."

"You ready to go, or do you need a minute?"

"I could use a pit stop," Sarah said.

"Celeste. Show Detective Kingsly to the facilities."

The woman didn't match the image her voice had put in Sarah's mind of a young, petite southern girl. She was tall, plump, with graying hair and circles of bright pink rouge on her cheeks. She stood, smiled, and gestured to Sarah. "Right this way."

Personal business taken care of, they were now on their way in the Sheriff's Land Rover Evoque. Burt had taken the backseat, so Sarah was riding shotgun. "Nice vehicle," she said. "Smooth. And hardly any engine noise."

"It's a hybrid."

"Really? Heard those were pretty pricey. How'd you get the county to spring for it?"

Goodman smiled. "We'll drive it until the wheels fall off. Figure what we save on gas will pay off in the long run."

"Can we quote you in our request for one at the DPD?" Burt said from the back seat.

Goodman nodded as Sarah laughed. "Like that could ever happen," she said.

Another two miles down the county road that wound lazily through green wooded areas interspersed with brief clearings, Goodman pulled off onto what could be a narrow gravel road or a driveway to a country home. The area was thick with trees, mostly pines of some sort with hardwoods mingled in. The leaves of hardwoods hung limp in the mid-afternoon heat. "Gunther's place is down this road," Goodman said. "There are three farms side by side. Mostly producing row crops."

"Row crops?" Sarah asked.

"Kind of what the name implies," Goodman said. "Lots of different vegetables that farmers sell at the markets. But we've always suspected Gunther sells more than tomatoes."

"Never caught him?" Burt asked.

"He's good at rotating his crops. Moves the illegal stuff frequently."

Dust from the gravel billowed in a huge white cloud behind the vehicle as they went about a half a mile further, then Sarah saw a small pickup pulled into a clear space just off the road. Goodman stopped. "That's my guy."

Goodman rolled down his window as a tall, lanky man

wearing Army camouflage and a bush hat exited the truck and hustled over. The acrid dust from the gravel wafted into the Rover along with a blast of summer heat, and Sarah knew that was just a small taste of what was ahead. She couldn't decide which was worse. Policing in the dead of winter when you'd freeze your balls off, if you had any, or risking heat stroke in the summer. "He still there?" Goodman asked.

The other man nodded. "Nothing in or out all day."

"Okay. Stick around for backup in case we need you."

"Got it." The man tapped the door frame, then turned and jogged back to his truck.

Goodman levered the window up, then turned to Sarah. "That's Andy Malcolm. Good guy to have in a pinch."

He eased the vehicle forward, going a couple of hundred yards further before pulling off the gravel as far as he could. "His place is in there."

Sarah looked but could hardly see anything through the trees.

"How far in?" Burt asked.

"About fifty yards."

A dented metal mailbox hung by wire from the cross-beam of a weathered wooden mailbox post, listing sharply to one side. Looking closely, Sarah finally spotted the faint outline of a dirt drive leading from the mailbox into the almost impenetrable thicket of trees. "Gunther's gotta drive in there, right? Let's go ahead."

Goodman gave a little chuckle. "Okay. But if he shoots my nice smooth ride all to hell it's on you."

"If he's going to shoot anything all to hell, better it be a vehicle than us," Burt offered.

Goodman turned the wheel and pointed the nose of the Land Rover into the narrow opening. After following the rough dirt track around a tight curve, a home that more closely resembled a shack came into view. It listed heavily to one side and part of the roof was missing. Goodman stopped the car but didn't turn off the engine.

It didn't take more than a few seconds for Gunther to appear on the porch, boards shifting visibly under his weight. "Whatta you want, Sheriff?"

"Just a few minutes of your time," Goodman said.

"Get the hell off my property. I know my rights."

Sarah touched the sheriff's arm. "I got this." She opened the door and stepped out, walking around the front of the Land Rover but staying close to the front bumper.

"Who the hell are you?"

"Sarah Kingsly. Dallas Police."

Shock registered on his face, but it was quickly covered with a sneer. "You think you got business here?" An edge of menace crept into his voice. "Get lost."

She heard doors opening behind her, but she didn't turn to look, figuring it was Burt and the sheriff.

Sarah held up a placating hand. "We just need to talk, Eric. About Dallas. You were there, right?"

He just stared at her for a beat then called out, "Yeah. I was there. So what? No law against me taking a little road trip."

"Appears you did more than just that."

"What do you think I did?"

Sarah slapped at a mosquito that landed on her arm. "Can we come in and talk Eric? No fun standing out here in the heat with the mosquitoes eating me up."

"Ain't letting no cops inside."

"Then come over here. We'll talk in the car."

In a flash, Gunther spun and tore back into the house.

"Oh, fuck." At the sight of the rifle barrel poking out of a hole in the wall just to the right of the door, Sarah made a dash for the Land Rover, yanking open the passenger door. Burt was scrambling into the backseat as Eric started to shoot. Goodman was already backing out as Sarah fell into the passenger seat of the vehicle. The ping of bullets sounded like hail raining down on the roof.

Goodman backed all the way to the road without stopping, tree branches scraping the sides of the Rover when he slid off the dirt while navigating a couple of tight curves.

"Damn! Sorry about your car," Sarah said.

Goodman just shook his head. "What do you want to do?"

"Can't storm the place," Burt said. "Really want him alive."

"You got tear gas?" Sarah asked.

Goodman got out and led them to the back of the vehicle, opening the hatch to reveal a large black metal box that resembled one used for tools. He opened it to reveal neatly arranged compartments that held tear gas grenades, boxes of ammunition, evidence bags, plastic wrist ties. There were four rifles along the bottom.

"How soon before sunset?" Burt asked.

Sarah and Goodman both grabbed their smartphones and answered almost simultaneously. "Two hours."

Malcolm hurried over. "Everyone okay?"

Goodman nodded. "Guy's still holed up in there."

"What's the plan?"

Goodman looked to Burt for the answer. "Your collar, your call."

"Wait until dark, then take him?" Burt posed it as much as a question as a statement.

"It's going to be black as pitch," Malcolm offered. "Only

a sliver of a moon tonight."

"Works in our favor," Sarah said. "No light reflecting off white shirts."

Goodman rooted in the tool box and pulled out two dark, long sleeved shirts. "Got these you can use."

Sarah didn't hesitate to grab one. "Works for deterring mosquitoes, too. An added bonus."

Goodman told his deputy to stay on watch until they came back. Promised to bring him a burger and fries. Then he motioned Sarah and Burt to get into the Rover. "Let's go grab a bite and count the bullet holes in my car."

Goodman pulled into the clearing off the road and killed the engine. He'd doused the headlights about a half-mile back, not wanting Gunther to be alerted to their presence. The deputy had been right, Sarah realized. The darkness was complete, but driving without headlights had given their eyes a chance to adjust. She could see faint variations of shapes in the depth of inkiness.

While at the Burger Barn in town, Goodman had loosened the overhead and hatch bulbs in the vehicle, so there was nothing to betray them as he slid out. He carried the sack of food to Andy, then hustled back. "He needs about five minutes, then he'll be ready. He said my other deputy is just a short distance down the road waiting for the signal."

"Okay." Sarah plucked at the sleeve of the shirt to pull it away from the sweat gathering in her armpit.

They'd decided earlier that she'd take the lead, even though Burt and Goodman both wanted to play the role of the gallant knight. When she'd frozen them with a glare at the suggestion, Burt had grinned. "Better we give in," he'd said to Goodman. "She can be quite nasty when she's riled."

Goodman had apparently recognized the tease, as well as the intent in Sarah's eyes, because he'd quickly acquiesced.

Now, he pulled two tear-gas grenades from the tool box and handed them to her. She tucked one in each front pocket of her slacks. Then Goodman gave them each a bullet-proof vest and took one for himself.

After the vest was secured, Sarah looked first at Burt, then at Goodman. "Ready?" she asked.

They both nodded, and Goodman said. "Deputies are in place."

Sarah led the way down the narrow trail to the run-down house, pushing aside low-hanging branches and holding them back from slapping Burt who was right behind her. The ground was soft, so their footsteps were muffled, allowing the night-sounds of crickets and tree frogs to take center stage. She paused when they reached that final curve in the driveway, and she could make out the shape of the building ahead. No lights were visible, and it was impossible to tell if the rifle was still in the same spot as before. Sarah hoped it wasn't. Her hope was that Gunther had given up the idea of a fight, but she knew that was most likely futile. Using hand gestures, she indicated that she'd go wide and move to the house from the left.

Both men raised a hand in acknowledgement and started their own wide berth to the right.

The tree frogs stopped their night-song as Sarah apparently came too close to the tall pine where they'd been singing. She froze, realizing that Gunther was enough of an outdoorsman to recognize the sudden silence for what it could mean. She moved a few feet from the tree and waited for the chorus to start up again before slowly making her way the last few yards to the house. Once there, she skirted the wide porch, only stepping up when she was close to the door. No sense having an old, creaking board give her away now. She flattened against the log exterior and side-stepped toward the left side of the door, hoping that this far out in the country there was no lock.

Drawing close, she caught the briefest hint of movement on the other side of the door, then a slight glint of metal in the pale moonlight.

The rifle.

Shit.

Earlier, they'd decided not to use voice communications. Goodman pointing out how far the smallest sound could carry on night breezes away from the noise of civilization. So, Sarah could only hope that the other officers were approaching with equal care and would spot the weapon before Gunther had a chance to fire.

Coming as close as she could, Sarah took a deep breath and reached across the width of the door to gently test the knob.

It turned.

Moving with practiced precision, she took a tear-gas cannister out of her pocket, activated it, opened the door, and lobbed the can in. There was a loud bang, then the rapid staccato of automatic rifle fire.

Apparently, Gunther had stayed right there with the weapon ready. But, damn. He should have been incapacitated.

Sarah ducked back against the wall, going so tight against the wood not even a bug could get between her back and the logs. She heard Gunther inside, screaming and cursing, but he still managed to keep firing.

Shocked that the first grenade didn't knock him cold, Sarah had the fleeting thought that he must be as tough as a fucking grizzly bear. She grabbed the second grenade that Goodman had insisted she carry and eased toward the crack of an opening in the front door. She had no idea where Goodman and Burt were, or the deputies. That not knowing increased the imperative that she stop the rifle fire.

Now.

Stepping away from the safety of the wall, she pushed the door open again with her left hand and tossed the tear gas inside with her right. In that split second a bullet caught her high on her shoulder. She spun away from the door, not feeling the pain yet. Adrenaline was coursing now, dulling the sensation, but she'd been wounded before and knew the searing pain was on its way.

She pressed against the outside wall, staying there for the agonizing minute it took for the firing and cursing to stop. Then she took a deep breath and charged through the door. Gunther was slumped just a few feet to her right. With her good arm, she grabbed the man by the back of his jacket and dragged him out to the porch. There she put a knee on his back and grabbed her handcuffs, that movement bringing a stab of pain she ignored while she snapped the cuffs in place.

Burt beat Goodman to the porch. "You okay?"

Sarah nodded, even though she knew he'd discover the lie. She was relieved to see that neither of them had been hit. "Your deputies okay?" she asked Goodman.

"Malcolm caught one in the leg. But it missed the big artery. ." He gestured to the manacled Gunther. "Slick work there."

"Yeah. Well. I was motivated. He pissed me off."

Burt chuckled. "You have to know her. She has a reputation."

Sarah winced as they tried to leverage the nearly unconscious man up, and Burt reached out to touch her shoulder. "Please tell me that's sweat dampening your shirt."

"Shit, woman. You been hit?" The break from Goodman's usual precise way of speaking was almost comical, but Sarah was sinking fast from the adrenaline high and couldn't appreciate the humor.

"Yes, sir."

Then she passed out.

McGregor sat in his recliner with his supper that consisted of meatloaf, beans, and mashed potatoes that he'd taken from a frozen dinner and put on a plate. He figured not eating from the cardboard heating container was a little like having the real deal. He rested the fork on the meat and flipped through TV channels before finally settling on "Wheel of Time." Nobody at the station knew he was a fan, and he planned on keeping it that way. It was his new addiction and beat the hell out of the bottle. No morning hangover.

He took a bite of beans, and then his phone clanged with an incoming call. He stabbed the fork onto the pile of potatoes to hold it in place and then muted the sound from the television before picking up his phone, pausing a moment to swallow the food and check the display to see who was calling. It was Burt. Shit! McGregor's heartbeat went into overdrive. A call in the evening was rarely to pass on good news.

"What happened?"

"Things went a bit sideways here. Sarah was shot."

McGregor tried to take a breath, but it wouldn't come. He could barely push words out. "Not another one."

"Don't panic. She's okay. She caught one in the shoulder. In surgery now to get the slug out. It wasn't through and through."

"Should I come? I know she doesn't have family in the area."

"No need. I'll stay the night. The sheriff has Gunther in his jail and will hold him as long as necessary. But I figure I can bring the perp to Dallas tomorrow, and maybe Sarah'll be able to come home in a day or two. Will know more later tonight."

"Oh geez!" McGregor set his plate on the table next to the can of Diet Coke, his appetite killed by the news. "I'll let Angel know. Then we'll figure out what to do for Sarah."

"As my buddy Simms is always reminding me, we just have to go with the river's flow."

"Yeah, right," McGregor said, but his heart wasn't in the words. Nothing was right when two of his officers had been shot. Granted, technically, Ryan was Webb's officer, but because of the many times Ryan had assisted Angel and Sarah, McGregor considered the vice cop one of his own. "Keep me posted."

"Will do."

With that, Burt disconnected the call, and McGregor slammed his phone down on the table. He stayed in his chair for long moments, staring at the television, but not focusing on the action flitting across the screen. Then he sighed and picked the phone back up. He didn't look forward to the call to Angel. She didn't need another kick to the gut any more than he did.

Times like this were what made him crave a drink, so the second call would be to his sponsor.

CHAPTER TWENTY-ONE

Wednesday, July 8 - Morning

Sarah opened her eyes and the first thing she saw was a pattern of white tiles above her head, each tile containing dozens of little dark holes. *What the hell?* She blinked and turned her head. Aluminum rails to the side. Okay. She was in a hospital, but she had no clue as to how or why.

She twisted a bit more, and the sudden pain in her right shoulder answered one of those questions. When Burt stood quickly from a chair in the corner, she figured that was the answer to the other question. He walked to the bed. "Hey, Sarah. Good morning."

She tried a smile, but the throbbing pain in her shoulder drove it away. "Not such a good morning after all."

Burt chuckled. "I know I shouldn't laugh, but the fact that you're alive makes it a great morning."

"Thanks." Sarah shifted as best she could, trying to get comfortable. "I don't remember getting here."

"Not a surprise. And probably not a bad idea that you don't recall much from last night."

"I do remember that son of a bitch shooting at everybody. Did anyone else get hurt?"

"Goodman's deputy, Andy, caught a bullet in the leg. But he's okay." Burt smiled. "And Gunther's got a few bruises from you slamming him on the porch."

"Good. I hope they hurt like hell. Gunther. Not Andy." Sarah closed her eyes for a moment.

"You want to go back to sleep?"

She opened her eyes. "Nah. Need to know about the asswipe."

"He's locked up in the sheriff's jail. Just waiting for me to haul him back to Dallas today."

"Do I get to go with you?"

"That's up to the doc, but I doubt it. You had surgery, so they may want to keep you another day or so."

"That sucks."

"Yup. But the good news is you'll probably have a full recovery."

"Probably?"

"You know doctors. They never make promises. But the doc said the bullet didn't mess up any bones. That was in your favor."

"Why the hell couldn't he have shot me in the other shoulder? It's gonna be hell trying to do stuff with my left hand."

"Bad aim?"

"Got his gun?"

"Yup. Bagged and tagged and ready to go."

"Then it was worth it."

Burt shook his head. "Woman. You are a case."

"That's what people keep telling me."

After Burt left, Sarah closed her eyes and leaned back

against the pillow, thankful that she was still here. Above the ground, that is, but wishing she wasn't stuck in the hospital with this hole in her shoulder.

The phone on the bedside table pealed loudly, and she reached with her good hand to grab the receiver, fumbling and almost dropping it before getting it to her ear. It'd been a long time since she'd used an old-fashioned landline telephone.

In response to her "hello," she heard the unmistakable voice of LaVon.

"Sarah. What the hell—"

"I'm fine, LaVon."

"It didn't sound like you were so fine when Angel called last night to tell me what happened. If I could've ditched my court case this morning, I would've been in Texarkana in thirty minutes."

"And risked a speeding ticket to mar your stellar driving record?"

The only response was a sharp intake of breath on the other end. Like McGregor, he didn't always find her humor all that funny. "Don't worry. It's just a minor wound."

"Jesus, woman. A bullet in the shoulder that requires surgery is not minor. I'll try to wrap things up by mid-afternoon and drive over. At a more leisurely pace."

It was good to hear his small attempt at a joke, but still. "There's no need for that, LaVon. I know you have heavy schedules for the next couple of days. And I really am just fine."

"You already said that, and I'm still not sure I'm convinced."

"Maybe this will help. There's a good chance I could go home later today or tomorrow." She hated the small lie, but as much as she'd love to see him, it was silly for him to come. She'd leave tomorrow regardless of what the doctor said.

LaVon let out a deep sigh. "If you're sure?"

"Go do your lawyer thing and let me rest. The more rest I get the quicker I get to come home."

"I'm not comfortable with this."

Sarah gave a slight chuckle. "Neither am I. Shoulder hurts like hell, but we'll get over it."

That was met with a chuckle from the other end. "Okay, then. I'll hang up and let you be."

Sarah almost dropped the receiver again as she struggled to replace it on the cradle. Her last thought as the pain meds and sleep overcame her consciousness was to ask the staff to move the table within easier reach.

McGregor faced the officers who were gathered in the conference room for the morning briefing. "For those of you who haven't heard yet," he said, "Sarah's in the hospital in Texarkana."

There was a collective groan around the room, and McGregor held up his hand to still the reaction. "She's going to be fine. She was shot taking down the guy we suspect was the shooter in the Abrams case."

"Geez. I almost forgot that one. We're juggling so many cases, it feels like we could be a circus act," Simms said.

McGregor gave a weak smile. "If we get a positive on that guy's weapon, we may be able to wrap this one up. What do we have on the CCTV from the night Ryan was shot? Could it be the same guy?"

Simms shook his head. "Doubtful. Chang and I looked at hours and hours of tape. Didn't see any white faces among the looters."

"Damn."

"When will Burt be back?" Chang asked.

"Later today. Bringing Gunther with him. We'll have to wait on ballistics, but it's almost certain he did the Abrams girl. Long shot on whether he shot Ryan."

"Long shot indeed," Simms said. "But he could have been a street over. He have any military training?"

Chang opened her laptop. "Give me just a sec."

They all waited in silence until she looked up. "Was in the army. Washed out of Ranger training."

"Reason?"

"Nothing specified. But he did qualify as a sniper."

"Raises the possibility we get a two-fer." McGregor checked the notes on the table in front of him. "Okay folks, that's all. Get back to it."

With a couple of hours to kill before Burt returned, McGregor decided to run by the hospital to check on Ryan and wasn't surprised to see Angel there. She was alone. He sat down in the closest chair that wasn't taped off for social distancing and inclined his head toward the ICU area. "Any change?"

"Marie thought Ryan was trying to wake up last night but didn't seem to be able to rouse himself."

"She go out?"

"Just down to the cafeteria. Getting a bite to eat, then she'll be back. What's the word on Sarah?"

"She could come home tomorrow."

"Maybe I should go there."

McGregor reached up to loosen his mask for a moment.

Damn thing was cutting into the back of his ear. "No need. Especially if she comes home later today."

"Okay." Angel shifted her gaze to the mural on the wall of the waiting room, almost as if purposely disengaging. "But her there and Ryan here ..."

When Angel didn't continue, McGregor waited a beat then sighed. "I can't imagine how difficult things have been for you lately. With all the shootings, and the protests, and ... " He paused. What the hell was he saying? She knew damn well he had no idea what it was like to live with any kind of discrimination. Let alone the Black experience. And while the seemingly unnecessary shooting of that teenage boy had hit him hard, it sure as hell must have slammed into her like a runaway truck.

On the other hand, while he did have to keep a certain emotional distance, he also had to let her know where he stood. "Okay, Angel. I'm just going to be straight with you. I know you were marching with the demonstrators."

Angel sucked in a breath. "How'd you find out?"

McGregor didn't want to increase the slowly growing rancor between the uniformed officers and the detectives, so he didn't tell her about the visit he'd gotten from Sylvia Prath, a young rookie who'd been on guard duty one night at the federal building. As one of the few Black women on the force, she'd taken special note of Angel some months prior at the station and recognized her when she saw her walking with the protestors. "It doesn't matter how I know. It just matters that I do. And while I understand your motivation, I can't openly condone what you've done."

"I get that."

"What you also need to get is how hard it is for me, and those above me, to keep the peace and try to protect everybody. That's a difficult balancing act to maintain. You must have some clue as to how hard that is."

Angel nodded. "Sarah and I've talked about it in the past. And I …"

McGregor waited for her to continue, but she again she let her thought trail off. "I haven't told Chief Dorsett."

Angel shot him a quick glance.

"And I won't. Unless I'm forced to."

She watched him as if wondering if there was more, but he knew she got the message. Finally, she said, "So, we're good?"

McGregor held her gaze for a beat then said. "Good is relative. But since we're so short-handed, I need you. You have the rest of today. Then I want you at your desk in the morning."

"Noted."

McGregor stood and stretched. "Want to check if I can get in to see Ryan before heading back to the station."

Angel pushed to her feet. "Maybe we can both get in. If that's okay with you?"

"Sure. Come on." McGregor walked down the hall to the ICU monitoring station and stepped to the desk. "Can we have a few minutes with Ryan McDonnell?"

A young nurse with a blonde ponytail looked up, bright blue eyes sparkling with what McGregor guessed was a smile, but she shook her head. "It's not time for visitors yet. Not for another twenty minutes."

"We'll just be a few seconds." He motioned to Angel. "We need to get back to work. His mother can have the regular visit time."

The nurse seemed to consider the request, then nodded. "Okay. But I'll be counting the seconds."

"Thanks." He quickly walked to the room, with Angel just a step or two behind. After entering, he moved to the side of the bed to watch the steady rise and fall of the young officer's chest as the machine pumped air in and out of his lungs. "Damn, Ryan. I hate to see you like this."

One of the machines on the other side of the bed started blaring an alarm. McGregor took a step back, almost bumping into Angel.

The young nurse raced into the room, ponytail bobbing, and hustled over to take care of the noise. "Is that a code again?" McGregor asked.

"No." She pointed to the bed. "Your friend is waking up. Fighting the machine."

McGregor looked at Ryan who now had his eyes open. Angel stepped closer. "Oh, thank God," she said.

"You need to leave while we remove the tube," the nurse said, her tone not inviting a debate. "Now."

McGregor and Angel obeyed as two other nurses hustled into the room and closed the door. A few moments later, the nurses stepped out, and the pretty blonde said, "He wants to see you."

"Great." McGregor started to push past her.

"But just for those few seconds you promised me, officer. And keep your masks on. He's still a very sick man."

McGregor held up two fingers. "Scout's honor."

"I'll hold you to the honor." The nurse moved aside to let them enter.

"Hey," McGregor said, keeping an awkward few feet from the bed. "Nice to see you looking back at us."

Ryan responded with a weak smile that grew a little stronger when he spotted Angel who stood a hair's breadth behind the lieutenant.

"Word is, you're going to have a full recovery," McGregor said. "We knew you were too tough to let a couple of bullets take you down."

"There were two?" Ryan aimed the question at McGregor without taking his eyes from Angel.

"Bullets, yes. Shooter, probably just one. The whole department's looking for the scumbag," McGregor said. "We, uh … It'd help if you could talk about that night. We'll be quick."

Ryan glanced from Angel to the lieutenant and gave a small nod.

"Did you see the person who shot you?"

Ryan gave a slight shake of his head. "It was all so crazy. So fast. One minute I'm talking to my CI. The next, this mass of folks comes rushing down the street like a human flood. Yelling and screaming and throwing bricks into windows. My CI runs, and all I can think is I have to stop the looters."

"All by yourself?" Angel asked.

Ryan glanced at her. "There were some Uniforms nearby. But I was closer. Made it to the store first and saw the guys climbing through the broken window."

"How many were there?" McGregor asked.

Ryan closed his eyes and took so long to answer McGregor panicked and turned to Angel. "Shit! Did we put him back into the coma?"

A hint of a smile crossed Ryan's face. "Just thinking, Lieu. Just thinking. I only saw five trying to gain entry. But didn't count now many were cheering them on."

"Any weapons in the crowd?" McGregor asked.

Ryan shook his head. "But I was focused on the looters. Didn't check the whole crowd. Happened too fast."

"What were you meeting your CI for?" Angel asked.

"He had info about a new distributor muscling in on the Crips' territory. Lots of talk on the streets about a possible gang war."

"Great," McGregor said. "Just what we need on top of all the other bullshit going on in the city."

Ryan closed his eyes for a moment, Angel touched his arm lightly. "You okay?"

"Just give me a sec."

"We could come back," McGregor offered. "Don't want to set you back."

"Hurts like a son of a bitch."

Angel waited to give him a moment to regain his strength, then asked, "But why meet so close to where the protests are happening?"

Ryan took a shallow breath, then said, "Not sure why he asked to meet there. But he's always given good info. Thought it was worth it."

"And was it?" McGregor asked.

Ryan tried to laugh but the attempt turned into grimace. A clear indication that the effort hurt too much.

"Sorry. That was a lame attempt at humor," McGregor said. "Take us through the sequence if you can."

"Okay." Ryan shifted in the bed and clenched his jaw in pain again.

"Is this too much?" Angel asked. "We can come back."

"No. It's fine." Ryan managed a weak smile. "My CI and I had just gotten to the little Irish pub on Main, where we'd agreed to meet. Hadn't even started to talk when we heard the gang of looters coming down the street."

"What exactly did you hear?" McGregor asked.

"Glass breaking at the Neiman Marcus store. Lots of shouting."

"No threats to cops?"

Ryan shook his head. "Then my CI bolted. Didn't blame him. In his shoes, I wouldn't want to be seen with a cop by all those angry people."

"Why didn't you run?" Angel asked.

Surprise registered on his face. "Would you have?"

Angel didn't have a chance to answer as the nurse stepped into the room, followed by Marie. "You'll have to leave now," the nurse said. "Give him a few minutes with his mother."

"Sure," Angel said. "I'll come back."

"Yeah, well, me, too." McGregor shifted his bulk from foot to foot, a sudden wave of awkwardness taking hold of him. When not able to ask questions, he never quite knew what to say at times like this. "We're pulling for you," he added as he moved toward the door, internally acknowledging how relieved he was that Ryan was out of danger.

Now if he could just keep the rest of his cops safe.

CHAPTER TWENTY-TWO

Wednesday, July 8 - Afternoon

After leaving the hospital, Angel stopped at a Subway for a quick lunch. She thought she was hungry when she ordered the six-inch bacon club sandwich, but after a few bites her stomach tightened, and she simply couldn't swallow anymore. She wasn't surprised at her body's reaction to the food. It had been that way for a little over a week now. And even the deep breathing relaxation techniques she'd learned from Randy at the dojo weren't making much of a dent in her level of stress.

Restless and out of sorts, she debated about what to do next. She wasn't up for another workout or having a conversation with Randy. Normally she welcomed his counsel, but today she didn't feel like talking. Or listening. And she definitely didn't want to simply go home to do nothing. An option was to meet up with that James guy, but she hadn't heard any more from Tyrell about an introduction.

Still, that didn't mean she couldn't go by the apartments in Hamilton Park to check out the area. And she was still in civvies. No better time to take a swing by.

After attempting a couple more bites of the sandwich, she gave up. She hated to throw food away, but her stomach had refused to give her an alternative, so she rewrapped the sandwich and carried it to the trash. The elderly lady at a table across from her gave Angel a disapproving purse of her lips. Angel shrugged a silent apology, grabbed her iced tea, and headed to the door. Heat slapped her in the face the minute she stepped out, and she quickened her pace to the car.

Ten minutes of driving brought her to the apartment complex. It was nice to see that the area was cleaner and appeared better maintained than the conditions during her last visit as a patrol officer responding to a domestic violence incident. Thankfully, that had been resolved with nobody getting hurt beyond a few bruises the woman gave her drunk husband.

Pulling into the main entrance, she followed her memory around the first set of buildings to a quad-type area that had playground equipment for kids, some picnic tables, and a few trees to offer shade for families wanting to cook outside. Easing slowly into one of the parking spots for visitors, she kept the engine running and glanced over to where a couple of guys sat at one of the picnic tables. They looked young. Early twenties or late teens maybe. They both wore sleeveless tees and had well-muscled arms on full display. One had skin so dark he could've been an ebony statue in a do-rag. The man with a Mavericks cap had skin that was even lighter toned than Angel.

She watched them for a minute, then got out of the car, put on her sunglasses, slung her purse over her shoulder, and walked toward the picnic area. She purposely didn't look at the guys as she approached, not wanting to spook them if they smelled cop on her.

Settling at a nearby table, Angel pulled her phone out of her bag and pretended to be very engrossed in something she found in notifications. She kept that ruse going for almost a full minute, then gave an exasperated sigh and put the phone down. Then she glanced around the little park area, finally letting her gaze settle on the two young men. She smiled. "How's it going?"

They didn't answer, but she didn't miss the slight tensing of the muscles in their shoulders. She shrugged and turned back to her phone to scroll through a few messages without actually reading them, letting a few more minutes elapse.

Then she tried again. "You guys live here?"

They took so long to answer Angel was afraid she might have spooked them, but then the guy with the Mavericks ball cap said, "What's it to you?"

"Looking to score."

The other kid stood abruptly, his height more than a little intimidating. "You a narc?"

Angel raised her sunglasses and gave him her best impression of an amused reaction. "Just chill, man. My friend Tyrell told me this was a good place to come for somethin' somethin'. I was to ask for James."

The two teens exchanged a quick glance, and Angel watched the tension in their bodies ease just a bit. Apparently, the mention of Tyrell's name still had cred around here.

"We heard Tyrell was straight," the other teen said. "Got himself all respectable."

Angel gave a little chuckle. "That don't mean he doesn't know the way things are around here. Tyrell and me. We go way back."

The big guy sat down again, and Angel waited a beat before she focused on him and asked, "So. This James. He around?"

The guy shook his head.

"You know when he might be around?"

Another head shake.

"Who takes care of business when he's not here?"

That question was answered with a shrug, and Angel wondered if she dare push any further. After considering for a moment, she decided it was probably better not to spook them. She could always come back tonight. More action took place after dark than in broad daylight.

She took a few minutes to again focus on her phone to keep the ruse of the casual stop in the little park going, then stood and sauntered toward her car.

Burt made it back to Dallas right around two in the afternoon. It had taken longer than anticipated to get all the paperwork in order so he could bring Gunther from Arkansas, but now the perp was securely stashed in the jail. Burt carried the rifle Gunther had used, as well as a Baggie with used shells, over to Hanks in Ballistics. "Any chance I can get a test on this this afternoon?" Burt dropped the plastic bag on the counter next to the microscope Hanks was currently squinting into.

The short man, whose bulk hung over the narrow stool he was using, didn't even look up. "Take a number."

That was a standard response here, as well as in Forensics. There were always too many cases ahead of the one that was most pressing to the detective now pestering the scientist.

Aware that it was a real longshot, Burt played the card anyway. "There's a chance these shells are from the gun that shot Ryan."

That got the portly man's attention. He turned from the microscope and pinned Burt with his rheumy eyes that were almost hidden behind thick glasses. "You blowing smoke up my ass, Detective?"

"Wouldn't touch your ass, Timothy," Burt said, softening the comment with a slight grin. "But I will buy you a beer sometime after work. If you ever leave this dungeon."

"I only drink scotch."

"Noted."

"Where'd this weapon come from?"

Burt gave him a condensed version of the perp in Texarkana and apprehending him, along with the gun, finishing with, "Pretty sure this is the weapon that was used in the July sixth shooting downtown. Not so sure about tying it to Ryan, but it would be good to know one way or another."

Hanks took his glasses off and used the tail of his lab coat to clean the lenses before putting them back on. "Get the slugs from the July six shooting, and I'll do the test in an hour."

~*~

Burt knocked on the open door to McGregor's office and poked his head in. "Hey, Boss. I got Hanks to rush the ballistics test on Gunther's gun. Perfect match to the slugs taken from Phyllis Abrams' body."

"And Ryan?"

Burt shook his head.

"Damn." McGregor leaned back in his chair and sighed. "And I'm guessing not for our first vic?"

"Nope."

"What's Gunther got to say for himself?"

"Nothing beyond a few racial slurs and spouting his right to have a gun."

"In this case that *right* just might land him on death row."

"I'm not a proponent of the death penalty, but for this guy I agree with you wholeheartedly. If we could've gotten him for Ryan, I'd shoot the bastard myself."

"I'm going to pretend I didn't hear that."

Burt chuckled. "You should have seen the guy's place. Goodman and I went through it and even I found all the white supremacy stuff offensive. Hate to think what Goodman felt with the n-word scrawled on the wall under the Confederate flag."

"Jeeze!"

"And there was a manifesto. Basically, urging all the pure whites to arm up and get ready for the fight. Got it processed into evidence."

McGregor sighed and motioned for Burt to come all the way into the room. "Good work on that. Now, where do we stand on the Cummings shooting? Any progress there?"

Burt pulled a metal folding chair from against the wall and sat down. "Momentum got stalled with this trip to Texarkana and all. But we do have a possible suspect. The husband of the hairdresser Cummings was seeing, Wanda. Husband has quite a temper, and the woman didn't know when he found out about her and Cummings. But she was pretty sure he knew. When we spoke to him, he said he had his woman under control. His words. Also gave us an alibi of sorts. First part checked out. Sarah was going to call Wanda to get verification of when her husband came home the night of the shooting. That's when the shit hit the fan with this second downtown shooting."

"Okay. See if you can sort it out."

"Sure thing, Lieu. I'll swing by the salon after filing my report from our Texarkana vacation."

McGregor waved one hand in a dismissive gesture, his mind obviously moving to another topic. He tended to do that. Switch tracks as smoothly as a train coming into a large depot.

Burt went to his desk to write up the day's report and was in the middle of that when a notification pinged on his phone. He glanced at the screen to see a news alert with the headline: Police Officer Formally Charged. Clicking on the headline, Burt was taken to the news story that included a photograph of the young rookie officer, Smithfield, with his attorney by his side. The two of them stood on the steps of the courthouse surrounded by members of the media. Burt looked closely at the recent widow, whose appearance and demeanor shouted business as usual. Not a glimmer of grief on her face or in her posture.

Granted, she had a job to do, but it had only been days since her husband had been shot. Wasn't she still in mourning? Or had she truly not cared for, or about, her husband? Was there a possible motive lurking there? That was an interesting thought. Sarah had voiced the same curiosity about the widow after the second interview. Could two hunches be right?

Burt shook that question off. If the lead they already had didn't pan out, they could take a closer look at Mrs. Cummings. First things first.

After typing the last few words of the report, Burt shut down his computer and left to go home, planning a detour to The Beauty and The Beast hair salon. When he walked in, a pretty young girl at the front reception counter smiled brightly at him. A nametag pinned to her blouse identified her as Melody. "Hello," she said. "Welcome to Beauty and the Beast. Do you have an appointment, sir?"

"Sorry. No." Burt took a step closer to the counter and showed her his badge. "Hoping to have a quick word with the owner."

"Oh." Melody's smile faltered just a bit. "She's not in this evening. May I be of assistance?"

Mentally berating himself for not snagging the woman's contact information before he left the station, Burt slipped his wallet back into his pocket. "Hopefully you can. I need her home phone number."

The young woman hesitated a beat. "I gave that information to the officers who were here the other day."

"Yeah, I know. Like an idiot I left the station without it. Any chance you can help a forgetful old man out?" He followed that question with what he hoped was his most charming smile, although it had been a long time since he'd had to try his charm on a lovely young lady.

There was silence again for another beat before Melody rearranged her professional demeanor into that of the helpful employee. "Certainly. I'll be happy to be of assistance." She grabbed a sticky note, wrote something on it, then handed the paper to him.

Out in the car, Burt dialed the number Melody had given him and after four rings the connection went to voicemail, where he was encouraged to leave a message. Remembering what Sarah had told him about how volatile Wanda's husband could be, he decided not to leave a message, and perhaps cause trouble for the wife. Verifying this alibi was important, but not worth that kind of risk.

CHAPTER TWENTY-THREE

Thursday, July 9 - Evening

In response to the knock on her apartment door Sarah pushed herself awkwardly from the sofa, cradling her arm that was immobilized with a sling. The doctor had told her to wear it for at least a week to let the surgery site heal. He'd also highly recommended she stay in the hospital another day. They could take good care of her there, but Sarah had been adamant. She had to go home. If she was supposed to rest so she could heal, resting would be a lot easier in a quiet apartment instead of in a busy hospital where she was interrupted every couple of hours for checks on her vitals or the level of water in her water pitcher.

Reluctantly, the doctor had signed the discharge order and turned her over to Goodman who was there for a visit and had offered to drive her to Dallas. He'd dropped her off less than an hour ago, at first hovering like some kind of macho mother hen until she told him to go home to his wife. She, Sarah, would be just fine. She could do a lot of things with just one hand. Including making herself a bowl of cereal for supper.

Anticipating that it might be Goodman at the door, coming back for something he'd forgotten, or to offer one last bit of assistance, Sarah was surprised when she looked through the peephole and saw Angel on her doorstep.

Awkwardly, Sarah undid the locks and swung open the door. Angel stepped inside, carrying bags of take-out that had the most enticing aromas trailing her. "I hope you like Thai food. I wasn't sure. But a dish of noodles can sit well when one is a bit under par."

"That's a delicate way of putting it. The under-par reference."

"Yeah. Well. So, what do you think?" Angel held one of the bags aloft.

Sarah hated to admit that she'd never tasted Thai food. So, she didn't respond to that question other than motioning Angel to bring the bags to the kitchen counter. "We could eat out of the Styrofoam containers," Angel said. "Or point me in the direction of your bowls, and I'll transfer the food."

"Wait a minute. I mean … I appreciate this. But we've never done the … you know …" Sarah gestured awkwardly at the food. "Casually sharing an impromptu meal like old friends."

Angel turned to look at Sarah for a long moment. "Maybe it's time we changed that."

Well, fuck a duck. Sarah had been trying to curb her propensity for colorful language, but right now she didn't care. She'd gladly put five bucks in McGregor's swear jar. After a moment of trying to figure out how to respond to her partner, she pointed to a nearby cabinet. "Bowls are in there."

"I thought LaVon might be here," Angel said. "I brought enough for three."

"Oh." They hadn't talked much about her brother and the

relationship in a while, so Sarah was surprised at the casual mention. Obviously, they didn't have to talk about the subject to keep an awareness. "He was a little worried about COVID. Apparently, someone on the judge's staff tested positive this morning. Didn't want to bring me any germs."

"Hope he manages to dodge them." Angel glanced at Sarah. "You want me to wear a mask?"

"We don't have to hug." Sarah added a smile, to let Angel know it was a joke, and the slight tension that had been in the room eased.

Angel served up the noodles that were swimming in a shimmering brown broth, and they both took seats at the small table. Sarah looked at her dish, not recognizing any of the green vegetables or what was supposed to be noodles. They didn't look like any noodle she'd ever seen. She took a tentative bite, chewed then swallowed. "This is good. What's it called?"

"Boat noodle soup."

"Really?"

"It has a Thai name, but that one's easier to pronounce." Angel gave her a quizzical look. "You haven't tasted Thai food before, have you?"

Sarah gave a little chuckle. "Busted."

Angel smiled. "Glad you like it."

For a few minutes the room was quiet except for the clink of metal against glass as they ate. Sarah wondered what had prompted this about-face with Angel, but she didn't want to spoil the moment by asking. If Angel had an agenda, she'd get to it when she was ready.

After a couple more attempts to get more of the food in her mouth than on her face, Sarah put her spoon down. "How's Ryan? McGregor told me he woke up."

Angel nodded. "He's definitely on an upswing."

"And how are you? With the protests and all?"

Angel shrugged. "Thanks for not telling on me."

Ah. So, McGregor did know. Sarah wondered how he'd found out, but maybe that was something she didn't have to know. She awkwardly maneuvered a few more spoons of broth to her mouth, then put the spoon down again, glancing over at Angel. "Going to go back?"

Angel shook her head. "McGregor made it clear what would happen."

Sarah waited another beat, then said, "For what it's worth, I'd consider marching."

Angel choked on a mouthful of noodles. "Really?!"

Sarah used her napkin to mop the juice that had run down her chin. Eating with her non-dominant hand was a bitch. Especially soup. Then she looked squarely at her partner. "Really."

"You'd risk your career for me?"

"Sorry. Not just for you. For all the victims of police brutality and the senseless deaths. And to tell the truth, I'm sick of having to be on one side of that thin blue line. Shit. I'm sick of the fact that we even have that."

Surprise registered on Angel's face in a widening of her eyes, then she asked, "What about you? When that line stood by you?"

Sarah stirred her noodles for a moment, using the time to formulate an answer. "I'd give anything to rewind that night. John would be alive. That kid would be alive. I wouldn't have to live with the guilt for all these years since."

Angel leaned back in her chair and cocked her head toward Sarah. "I didn't know it still bothered you."

"You don't get over shooting a kid. Ever. Bad enough to

shoot a scumbag. But a kid ...? Shit." Sarah pushed her plate aside and stood, averting her face so Angel couldn't see the tears threatening. "Be right back."

After closing her bedroom door, Sarah went to the adjoining bathroom and grabbed a washcloth. Awkwardly, she used her good hand to wet the rag with cold water and wiped at the tears she hadn't been able to hold back after leaving the table. Maybe the cold water would keep her face from getting all splotchy, which is usually what happened when she cried. She didn't know why she was having the emotional breakdown, but could guess at a few reasons. Number one on that list was being shot, followed closely by pain meds that messed with her ability to hold it all together. Number three was this unexpected kindness from Angel.

Damn, that woman never failed to surprise her.

She took another minute or two to try to erase any sign of the meltdown, then went back to the kitchen. Angel was on her cell phone, talking in low tones, and she quickly hung up when she saw Sarah. "You okay?"

"Just dandy." Sarah sat down, avoiding eye contact. She didn't want sympathy from Angel because that would only shatter the calm that she'd managed to achieve before coming back out. "But I'm not very hungry. I think the antibiotic and the pain meds aren't sitting well."

"Then I should go." Angel stood. "I'll clear this up first."

Sarah nodded to the phone that was face down on the table. "Something come up?"

Angel took the bowls to the sink and scraped the leftover food into the disposal. "What do you want me to do with these? Handwash them?"

"They can go in the dishwasher." Sarah waited until Angel had stowed all the dirty dishes and came back for her phone and purse. Then she asked again, "What is it?"

Angel paused, an internal debate clearly registering in her eyes, then she said, "Meeting someone who might have information on Ryan's shooter."

"Now? Alone?"

Angel nodded.

"Is this person a CI?"

"No."

"Who is it?"

Angel hesitated a beat then said, "Guy who controls Hamilton Park."

"What the hell?" The thought of her partner going to that neighborhood alone ... Sarah stood. "I'm coming with you."

"You're in no con—"

"No arguments. I'll just use my good arm."

"For what?"

"To hold a gun if I need to." Sarah paused a beat then offered a crooked grin. "Just don't tell anyone that it's not my good arm. Perps should think I can still shoot straight."

Angel opened her mouth. Probably to protest, but Sarah stopped her. "Not open to debate."

"Okay. But I'm driving."

"Good. I sure as hell can't."

Angel pulled her car into the same parking area she'd used the other day when she'd come here, but everything was so different in the darkness. Some of the streetlights were out, and lights on buildings were sporadic, leaving sections of the complex in shadows.

"This doesn't look inviting," Sarah said from the passenger seat.

"Should be better illumination at the park. That's where I was told to meet James."

"Who's your informant?"

"Can't tell you. Promised I'd keep the identity secret."

Sarah awkwardly twisted her left arm until she could push the seatbelt release, then tried to reach across her body to the door handle. "Um. Need some help here."

Angel chuckled. "Be right there." She got out and walked around the front of the car to open Sarah's door. After locking the vehicle, Angel led the way to the park, wondering briefly if the same guys she'd seen the other day might still be hanging out.

The picnic benches were empty, but several young men were clustered in the walkway between two building. One, wearing low-slung jeans shorts and a sleeveless white tee weighted down with several gold chains, was leaning against the wall. Definitely a different breed of small-time hustler than the two she'd seen earlier, and maybe not small-time at all.

This man, all full of attitude and bravado, pushed away from the wall and swaggered over to Angel. "What do you want here, ho?"

"Sure as hell didn't come here to suck your sorry-ass dick."

That comment was met with a few hoots of laughter from the other others that was quickly quelled when the guy whirled and shot them an angry glare. Then he turned back to Angel. "If not for those," he mimed holding a big set of boobs, "I'd think you were a dude with more balls than good sense. You know who you just dissed?"

"Do I look like I care?" Angel heard a slight intake of breath from Sarah who was slightly behind her, but she didn't turn. She held the steely gaze of this guy who was trying his best to disarm her with all this attitude and the "look."

He broke first. "You got business here? Looking for something?" He mimed taking a toke.

"Not here for that," Angel said. "And unless your name is James, you're not the person I'm looking for."

The guy sized her up again, then did the same to Sarah, before a slow realization flickered in his eyes. "Oh, fuck. You're cops!"

At that pronouncement, the others scattered like gamblers caught in a raid. Angel watched them run, then turned back to the tall man who was twirling one of his necklaces as if he didn't have a concern in the world. "You lost your posse."

"Ah, they be okay. Close enough if I need them." He did a chin nod to Sarah. "What happened to your partner."

"Surgery," Sarah said before Angel could answer. "Rotator cuff."

"Bad business." He rolled his shoulders. "Mine are both good."

"I'm sure they are," Angel said. "But we didn't come here to trade surgical war stories. Do you know James? Where he is? I was told he was here."

"He was. Now he gone."

"Where?"

The loud report of a gunshot drowned any response the man was going to make, and he whirled to tear off into the darkness in the opposite direction of the shots. Bullets pinged off the concrete at Angel's feet. She drew her weapon and ducked around the corner of the building, Sarah right behind her.

More shots rang out and Angel turned to Sarah. "Can you reach your phone?"

"Got it. Calling it in."

Not knowing exactly where the shots were coming from, Angel didn't want to indiscriminately fire back. No telling where civilians were, and she sure as hell didn't want to be another cop who shot an unarmed man or woman.

A few minutes later, the wail of a siren could be heard, and Angel decided it was the best thing she'd heard in days. At the same time, the shooting stopped, so she figured that whoever was behind the gun heard the approaching backup and decided to flee.

Vehicles screamed into the area, blue and red and yellow lights chasing away the shadows. Once it was clear that the shooter, or shooters, wouldn't take on the new cops, Angel and Sarah moved from the cover of the building and walked toward the first patrol car.

McGregor stepped out and slammed the door. "You okay?"

Angel nodded.

"Jesus Christ, Angel. What the hell were you doing?"

"Following a lead on somebody who might've been Ryan's shooter."

"And you decided maybe you could be a victim of that same shooter?"

Angel stood firm against the force of the anger that drove his words like tiny fists hitting her in the stomach. "We don't know it's the same guy."

"Sure. We just have a bunch of assholes out there taking pot shots at cops."

The comment dripped with sarcasm, but Angel didn't

react to it. She took a few breaths then said, "Lots of people in the city are angry. And too many of those angry people have guns."

He took so long to respond, she wasn't sure what her boss would say, then he sighed. "You're right."

Not waiting for her response, McGregor then turned to Sarah. "And you? Getting shot once wasn't enough?"

"With all due respect, sir, we didn't come here for the fireworks."

McGregor glared.

"Sorry, sir. Didn't mean to be flippant. Just the adrenaline talking."

He glared for another few seconds, before saying, "Get back to your apartment and stay there." Then he poked a finger at Angel. "Be at your desk tomorrow morning. Don't move from there until I decide whether fire your ass. Hell, maybe I'll jettison both of you. Lower my blood pressure significantly. Now, get out of my sight."

"Yes, sir."

On the way back to Sarah's place, Angel drove for a few blocks in silence, then asked, "You think he's really going to fire us?"

"Nah. He's shorthanded."

CHAPTER TWENTY-FOUR

Thursday, July 9 - Night

After helping Sarah get settled, Angel left the apartment with the intention of going home. Now that the adrenaline surge had flattened, exhaustion dogged her. She'd just pulled out of the apartment complex when the ring of her phone punctuated the nighttime silence. It was tempting to just ignore the call, but then it might be news about Ryan. She slowed and pulled over to answer. "Hello?"

"Tyrell said you wanted to meet."

James? Must be. "Thought that was happening earlier this evening."

"You didn't come alone."

"You really expected me to walk into that den of thieves without someone to have my back?"

"You don't understand. I don't *expect*. I *demand*."

The emphasis wasn't missed despite the rather bad connection, and the force of the words sent a chill down Angel's spine. According to what Tyrell had said, this guy was supposed to be a mid-level drug dealer, but he sure as hell didn't sound like someone that far down the food chain. She almost gave in to the impulse to hang up, but too much was riding on this. She took a breath and let it out slowly, then said, "Okay."

"I'll meet you alone. For five minutes."

"Same place?"

"No. At the old high school football field."

Angel had no doubt about the reference. If James and Tyrell were friends, then he could only mean the field by the old high school she'd attended. The field that had played an important role in her youth when she'd gone to watch Bobby play ball, until he'd thrown it all away with drugs. His hopes for a scholarship, and her hopes for the whole marriage, kids, family thing with him. She didn't remember someone named James in their class, but it was a large school, and got even larger in the years after she'd graduated. A new school, with a new football field had been built three years ago to accommodate a growing number of students, and the timeworn classroom buildings with the broken bricks and the sagging roof had been razed to make way for the new. The old field, skirting the edge of the school complex, had stayed empty, grandstand starting to crumble, as well as bleachers. Not the best place to meet, but ... "Okay. When?"

"Now."

The line went dead.

That must mean he was either there, or close. Angel did a quick mental calculation. This time of night with little traffic, she should be able to make it in fifteen minutes. She pushed her accelerator hard, screeched out of the parking lot, and jumped ahead of what looked like a slow-moving car to tear down the street.

Hoping she wouldn't get stopped for speeding, she raced

as fast as she dared until reaching the site of the old Samuel Perkins High School. There, she doused her headlights and eased off the gas, pulling to a stop a block away from the abandoned field. She flicked the switch that turned off the interior light, then slowly eased out of the car, closing the door with a soft click. Unlike Hamilton Park, this area was not under the control of D-Town gang members. There was no regulation, no hierarchy to keep order, no checks and balances, even if those weren't always of the lawful nature. People who tended to gather here were washouts from the different gangs, druggies, homeless people with varying degrees of mental illness. In short, a lot of dangerous folks in a concentrated area, with no police presence and very little illumination. Reaching around, she touched the butt of her weapon stuck in the waistband of her jeans.

Protection. But would it be enough if things went south?

Momentarily regretting not asking Sarah to come with her again, Angel tamped down her fear and walked toward the field, almost bumping into a figure who emerged out of the deepest shadow like some apparition. She stepped back, instinctively grabbing for her weapon.

"Hands in front." The voice was unmistakable.

Still, she asked as she slowly held her hands out in a non-threatening pose. "James?"

"Yes."

He wasn't at all what she expected. The faint glow of a crescent moon reflected on glasses rimmed in black, and his jeans, while baggy, were closer to his waist than his knees. Face a dark brown, he was of average height, and his demeanor was anything but menacing.

"We going to talk here?" she asked.

"Be quick."

"Tyrell tell you what this is about?"

James nodded, then tapped his wrist as if he had a watch. Which he didn't. "Time's wasting."

Okay. That's the way this was going to be. "Were you out there with the rioters that night the cop was shot?"

"Yes."

"One of the looters?"

"You gonna arrest me?"

"No. Just want information."

"I was with them. But I didn't have a gun."

"You know who the shooter was?"

James took so long to answer, Angel started to wonder if he ever would. Then when he did, there was a slight hesitation in the words. "If I name him, you gotta make sure nobody knows."

All semblance of tough-guy evaporated for a moment, and James was just a young guy that Angel could almost feel sorry for. "How deep are you into this?"

"Far enough that my ass'll fry if word gets out."

"I'll do my best. But you know I can't promise."

"No promise. No information." The tough guy was back, steel in his eyes again.

A cloud passed over the moon, momentarily casting them in total darkness. When illumination returned, James was still staring at her, unblinking. "That's the way it's gotta be."

"Other than not revealing identity, what else do you need?"

"Protection."

Tall order, but what choice did she have?

"Give me a minute." She held her hands out, palms facing him. "I'm getting my phone to make a call."

"Okay."

Moving slowly, Angel took her phone out of the pocket of her slacks, took a few steps away from him, and tapped the number for Sarah. "You still awake?"

"Angel? What the hell?"

"I've got a situation."

"Thought you were going home."

"I was. Listen. I need your help."

"Are we getting shot at again?"

"I have a serious lead on who shot Ryan."

There was a quick intake of breath from Sarah, then she said, "Okay. Call for backup. You heard McGregor."

Angel turned to make sure James was still there. "I will. Listen. I need to bring my informant to your place."

"What?!"

"He could be in danger."

"Take him to the station."

"You're closer."

"Oh geez." There was silence for a long moment, then, "Come on."

Angel hung up and walked back to James. "I'll take you to a safe place. Now the name."

"Frank Purcell."

"Know where he lives?"

James nodded.

"Come on. You can tell me on the way." She reached out and grasped his arm, holding firm when he tried to pull away.

CHAPTER TWENTY-FIVE

Same Night

A ngel's phone pinged with a message as she stepped out of the elevator at the station. She'd stashed James with Sarah a half hour ago. Talked her partner out of the desire to be part of whatever was going to go down with the Purcell guy. And called McGregor to tell him about the lead.

The text was from McGregor.

My office. Now.

There was no need to respond. He wouldn't expect it.

Angel headed toward the office and entered through the open door. Lieutenant Webb, looking like he'd just stumbled out of bed, was sitting in one of the metal folding chairs in front of McGregor's desk. She gave him a nod before glancing toward her boss.

McGregor was equally rumpled, and there was nothing welcoming in his expression. He didn't have to tell her how much he hated a midnight rendezvous, but, still, there was a hint of excitement in his eyes. The same kind of excitement she'd felt when James called her. Angel hoped that meant

McGregor would be onboard with the demands from James. "How sure are you about what you told me on the phone?"

"Reliable sources." Angel said.

"Names?"

"I can't say on the first. But the informant is James."

"James …?" McGregor let the sentence fade, inviting her to fill in the blank. When she said nothing, he sighed. "Okay. Where is this James guy?"

"He can't be seen at the station."

McGregor glared, and Webb jumped in with a question. "How connected is he?"

Angel turned to Webb. "Deep enough to be in danger because of this. I promised him protection."

"On whose authority?" McGregor asked.

Angel gave him a level look. "Mine, sir."

Silence descended on the room like a deflated balloon. Angel wasn't sure if McGregor was going to explode or fire her right now for insubordination. But she was oh, so very tired of the politics. Of trying to get along in the department. The power struggles. All of the things that had made her afraid to stand up as a proud Black woman.

No more.

Finally, Webb gave a little cough then said, "That might be a good idea." He waited a beat until McGregor broke eye contact with Angel.

"I'm listening," McGregor said.

"If Ryan's CI was right about the threat of a turf war, this James could be in real danger. Everyone's on edge. Watching their soldiers for the slightest wrong move. Even the hint of suspicion can get a guy killed."

McGregor leaned back in his chair and slowly rubbed a hand across a cheek heavy with a nighttime shadow of beard.

It was a familiar thinking posture. Then he sat forward and pointed at Webb. "Call Grotelli and see how many Uniforms he can spare. I gotta notify Dorsett to arrange for the marshals to pick up the informant. Then call SWAT."

Turning to Angel he said, "You. Go home."

Angel didn't move. "With all due respect, sir, I—"

McGregor held out a hand to stop her, his face turning an alarming shade of red. "You have a death wish like your partner?"

"No, sir." Angel was careful to keep her voice level. "Just want to do my job."

Tension strained between them as if they were opponents in a tug of war contest. Angel held firm and didn't break eye contact. She also didn't let go of her end of the rope. She was going to win this one.

After a few agonizing moments, McGregor gave a slight head nod, then said. "Get your gear. You know the drill."

"Yes, sir."

Angel habitually kept her vest in the trunk of her car along with her uniform for Tae Kwon Do. Her extra weapon was in a lock box, also in the trunk. She donned the Kevlar. Changed into cargo pants right there in the parking lot. If someone saw her yellow undies it was their good luck. That fanciful thought brought a smile for a moment, then it was all business again.

She unlocked the gun box and checked the Glock. Fully loaded. Then she put two extra magazines in the pockets of her pants.

Ready. Set. Just waiting for the communications gear and the signal to go. She was beyond tired and wished she could take advantage of the wait to get a short nap, but the adrenaline racing through her body was as good as a double espresso for keeping her awake. And she wanted this bastard. Wanted him real bad.

Unlike the last time Angel had been involved in a suspect take-down a few years ago, this was deep night and the residential street had no traffic. Coming into the area where Purcell lived in a one-story frame house, a shabby intrusion between two well-kept homes, she'd noted the patrol cars parked at the top and bottom of connecting streets. No traffic would make it through to disrupt the arrest.

Driving past the house, Angel pulled to a stop two blocks down where other vehicles were parked, got out of her car, and waited until she saw McGregor moving toward her. "SWAT's in position," he said quietly. "Behind in the alley and across the street."

Angel wasn't surprised she hadn't seen those officers. She wasn't necessarily supposed to. Any interaction would go through their communication devices.

"Grotelli's got Grantham coming with the ram. Should be here about now."

Angel nodded, sweat pooling on her back under the vest. She wasn't sure if it was because of the heat that was still oppressive despite the hour, or if nerves were causing the waterworks.

The minute Doug and another uniformed officer arrived, McGregor let the SWAT team know they were ready to go. No hesitation. No waiting. Everyone sprinted toward the house, and as soon as the door was breached, Angel followed McGregor inside. They faced a long hallway with doors on both sides. McGregor moved to the left, so she hugged the right side, letting her flashlight and gun lead the way around doorframes.

First opening was to what looked like a living room. Sofa. Tables. Chairs. Fireplace. All clear.

Next was a small room. Storage? Boxes stacked tight against walls. No spaces in between for anyone to hide.

McGregor signaled with his flashlight toward a closed door further down. Angel nodded and followed him, each keeping to opposite sides of the hallway.

When the door of that room suddenly opened, a jolt of adrenaline took Angel precariously close to squeezing the trigger. A half-dressed woman burst out, sprinting despite the sagging jeans that threatened to trip her up. The beam from McGregor's flashlight caught the woman square in the face, and she held her hands high. "Don't shoot," she screamed as she ran. "Just let me get out of here."

In mere seconds she was past them, and Angel turned, ready to take up pursuit.

"Let her go," McGregor whispered. "She won't get far."

Angel acknowledged with a chin nod and focused on the door the woman had slammed shut, moving in tandem with McGregor, inching closer to the room. Probably a bedroom if the state of the woman's undress meant anything. "Purcell," Angel called out. "This is the police. You're surrounded. Come out with your hands up."

A barrage of bullets splintered the wood of the door and poured down the hall. Instinctively, Angel pressed her body to the wall. Across from her, McGregor did the same, but one caught him, knocking him to his knees.

An eerie silence followed.

"Lieu! Where are you hit?" Despite the distinct possibility

more bullets were about to fly, Angel dashed to him and moved her light around, checking for blood.

"Caught me in the chest," McGregor said, voice hoarse with the effort to breathe. "Thank God for Kevlar."

"We can't just sit here."

"Give me a second."

Angel activated her walkie-talkie. "Webb? You there?"

"Yeah. Everyone okay inside?"

"We're good. Suspect in back room on my left facing it. Is there a window?"

A few seconds later, "Affirmative."

"If the bastard tries to escape, have the SWAT sniper take him out."

"Affirmative."

Then Webb clicked off.

Angel patted McGregor. "Stay here and breathe." Then she moved a few feet closer to the door. "Hey, Purcell. Snipers are out there. Ready to take you down. So, you got two choices. Bail out that window and get shot. Or come at us with gunfire again and get shot. Which will it be?"

Silence.

She tried again. "Come out with your hands up, and we'll all manage to live through this."

Nothing. Then a slight whisper of a sound. Not sure what caused it, Angel pressed tight against the wall and waited.

Then there was a single gunshot, followed by a voice on her walkie-talkie. "He's on the run."

Angel turned and raced toward the front door. McGregor running in an awkward shuffle in front of her. She passed him in three strides, blasting out the door and sprinting around the house to find Webb in the alley. He pointed to the house across the way. "Through there. Sniper got him in the shoulder, but he managed to evade a second shot. Grotelli has cars blocking nearby streets."

Angel didn't have to ask, and Webb didn't have to explain why he didn't take up pursuit. He'd just been back a month after triple bypass. No running in his near future. In fact, he wouldn't even be here if it wasn't for the fact that Uniforms were spread so thin because of the protests downtown. She just gave Webb a nod and took off between the two houses in front of her.

Coming out on the next street, she spotted Grantham two houses down. "See where he went?"

Doug shook his head. "Elusive little bastard."

Before Angel had time to even take a breath, let alone respond, a figure jumped out from behind a tall bush that flanked a porch several houses to her right. A security light had popped on, which was the only reason she caught the movement. The man turned and raced down the street away from her and she tore after him, Doug close behind.

Legs pumping hard and fast, Angel thanked her frequent workouts for the strength and stamina, hoping that the man she was chasing was a lazy slug. He didn't dodge and weave, just kept a straight line ahead of her, and the distance started between them slowly started to close. Maybe not a slug, but close to it.

They were still ahead of Doug, but he was keeping up. No sound of fading footfalls.

Inexplicably, the perp started to pull away. *Where were the patrol cars? Where were the other uniforms? Where was McGregor?*

Angel pushed harder, muscles burning in her legs along with pain in her lungs. No way was this bastard getting away.

After another half a block, the man's pace started to falter and he suddenly went down. Why? Angel didn't care. She closed the distance, shoved him the rest of the way to the ground face first, putting a knee to his back and her Glock to the back of his head. "Give me a reason, motherfucker."

The man remained still and quiet.

She pushed the gun harder into his skull. Then she heard Grantham shout, "Angel! Don't do it."

"He shot Ryan."

"We don't know that for sure." Grantham waited a moment and when Angel didn't move her weapon, he came a little closer. "Think about it. We'll never know if you kill him."

"Nobody will blame me."

"You're right. If he's the bastard who shot Ryan, we'll all celebrate. But what if he isn't?" Doug sidled closer and got down on one knee beside Angel. "What if this isn't the guy? And you kill him. And we're all left wondering."

The barrel of the gun wavered ever so slightly in Angel's hand. Doug reached out, not touching the gun, but ready. "Let me have it, Angel. You do this, you'll spend the rest of your life doubting. Maybe never having another good night's sleep."

For one agonizing moment Angel considered doing it anyway. It would be so easy. Just one little squeeze. Then thoughts of the aftermath flashed through her mind. Her parent's disgust. Possibly being suspended. Or worse, fired. Her brother's disappointment. And maybe her partner's, too. This scumbag wasn't worth it. Without moving the weapon, she turned to Doug. "Got your cuffs?"

After the suspect was cuffed, Doug keyed his mic and called for a patrol car. One flew around the corner within moments. Angel hauled Purcell up and pushed him into the backseat of the cruiser, not being the least bit careful about his head and the doorjamb. If she couldn't shoot the bastard, she could at least hurt him.

"Feel better?" Doug asked with a slight grin.

"Yeah. A little." She pointed over her shoulder. "Going back. Want to see if he left a confession."

Doug chuckled. "As if."

When Angel got back to the perp's crib, she found McGregor alone, waiting for CSI and forensics.

"You okay?" Angel gestured toward his chest.

"Ribs'll be sore for a while. But better than being dead."

Angel flinched.

"Oh, man. Sorry."

"Yeah. We all are."

Angel glanced around the room. "You got this?"

McGregor nodded. "Forensics are on the way."

"You find his gun?"

McGregor held up a plastic evidence bag with a weapon in it.

"Wonder why he didn't take it," Angel said.

McGregor smiled. "Out of ammo."

Angel wished she could return the smile, but she just couldn't. "I'm going home."

If McGregor wanted to make something of the fact that she didn't ask – she told - Angel didn't care. Now that it was over, at least for tonight, fatigue hit her hard. Emotionally battered, with grief, anger, and frustration all slamming into her at once like storm waves pounding a sea wall, she wasn't sure how much longer she could stay upright.

And maybe exhaustion would finally bring sleep.

Maybe.

CHAPTER TWENTY-SIX

Friday, July 10 - Morning

T wo officers from the U.S. Marshals had come to Sarah's apartment last night close to midnight to get James and take him to one of their safe houses. She didn't know what was going on with Angel and McGregor, but by the time those officers left, she was too wiped and in too much pain to even check. She took a pain pill and went to bed.

She felt marginally better in the morning, and when she got a text from Burt that Gunther was being questioned today, she decided to go to the station. Which she did after washing up as best she could with one hand. Being wounded was a bitch.

An hour later, she went to McGregor's office first, hoping to get an update on last night, but it was empty, save for his desk that was overflowing with papers and file folders. Turning to leave, she bumped into Chang. "Where's the boss?" Sarah asked.

"Interrogation," Chang said. "Are you supposed to be here?"

"Technically. I work here." Sarah smiled so Chang would catch the joke and not think it was a sarcastic remark. "But will McGregor be happy? Probably not. But I want a crack at the guy who shot me."

"Hurt much?" Chang gestured to the sling.

"Like a son of a bitch. But don't tell anyone."

Chang touched her lips with a finger. "Our secret."

Downstairs, Sarah entered the interrogation viewing room and saw McGregor in front of the one-way window. At the sound of her footsteps, he turned and when it registered who it was, he glared. "What the fuck are you doing here?"

Sarah cocked her head. "Got a dollar to drop into your curse jar?"

"Yeah, well, it's either swear or drink. It'll be easier for me to stop cursing once this is over. And that's the end of any deflection you get. Tell me why you aren't still at home?"

Sarah nodded to the scene behind the window where they could see Burt sitting across a small metal table from Gunther who had one hand cuffed to a thick metal ring attached to the top. "Burt told me Gunther was here. Figured I'd come down and see what the dipwad has to say for himself."

"Dipwad? That's a new one for you."

"I'm all out of single dollar bills. Otherwise, I'd call him a fuckin' asshole." She paused a beat then asked, "How'd it go last night? Angel didn't answer my text this morning."

"Managed to get the guy in one piece. But Grantham told me he had to talk Angel down. She was ready to shoot the guy."

Inwardly, Sarah was thankful that Angel wouldn't have a deadly shooting to deal with for the rest of her life. "The guy here?"

"Walinski's got him. And ballistics are being checked.

We'll know soon if he's the one who shot Ryan."

"What about him?" Sarah canted her head toward the one-way mirror. "Burt getting anything?"

McGregor turned back to the interrogation. "So far nada."

"Can I take a crack at him?"

McGregor turned abruptly. "You armed?"

Sarah feigned shock. "Don't want to hurt him, Boss. Just persuade him to tell all."

McGregor eyed her thoughtfully for a long moment, then nodded.

When Sarah stepped into the interrogation room, Burt looked up with a smile. "My reinforcements have arrived."

"Just here to observe my friend." Sarah grabbed the third chair from the corner of the room and pulled it to the table, then looked at Gunther. "How you doing?"

"You observing with your mouth?"

"Ah, funny. Did you know we had a comedian here, Burt?"

"I wouldn't pay to see him. But I do like that line better than, 'Lawyer.'"

"That all he's said?" Sarah asked.

Burt nodded.

"Huh. And you told him how cooperating could help him?"

Burt nodded again.

Sarah turned her gaze back to Gunther. "You do understand the deep hole you're in, don't you?"

Nothing.

"Just for this," she pointed to her sling, "you're going away for a long time. But if we tie you to a murder here in Dallas ..."

Nothing.

"We do like to execute scumbags like you in Texas."

"Eat my shit, Pig." Gunther spit across the table, the spittle just missing her face and landing on her hand.

Sarah clenched her jaw and glared, squeezing out two words, "Not hungry."

Gunther pulled violently at the handcuff and his face turned crimson. "I don't care what you do to me, you dirty fascist pig. One day we'll rise up and—" Gunther abruptly stilled and clamped his lips shut.

"You'll what, Gunther?" Burt asked.

After a long moment, Gunther said, "Lawyer."

"Last chance, buddy," Burt said.

Gunther leaned forward and for a moment Sarah thought he was going to lob another blob of spit at her. But he didn't. "Not your buddy, pigs. I want my lawyer."

Burt nodded to the officer who was standing in the corner. "Get him out of here."

Sarah stood and put the chair back, then walked out with Burt. They joined McGregor in the viewing room. "Good work," he said, nodding to Sarah. "I'll have Chang dig deeper into his background. See if she can unearth this group he was so quick to shut up about."

"You think this is all connected? Gunther and your guy from last night. And our first vic. Or just random?" Sarah asked.

McGregor shrugged. "Hard to say. We've got more than a few radical groups playing in our back yard lately."

"You should have seen Gunther's crib," Burt said, leaning a hip against the wall. "Confederate shit all over the place. And the weapons? Enough to outfit a good-sized posse."

At a sudden flash of pain in her shoulder, Sarah held her injured arm tight against her body, hoping McGregor hadn't seen her wince. She did *not* want to go home. She deflected by asking Burt. "You think Purcell knows Gunther?"

"Could be." Burt turned to the Lieu. "What was the Purcell guy's place like?"

"Basically a dump. But I didn't see anything that screamed White Supremacist. Left before Forensics was finished, though."

"Maybe a visit to Roberts is in order," Sarah said.

"Burt can go," McGregor said.

Burt shook his head. "Got to be in court at ten this morning. That rape case finally came to trial."

That case involved a man who worked at a care facility who had raped a young girl with Down Syndrome. Burt and Simms had broken the case after the mother had come in to report that the facility was protecting the man.

McGregor waved him away. "Ok. Go."

"Glad to. That's one scumbag that we know for sure is going away for a long time."

"You're on," McGregor said to Sarah.

Following the directions the ICU nurse had given her, Angel had no trouble finding the room Ryan had been moved to last evening. That was good. Progress in the right direction. She tapped on the closed door, then pushed it open when she heard his voice call out, "Come in."

Ryan looked so much better without all the monitoring equipment and tubes, and he greeted her with a smile. She returned the smile, hoping he could see it in her eyes above the mask, then looked toward the empty visitor's chair.

"Where's your mom?"

"At the motel with Dad. Both needed a good rest. Said they'd be back after dinner."

"Good." Angel lightly touched his arm. "We caught the guy."

She didn't have to explain what guy.

"Hot damn!" His smile broadened. "How? When?"

"Last night." Angel sat down in the visitor chair and told him the whole story. Everything from the moment she decided she was going to find the person who'd shot him to the events last night. When she finished, Ryan didn't speak for several minutes.

She waited, not moving. Barely breathing.

"You did all that? For me?"

Angel nodded. "And some for Lady Justice."

Ryan sighed. "Does she even exist?"

"That's questionable. But we have to hope."

Ryan reached for his water glass on the tray table.

"You got it?" Angel asked.

"Yeah." He took a long swallow, then set the glass back. "Doc says I can go home soon. In a day or so."

"That's good news."

"Do we know motive yet?"

Just like she didn't have to explain about what guy, Ryan didn't need to clarify his question.

"Nothing so far. He's being questioned so maybe we'll know later."

Ryan shifted in the bed, making room if she should choose to sit next to him. An invitation, not a demand. "Are things with us … you know …"

Angel rose and stepped closer to the bed. "Is this allowed?"

"Nobody in here but us."

"Just for a minute. Don't want to lose visiting privileges."

She sat next to him and traced her fingers along the muscle in his forearm. "To answer your question. I'm not sure what okay means anymore. Not a lot is normal for either of us at the moment."

"That's true. But I'll never give up on you."

Tears warmed her eyes, and she blinked hard to keep them from slipping out. "Are you sure? That old Angel is gone."

"So is the old Ryan."

Not a surprise after all he'd been through. She took a moment to absorb the full meaning of the words, those spoken and unspoken. Looking into his eyes that had gone dark with emotions that didn't have to be voiced to be grasped, she realized she wanted more, too. She could no longer sidestep the fact that something was happening between her and Ryan. Something that had been happening for a long time, while she tried to pretend it wasn't. And she had to trust that this man was different from the one she'd loved as a young woman. The one who'd made all the wrong choices. This man was ready to make the right choices.

She cleared her throat and stood before she did more than sit quietly beside him on the bed. "Can't stay much longer. I need to get to the station. Haven't been in yet."

He smiled as if he knew the real reason she was putting distance between them. "What happened to nine-to-five?"

Angel laughed. "When have we ever had that?"

She stood for a moment, uncertain. Felt weird to just walk out. Then she glanced quickly at the door, pulled her mask down and kissed him lightly on the lips.

He smiled. "Can we try that again?"

"When you're better, and I pass another COVID test. Don't want to make you sick."

Ryan leaned back and let out a soft sigh. "Appreciate that."

~*~

Roberts, his white lab coat neatly buttoned beneath his trademark bow-tie, handed a plastic evidence bag to Sarah that held a scrap of paper. "What's this?" she asked.

"Part of a leaflet. Could be something used for recruiting to one of those neo-Nazi groups. Reads like it could've come from a KKK handout."

"Really?"

"Would I lie to my favorite detective?"

"I don't know. Am I really your favorite?"

Roberts put a hand over his heart. "You wound me."

Sarah smiled. "Okay. I take it back."

He returned the smile and walked to a side table where he brought his computer and monitor to life. "Let me show you. Here's some wordage we were able to isolate."

Sarah looked at what was displayed on the screen:

Pro-White. Protect. Resistance. Action. Call.

"No number?" Sarah asked.

"Nope. Looks like the guy was trying to get rid of the papers in a hurry. Tore them into small bits. Maybe flushed the scraps. But dropped this piece."

"Where'd you find it?"

"Bathroom. Which is why I think he was trying to clog the toilet."

"Find anything else that rang your bell?"

"You're going to love this." Roberts went back to the table that held the microscope. "Turns out our guy's been to Arkansas recently. Found fragments of clay in his carpeting."

Sarah followed him. "Hate to point out the obvious. But you do know we have clay here. Right?"

"Yes indeed. But ..." Roberts held up one finger and grinned. "Components of clay can be unique. That found in Arkansas is kaolinitic. Most of north Texas is in the Blackland Prairie area. That's what contains the dark alkaline clay."

"Huh."

"Bottom line is that the kaolinitic clay is light in color, sometimes whitish, and our friend in lockup couldn't have tracked it in from anywhere near us. Take a look."

Sarah obliged but wasn't sure what she was looking at other than a blob of a white substance. "Okay," she said standing up. "This means you can absolutely prove he's been to Arkansas?"

"Science doesn't lie. However, there's nothing that shows an exact place. This clay can be found over large areas of Arkansas."

"Well, damn." Sarah shifted the sling, suddenly aware of a deep throbbing ache deep in her shoulder. "For a minute I dreamed that our two guys might be buddies."

Roberts turned off the light on the microscope. "They very well might be. We just have to find that 'very well' another way."

"Even if there's no connection. We still need to nail their asses."

"No argument from me. And to that end, this has all been forwarded to our computer wizard. Plus, she's checking Purcell's phone. Might have something for you later."

"Thanks." Sarah turned to leave.

"How's the shoulder?"

"I'll live."

"Good to hear. I'd miss our little science lessons here in the lab."

Sarah chuckled. "Me too."

CHAPTER TWENTY-SEVEN

Friday, July 10 - Afternoon

Putting her head under the faucet in the restroom, Sarah swallowed a couple of pain pills, dried her face and hands, then went to her desk. Angel was already there, busy with something on her computer and glanced up with a smile. "Saw Ryan today. He's out of ICU."

"Great." Sarah lowered herself to her chair, not able to hide a grimace of pain.

"Maybe you should go home. Nobody will fault you for that."

"I know. Just want to fill out a report on what I learned from Roberts today."

"Good stuff?"

"Yeah." Sarah started to tell Angel about the possible connection between Purcell and Gunther, but was interrupted when Chang bustled in, clutching her laptop to her chest like a mother holding a baby.

"Ladies," Chang said. "Awesome Asian woman comes through for you again."

"We'll give you a medal later," Sarah said. "What do you

have?"

Momentarily Chang's exuberance slipped and Sarah quickly added. "Sorry. Blame it on the pain and the pills."

"Okey-dokey." Chang pulled a chair from an empty desk over and sat down. Angel rolled her chair to join them. Then Chang activated her computer and said, "First. I found that Eric Gunther and Frank Purcell belong to an extreme racially-motivated group."

"That supports the paper evidence found in Purcell's crib," Sarah said.

Chang nodded. "I'll get to that in just a bit. First, how much do you want to know about these groups?" When neither Sarah or Angel answered right away Chang added, "Or maybe I should ask how much you already know."

"I've been getting educated a lot more lately," Angel said.

Sarah decided to let that comment stand without a direct response. She nodded to Chang. "Give us a condensed lesson."

"Okey-dokey. These groups like to think of themselves as a militia. Some people simply call them a movement, and they all share similar ideologies. Mainly that they think the White race is the supreme one, and they all hate authority. But each group sets their own policies and leadership structure. Some of those are totally independent, but others are like a branch of the national ones. You've heard of them, I'm sure. The Proud Boys. Oath Keepers. Three Percenters."

She paused and Sarah said, "Hard to ignore them since what happened in D.C."

"You got that right." Chang said. "These groups that are motivated by a sense of white supremacy are listed as the most lethal domestic violence extremists. And they're the most likely to commit mass-casualty attacks."

"You think they're organized here in Dallas?" Angel asked.

Chang nodded. "There's this group, The Patriot Front. It's an American white nationalist and neo-fascist hate group. Once it was part of the broader alt-right movement but split from the neo-Nazi organization Vanguard America in 2017. Patriot Front espouses, well, patriotism, but with a lot of fascist beliefs."

"I've heard of them, too," Sarah said, "But aren't they also national in leadership?"

Chang grinned. "I went on the Dark Web and what did I find?"

The other detectives didn't say anything, so Chang continued. "Okey-dokey. No joke. There's a group here in Dallas called Texans for Liberty. Sounds pretty harmless, right?"

This time she got nods, so she continued. "The leader calls himself Happy Camper and the material on their website is anything but harmless."

Chang hit a few keys and a site opened with a banner sprawled across the top that had Confederate flags next to Nazi flags. The wordage across the bottom of the image read: "Hitler had it Right."

Sarah shook her head. "And here I thought all the scumbags we were up against were just your run-of-the-mill murderers and burglars."

"We have a whole new world of scumbags," Angel said.

Chang clicked on the "Save America" tab under the banner at the top of the website. The tab opened a new window with what appeared to be a manifesto. "This is pretty nasty stuff, and it has the N word, but I'll read it if you want."

"Not sure I 'want,'" Angel said. "But I think we need to

know what's being propagated."

Chang glanced at Sarah who nodded, then she read: "It is our belief that, if left to continue, the Black Lives Matter and other organizations supporting the niggers and wetbacks will take over the country.

"White Lives Matter.

"Democrats are now in power, supporting all these niggers, ready to take away our guns, and everyone who believes in our God-given supremacy is in danger.

"Mark our words. There will be a civil war here in America again. Blood is going to be shed on the streets and you and your family could be killed. No matter what you think the "others" will do, the war is coming."

Sarah leaned back in her chair with a deep sigh. "Can we find this guy and throw his ass in jail?"

"I'd just like to shoot him." Angel delivered the statement without even a hint of a smile, and Sarah had no doubt this was hitting her partner particularly hard. Sarah refrained from trying to offer anything to mitigate Angel's feelings. She had a right to be as angry as all hell.

Chang closed her laptop, also seeming willing to let Angel's comment just sit there. "As for the question of a possible arrest. That's a tricky one. Maybe see what the DA has to say. But as nasty as this is, what's on this site and all the others is all protected by the right to free speech."

"Have you filled McGregor in on this?" Sarah asked.

Chang nodded. "Sent a full report just before coming here."

Angel stood, ready to go back to her desk, and Chang held up a hand to stop her. "That's not all this awesome Asian woman found."

The bit of levity was like a slight breeze blowing through

a stuffy room that took out the heat and odors of sweaty bodies and stale coffee. Even the pain her arm eased a little, and Sarah smiled.

Chang returned the smile. "Now. About that evidence Roberts found. Using the few words he was able to pull from the paper, I dug around the web and found this." Chang opened her laptop again, changed the image on the screen, then turned it so both women could see a flyer that read: "The Nationalist Social Club. A pro white, street-oriented fraternity dedicated to raising authentic resistance to the enemies of our people in North Texas. This takes the form of networking, training, activism, outreach, and above all, action.

"No matter how you find this, if you are a man of European descent in the North Texas area that wishes to see a better future for your people, contact us to get to work. For any and all inquiries, questions or concerns call: 214-555-6640."

"Holy shit," Sarah said.

"Yes, ma'am. Holy poopoo indeed," Chang said. "And, when I looked into the phone records of both our friends in lock-up, guess what number I found."

"That means we can connect them both to this hate group," Angel said. "So maybe they were part of a larger plan to disrupt the protests downtown."

"Or just talked to each other and decided for themselves without a formal plan." Sarah posed it as part statement and part question.

"These groups are careful about plans," Chang said. "They don't post specifics about dates and times, or targets. Just this general hate speech."

Sarah eased out of her chair and stood. "I think we need to finish this discussion with McGregor. He'll know more about whether we can go after this Happy Camper guy. Maybe even have Jessica sit in on it."

"Okey-dokey." Chang stood. "Text me when you're ready."

"Hopefully, we can do it this afternoon." Sarah said. "I'll call McGregor and see if he can check with Jessica on the legal questions of arresting Happy Camper."

"What a stupid name." she added.

"Maybe he try too hard to seem harmless." Chang delivered that with an exaggerated accent that made Sarah smile.

In the breakroom, Angel opened the cooler and grabbed a bottle of water to go with the snack bar from the vending machine. Water was provided for the officers, but they had to buy food. Sarah stepped in just as Angel was about to leave. "Heading to conference room B," Angel said. "You get the message?"

Sarah nodded. "See you there in a few."

Chang was already in the room, and Angel noted that Burt was there, too. "Sarah's on her way," Angel said.

"Chang already briefed me on the new information," McGregor said. "And Burt has some new stuff, too."

Sarah walked in, awkwardly carrying a Styrofoam cup of coffee that was dripping down the sides. Angel jumped up and grabbed the coffee before it sloshed any more.

"Okay." McGregor took a seat at the head of the table, then nodded to Burt.

"Simms and I spent a couple of hours today looking at

some tapes from the security cameras around the Federal Building. Bad news is we didn't see the person who pulled the trigger on Cummings. But we did see a guy moving through the crowd with a revolver in his hand. Each time we spotted him, he had the gun down by his side. Then once we saw what looked like him poking the gun in someone's back. Then he quickly dropped his hand and turned away."

"So that first shooting could've been from that douchebag?" Sarah asked.

Angel leaned forward. "Any possible ID on this guy?"

Burt shook his head. "We never saw his face."

"Anyway, can we get a list of the members of this group here in Dallas?" Angel directed that question at Chang.

"I've never seen anything with names on the sites. Most of these folks like to keep their identity secret."

"I checked with the ADA," McGregor said. "We have no grounds for an arrest of this Happy Camper guy, even if we could locate him. But we can use what Chang found against the two perps we have locked up."

"And maybe one of them knows this random guy you saw, Burt." Sarah said. "We should push them again."

"Let me have a go at Gunther," Angel said. "Maybe rile him up over having to talk to a bitch nigger."

The room went deathly silent for a moment. Nobody expected words like that from Angel, but she tilted her chin up as if defying anyone to challenge her.

"I think she's right," Sarah said into that void. "That would push all kinds of buttons with him."

CHAPTER TWENTY-EIGHT

Friday, July 10 - Late Afternoon

Sarah was ready to follow Angel out of the conference room, wanting to watch her partner tear into Gunther, when her phone rang. She held up one finger to Angel in that universal wait a moment gesture, then answered. "Kingsly."

The voice on the other end had an edge of panic in it, yet the words came in a soft whisper. "I need help."

A cold shiver ran down her back as Sarah saw the caller ID. Wanda, whose voice was laced with fear.

"Wanda. What's happening?"

"He has a gun. Said he'd kill me."

"Who??"

"Francisco. He is drunk. Very angry."

God! No! "Okay," Sarah said. "Where are you?"

"Bathroom. Door is locked. But he can break it."

"Hang on. Help is on the way."

Sarah quickly pocketed her phone and looked at the other officers still in the conference room. "We've got a hostage situation. Home of Francisco Lopez. He's armed and threatening to kill his wife."

McGregor jumped up. "I'll get Grotelli to mobilize some uniforms, and we'll get the SWAT team out there." He pointed to Chang who had immediately turned to her laptop when Sarah made the announcement. "Got an address for us?"

She rattled off a street number and the room buzzed with urgency as others in the room quickly pushed chairs back from the table and hustled out.

"I'll head over there now," Sarah said.

McGregor glared at her. "Really? You're in no shape to face a shooter."

Sarah didn't blink. "She called me."

"You should go home."

"Is that an order?"

McGregor swiped a hand across his cheeks, and before he could answer Angel said, "I'll go with her. Make sure she stays out of the line of fire."

Silence hung in the air for almost a full minute while McGregor looked from Angel to Sarah then back to Angel. Then Sarah turned and strode toward the door. "Time's wasting, Lieu."

Angel followed and McGregor called out. "Don't either of you get shot."

Sarah suppressed a smile as she kept walking. She certainly hoped not.

~*~

The Range Rover tore down the street, siren blaring, Angel at the wheel, and Sarah braced her feet against the floorboard.

Not that she minded going this fast, she just wished she was the one slamming the gas pedal to the floor. She had her phone open on her lap, set on speaker. Wanda had called back right after the detectives had commandeered the car and left the station. Loud thumps could be heard from Wanda's end. "What's happening?" Sarah asked, hoping Wanda could answer.

"Something heavy hitting the door."

"Is it still holding?"

"Not for long."

"Officers should be there any minute."

Silence for a few beats, then Wanda said, "Before I ..." There was a hiccup. "He's going to kill me. But before ... I think he killed Fred. He said he saw the text ... Oh, God. No!"

"Wanda! What text?"

A loud crashing sound prevented an answer, then silence. Had Francisco broken the bathroom door? Where were the officers?

"Shit! That doesn't sound good," Sarah said.

In response, Angel floored the accelerator and Sarah braced herself as Angel spun around the corner to the Lopez house, tires screaming, then came to a screeching stop behind a patrol car. Another patrol car faced them from two houses down, and officers were crouched behind open doors.

"Let me out," Sarah yelled, awkwardly trying to reach across her body to get to the door handle and failing.

"Nope. We stay here."

"And do nothing?"

Angel gestured to the phone now in Sarah's lap where she'd dropped it in her ill-fated attempt to get out of the car. "Keep the line open to Wanda. If he's breached the bathroom, maybe the husband will pick up. I'll pass any intel to

McGregor by text."

Ahead, Sarah watched the SWAT truck swing in behind the patrol car. Lloyd, the senior officer, piled out in full armor gear, along with two other officers. He gestured for them to approach the house from either side, and the men scurried to their assigned places, keeping low behind the hedge on one side and trees on the other.

"Remind you of anything?" Angel asked.

Angel's tone had been flat, no real emotion in her voice, but Sarah knew. "Hope this one ends better."

"Yeah."

The last time they had been in a similar situation with a shooter who had little to lose, it hadn't ended well at all. It was the first case they'd worked as partners, and the shooter had splattered his brains all over Angel.

Sarah's phone crackled to life. "This the dee-tective my whore of a wife been talking to?"

An underlying threat in the gravelly male voice made Sarah's heart thump wildly, but she forced her voice to be calm and conversational. "Hello, Francisco. How's your wife doing? Can she talk to me?"

"No concern for me, Dee-tective?"

"Not a whole lot."

"All those cops out there. Somebody gonna take me out?"

Sarah wished one of the snipers could just end this, but she was betting there wasn't a vantage point to the bathroom. "Not planning to, Francisco. Let Wanda go. Walk out with your hands up. And everybody lives." Sarah glanced over to see that Angel was frantically texting. "Can we do that, Francisco?"

No response.

Sarah waited a beat, then said, "Is your wife okay,

Francisco?"

"Stop saying my name."

Harsh words laced with a tinge of hysteria, that drove Sarah's heartbeat into overdrive. She took a breath, then said, "Okay. I need to know how your wife is. Is she able to talk?"

"Of course. She ain't dead."

"Okay. That's good."

"Thing is. She can't come to the phone. She's ... how do you say it? Incapacitated."

"What did you do?"

Silence again for a beat. Sarah exchanged a worried glance with Angel, muted her phone and whispered, "Any word on when someone might go in?"

"Lloyd told McGregor it's too dangerous. Chances are the hostage will get shot if they enter by force. And neither sniper has a visual."

"Not a surprise. But somebody has to do something."

"What are you thinking?"

"Not sure yet. Let me talk to Francisco again."

Sarah unmuted her phone and immediately Francisco started to talk. It was clear that in some sick way, he was enjoying the attention. "Where you been, Dee-tective? Off planning on how to kill me?"

"Told you, nobody wants to do that. Just come on out, and let us clear this whole mess up."

"Well, see, here's the thing. I heard Wanda tell you that I killed her lover-boy. Guess I'm not gonna get out of that one."

"It can go down easy if you don't make things worse tonight."

"How so?"

"Let Wanda come out."

"I don't mean what I should do, bitch. Whatta you gonna

do for me so things don't get *worse*?"

Sarah took a deep breath to keep from saying something that would set him off. She had a feeling he could explode at any second. "I don't have the authority to make any promises."

"Then you better get the authority."

At first Sarah thought he'd hung up, but then she heard soft moaning over the line. She was about to ask him again if Wanda was okay when she saw Angel frantically waving a hand, then gesturing to the phone and shaking her head. It took a few seconds, but Sarah finally realized her partner was telling her to switch off the speaker.

"McGregor said to promise the perp anything to keep the hostage alive."

"But he doesn't have the authority any more than we do."

"This wacko doesn't know that."

"Hey, Dee-tective lady. You still with me?" The voice was loud, even with the speaker off, but Sarah switched it back on anyway.

"Had to check with my boss. We can make a deal."

"What kind of deal?"

"Definitely take the death penalty off the table."

Silence for a beat then, "How 'bout I just get in my car and head south? Don't stop until I get to Mexico. Then I stay there."

"No can do."

"Then I ain't got nothin' to lose."

The phone went dead and Sarah shot a frantic glance toward Angel. "Get me out of this car."

"What do you plan to do?"

"No plan. Just get me out of this fucking car. Wanda can't die."

"There's no guarantee she isn't already dead."

Sarah stabbed her partner with a glare. "You willing to take that chance?"

"We'll lose our badges over this."

"So be it." Sarah slipped her arm out of the sling and reached to open the car door, pain shooting through her shoulder as if someone had punched it.

"Jesus Christ, woman. Stop!" Angel jumped out and ran around to open the door. Sarah scooted out, cradling her lame arm. She nodded to the phone Angel had pressed to her ear. "Still connected to McGregor?" Angel nodded. "Hang up."

Angel slowly lowered the phone. "You're nuts."

"I know. You keep reminding me."

Sarah lowered her right arm and carefully put her phone in her right hand. "See. It doesn't hurt at all."

Angel snorted as Sarah gingerly held her phone and used her left hand to push the redial button on the last call and open the speaker. Francisco answered after three rings.

"Gonna let me go, Dee-tective lady?"

"Here's the new deal, Francisco. I come inside. Make sure Wanda's okay. Bring her out. Then we talk about your road trip."

"I'm not stupid, lady."

"Well aware of that. You're a very smart man. So, you know the only chance you have is if your wife lives. I'm coming in with my partner. No guns. Nobody getting hurt."

Without giving him a chance to respond, Sarah disconnected just as Angel's phone rang. Angel glanced at the caller ID. "It's McGregor."

"Don't answer."

"You're going to get us fired."

"We're too damn good to get fired."

Again, Angel shook her head and followed Sarah toward the front of the house. Sarah called out to the cluster of officers by the SWAT vehicle and the uniformed officers by patrol cars. "Hold fire. We're going in."

"Wait for the hostage negotiator." A voice called out. Maybe McGregor. She wasn't sure, but she also didn't care.

"Fuck that," Sarah mumbled as she walked up the front steps to the porch. Once there, she reached out with her good hand and grasped the door handle. It turned, so she slowly pushed the door open and slipped inside. Angel came in behind her. Ahead was short hall with a large living area to the right. Sarah moved in that direction, gesturing to Angel to move away to her left. Then Angel's phone rang again, the ring tone too loud in the otherwise quiet space. "Silence that damn thing." Anger made Sarah's voice a harsh whisper.

"Sorry." Angel fumbled with her phone.

"That you, Dee-tective?" A voice called out.

"Yup. Me and my partner. Nice digs you got here."

Francisco appeared in a doorway at the other end of the room, brandishing a gun. His hair was in wild disarray, and his face twitched like he had Tourette's. Sarah sucked in a breath as she realized the danger. Then she quickly raised her hands shoulder high with her palms out. "We're unarmed." The position made her injured shoulder hurt like hell, but she did her best to ignore the pain. Put it somewhere else than in this room with this man who would just as soon kill them both as breathe. She gave a slight nod to the weapon he was holding. "Thought you said your gun had been stolen."

"Maybe I lied."

"Lot of that going around. Let my partner go check on your wife."

"You really do think I'm stupid. Not gonna let a cop go

anywhere but right here in front of me."

"That's part of any deal, Francisco. Wanda has to be okay. And Wanda has to come out alive."

"Bitch is still breathing. That's all you need to know. Which one of you talks to the boss man?"

"It's me," Angel said.

"Here's my deal," Francisco said, not moving from the doorway. "Tell him I'm getting my car from the garage out back and driving away. Nobody stops me. Otherwise, everybody in here dies."

Sarah shook her head slowly back and forth. "Now you're insulting us, Francisco. You think we're stupid enough to believe you won't just shoot us before you take off?"

Angel had started to move to her left, putting more space between her and Sarah, and Francisco suddenly turned the gun in her direction. "Stop!" He gestured with the barrel of the gun for her to go back toward Sarah. "You two over there by the sofa and keep your hands up."

Never taking her eyes off Francisco, Sarah sidestepped to the sofa and sat on the edge of one of the three cushions, Angel on her far left. He didn't move any closer, so he could still take them out in two quick shots before either one of them could move.

He gestured to Angel with his free hand. "You. Call the boss man and tell him my conditions."

Angel fumbled her phone with one hand and Sarah knew she was purposely stalling.

"In three, or else." Francisco said. "One. Two—"

That's when Wanda staggered up behind him, brandishing an old blue hairdryer that she slammed onto his head. The blow wasn't enough to bring him down, but it stunned him and he faltered. Angel burst from the couch and raced toward him in a few quick strides. Without stopping her forward momentum, she raised one leg and kicked his arm that was holding the weapon hard enough that the gun skittered across the hardwood floor. Sarah bolted up a split second after Angel and scrambled after the gun, snagging it with her left hand.

The bastard didn't have to know she was right-handed.

He sank to one knee, holding his injured arm. "Bitch! You broke it."

"Good." Angel said making a wide berth around him to get to Wanda who had collapsed after her efforts. She was battered. Beaten. But bless her heart, she was there at the right time. Angel glanced at Sarah. "Calling for an ambulance. And letting McGregor know."

"Thanks. I'll watch hubby, here. And maybe we'll get one for him, too."

A moment later, McGregor burst into the room, followed closely by Lloyd and a uniformed officer who took Francisco out. "I'll deal with you two later," McGregor said before he left.

Angel nodded and Sarah hurried to Wanda who was still slumped on the floor. Her eyes were closed and she looked … well, dead. Fear clutched at Sarah as she hunkered down and felt for a pulse. It was there, but barely. "That ambulance had better hurry up."

As if in answer to her silent prayer, a distant siren came closer and closer.

CHAPTER TWENTY-NINE

Saturday, July 11 - Morning

S arah didn't roll out of bed until almost nine, and that was only because Cat was walking all over her, demanding breakfast. Last night, after the EMTs had done their thing and taken Wanda to the closest hospital, and the uniformed officers had taken Francisco to the station, and they'd endured McGregor's wrath, Angel had driven Sarah home, promising to pick her up this morning to take her back to the station where her car still sat in the lot.

"Shit!" Sarah sat up and quickly fell back to the pillow, head swimming with dizziness. Must have been the pain pill she'd taken last night. Despite her protestations to Angel and McGregor that the midnight adventure hadn't been too much, it had been too much. Her incision was barely healed on the outside, let alone whatever had been torn up on the inside by a bullet rattling around in there.

She groaned, rolled over on her left side and slowly swung her feet to the floor. So far so good. Then she eased to a sitting position and, thankfully, the room didn't turn into a carnival fun house. What time did McGregor want them in today? Ten? She glanced at the clock. Shit! She'd better get a move on.

Her move-on was slower than normal, but after cleaning up as best she could she felt a bit clearer of mind. She put her arm back in the sling. *Won't take that puppy off again for a while.* Then she headed to the kitchen where Cat was sitting on the counter in front of the cabinet that held his food. "Trying to tell me something, buddy?"

Cat did not deign to answer. He merely glanced at the cabinet door, then watched carefully as Sarah grabbed the bag of kibbles and toted it over to his bowl. Then he jumped down and strutted over with an air of 'it's about time.'

Without her own ride to stop by Hussein's gas station for coffee on the way to work, Sarah opted for her old standby. She ran the tap until the water was as hot as it would get. Put a hefty teaspoon of instant coffee in a mug, and made her morning coffee. After a few sips, she remembered why she'd started going to the gas station in the first place. What had once been an acceptable cup of coffee when she'd first moved into this apartment had long outlived acceptable.

Sarah dumped the dregs down the drain, then foraged for a breakfast bar. Her phone buzzed with a text from Angel.

You ready?
Yeah.
I'm outside your apartment.
Be right out.

Sarah opened the door to the interrogation room, where Francisco sat handcuffed to the metal table. One hand was secured. The other was encased in a sling. He looked up and nodded toward the sling on her arm. "Hello, Dee-tective. That crazy nigger bitch kick the hell out of you, too?"

Biting the inside of her cheek so hard she tasted blood, Sarah walked as calmly as she could to the table and pulled the chair opposite him out so she could sit. *I will not rise to his bait. I will not rise to his bait.* She repeated that line as many times as needed until she could speak without jumping across the table and ripping his throat out. She shot him an icy glare. "That's 'crazy motherfucker bitch' to you."

"Whoa, lady. Didn't mean no harm."

"Yeah. That's what they all say."

For a beat, it appeared that he didn't seem to know how to process that last statement. He just looked at her with a blank stare, then he relaxed and smiled. "You dragged me out of my luxury room for a reason, Dee-tective?"

The way he said that word grated on Sarah, but at least it wasn't as bad as what he'd called Angel, so she decided to let it pass. "I'm here so you can tell me exactly what happened the night you shot Fred Cummings."

"What? I didn't shoot nobody."

"That's what you want me to believe?"

"It's the truth."

"That isn't what you said last night."

"Hell." He laughed like he didn't have a worry in the world. "Last night I was so drunk I would'a said I shot the pope."

"As far as we know the pope is in fine health. Sadly, Fred Cummings isn't."

"Fred? That's the guy who got shot? I don't know nothing about no Fred Cummings."

"Oh. How convenient. You forgot the man who was

fucking your wife?"

Francisco leaned back as far as the handcuff holding him to the table would allow and offered an insolent smile. "Lady, as far as I know I'm the only man fucking my wife. Now, I told the officer who brought me here that I want a lawyer. So, this is a good time for me to make that call."

Holding any reaction for a long moment, Sarah hoped it would make him wonder when he went back to his cell. Did they have anything on him? Then she nodded to the officer who'd brought Francisco in. "Get him out of here."

She pushed away from the table and stood, ignoring his parting shot. "Not even a polite adios, Dee-tective?"

Out in the hall, she turned to her right and stepped into the viewing room, where Angel and McGregor had watched the interview.

"That was a bust," McGregor said. "Waste of our time."

"We've got what he said to me before," Sarah offered.

"Right. But his lawyer can diffuse that. 'My client was drunk out of his mind. Didn't know what he was saying.'" McGregor sighed. "Let's hope Wanda wakes up and is willing to testify against him."

"I'm sure she will. He really did a number on her."

"Speaking of numbers. How come this text he purportedly saw to his wife didn't show up on Fred Cumming's phone?"

"Maybe Fred used a different one when texting Wanda?" Angel offered that as a half statement, half question.

"Why would he do that?" McGregor asked.

Sarah shrugged. "Keeping his 'dalliances,' as his wife referred to the extra-curricular activity, separate from other personal or business stuff?"

"Could be. Let's see what Chang can dig up when she

finishes going through Wanda's phone."

When McGregor walked out, Sarah put a hand on Angel's arm to hold her back. After the door clicked shut and they were alone, she asked, "You okay with what I said in there?" She nodded to the room that was now dimly lit and empty.

Angel smiled. "Kinda like being considered a crazy motherfucker bitch."

"And the fact I didn't call him out on the 'N' word?"

"Wouldn't've done any good. Not with people like him. And it was enough to see how much you wanted to fly across the table and kick his balls so hard he had to eat them."

Sarah was contemplating going home. Her shoulder ached and she didn't think she was doing any good at work. Nobody left to interrogate and nothing else coming from forensics. Might as well hang it up for the day. When she stood from her desk, her phone pinged with a message. She fumbled the phone from her jeans pocket to see that the message was from McGregor:

All hands on deck in conference room B.

The naval reference made her smile. Sometimes he liked to channel his former military service, often using some Navy phrase when he was feeling particularly good. It was way past time for them all to feel good.

Burt and Bruce Walinski from SIU were already in the room when Sarah got there, and she was a little surprised to see Grotelli. Angel came in right behind her, followed closely by McGregor and Chang.

Everyone took seats around the long conference table that

had a pitcher of water and several glasses on a tray acting as a centerpiece.

McGregor pulled out the chair at the head of the table and sat with a satisfied sigh. "First, an update from Chang."

She pulled papers from a folder she'd dropped on the table in front of her and slid copies to each person at the table. "The top one is for the Cummings case. On Wanda Lopez's phone I found this text," She read, "Can't come yet. Going downtown to march for an hour. Free later if you are."

"Still nothing on his phone that shows him sending the text?" Sarah asked.

"No," McGregor answered before Chang could. "But Grotelli has some good news."

"Things've been relatively quiet downtown the last couple of days, so I had some of my guys canvas stores around the Cummings house, and where he worked. Looking to see if he mighta bought a throw-away phone. And he did. Back in January."

"Did you locate the phone?" Angel asked.

Grotelli shook his head. "He mighta tossed it. Or it fell out of his pocket when he hit the pavement and someone in that crowd that night nabbed it."

"Why would he toss it?" Angel asked.

"Who knows? Just a theory."

Chang leaned forward in her chair. "If this is the text that Wanda's husband saw, and it probably was, it shows that he knew Cummings was going to be downtown."

"Just need ballistics to confirm that the gun he had last night is the one that fired the bullet that killed Cummings," McGregor said. "And we can send the case to the DA."

"Then it definitely wasn't the guy Simms and I saw on the tapes?" Burt asked.

"Probably not," McGregor said. "Looking better and better that Lopez is our shooter."

Sarah asked, "What about Gunther and Purcell?"

McGregor gestured to Walinski. "You want the floor?"

"Sure." The reed-thin man leaned back in his chair. "Had to really push him hard, but I finally got a confession from Purcell. That nails him as Ryan's shooter."

"How'd you manage that?" Sarah asked.

"Described in detail what it's like to die by lethal injection. Followed that by what happens in prison to cop-killers if he dodged the death penalty. Neither option appealed to him."

"Where do we stand with that hate group here in Dallas?" Sarah directed the question to Chang.

"Still can't find a name for whoever heads it up."

"What about Gunther?" Sarah asked. "From what you told us the other day, he was talking all over social media about white folks being the superior race. And what he wanted to do to people who didn't fit that image."

"True. He doesn't appear to be very bright," Chang replied. "But back to that local website. Texans for Freedom is loosely organized. No membership lists. No physical location for a headquarters posted on the site. Only the manifesto, copied almost word for word from other groups."

"Absolutely no trace of that guy who calls himself Happy Camper?" Angel asked.

Chang shook her head. "His accounts are routed through numerous proxy servers in Europe. Asia. South America. He may not even be in the States."

"But he's still orchestrating a lot of the unrest here?" Burt asked.

"Yes. And not just here in Dallas. All over the country. Maybe even internationally."

"Well, that sucks big time," Burt said.

"You know what sucks even more?" Sarah asked. "The fact that we can't nail the bastard and shut him down."

McGregor nodded. "But someone will. Matthew from Homeland Security said the intel we gathered is good stuff." He raised his water glass to Chang. "Good job."

Burt tapped the paper in front of him with the information Chang had brought to the meeting. "Does that mean this line of investigation's a dead end?"

Chang looked to McGregor before responding, and he nodded to indicate she should go ahead.

"Not for the feds, but for us. Yes."

"Too bad," Sarah said. "Looked forward to catching that bastard."

CHAPTER THIRTY

Saturday, July 11 - Evening

Sarah settled on the couch next to LaVon. Dinner that he'd prepared from groceries he'd brought with him, thank goodness because her cupboards were bare except for kitty chows that didn't make for a good dinner, was over and they were ready to watch TV for a while.

LaVon leaned in to snag a kiss that quickly started to heat up for both of them. Sarah let the passion build for a moment, then pulled back. "Unlike in fiction where cops get shot and then miraculously get healed enough to jump up to kill a bunch of bad guys, followed by a night of wild and exciting sex with no pain, this is real life, and that doesn't happen. Sorry."

Lavon ran a thumb down her cheek, a touch so soft it was almost as erotic as the kiss. "No need to be sorry. I get it. Do you want me to leave so you can rest?"

"No. This is good. Want to watch your favorite?"

"Sure. Why not."

LaVon reached for the remote on the coffee table and switched on the TV. Sarah's phone that was also on the table vibrated with a notification. She idly picked it up to check the message while he was scrolling though channels. The message was from Jolene:

We missed you at the funeral today.

"Oh, shit."

LaVon looked at her in alarm. "What?"

Sarah closed her phone . "It's my cousin. Her daddy died and they buried him today."

"I'm so sorry, Sarah. Were you close?"

"To my uncle? Once upon a time. But not for years." She paused to take a ragged breath. "My cousin and I ... we were ... I should call her."

"Go ahead. I'll clean up the dishes from supper." Lavon gave her another kiss on the cheek and then pushed his tall body off the sofa.

Sarah waited a moment and then opened her phone and pushed the redial button, hoping that Jolene would understand all the whys of Sarah missing the funeral. Not even acknowledging the funeral if Jolene had sent her the date and time.

"Hey, Bug," Sarah said when Jolene answered, using the pet name from their childhood. Sarah did that on purpose hoping that using the endearment would be a good thing. "I'm so sorry I couldn't be there for you today."

There was only the soft sound of crying from the other end of the call, so Sarah went on. "And I really should have taken a moment to let you know what's happened here that prevented me from coming."

"That would've been nice," Jolene said with an edge to her voice that Sarah remembered from the arguments of their teen years.

At this point, Sarah debated the wisdom of telling Jolene

about being shot. Would her cousin see that as an easy ploy for sympathy? *And really Jolene is the one who needs sympathy right now. Not me.* Still, being shot was a big deal and it was the main reason that she hadn't checked to see if there was a message from Jolene in the past few days.

Sarah took a deep breath and said, "Here's the deal, Jolene. I got shot last—"

"Oh, my God! Oh, my God! Are you okay?"

Sarah fought the urge to laugh at the quick transformation from anger to concern. "I'm fine. It was just a shoulder wound. But I was in the hospital for a couple of days following surgery—"

"Surgery?! You had to have surgery? Holy cow, Sassy."

Sarah smiled at hearing her long-ago nickname. "Just chill. It's all fine. But it's why I was silent for a few days. Then I was distracted by this big case we've been working."

"But you're fine now?"

"Yeah. The wound was in my shoulder, and it's healing. And the case is basically over except for the trials."

"That's good to hear." There was a note of sadness back in Jolene's voice that touched Sarah's heart.

"Hey, Bug. Now that things are calming down, maybe I could swing a short vacation. Come for a visit sometime soon."

"That would be good," Jolene said. "That would be real good."

After affirming that she really did mean she'd come visit, Sarah closed her phone and looked up to see LaVon leaning against the counter that separated her small kitchen from the living room. "Things okay?" he asked.

"As okay as they can be."

"Couldn't help but hear." He gestured to the short

distance between them. "If you want to take a road trip, I'd be happy to do the driving."

The offer, and the thought, stunned Sarah for a moment. What would her family think? While she was sad that Uncle Homer had died, he was one of the main reasons she'd never dreamed of taking LaVon to her hometown. But the rest of them? Depending on how indoctrinated Jolene had been by her father and her husband, that might be one person who would smile and welcome LaVon and really mean it.

Sarah considered. Should she? It was so tempting to just take a week or so to travel with LaVon.

She smiled at him. "Let me think on it."

Angel walked up to the front door of her parent's house with trepidation. Man, when was the last time she'd felt this way? When she was fifteen and was trying to sneak back in after a night that went way too late with Bobby. That was the last time. Her father had been sitting in his favorite recliner in the living room when she'd tiptoed in, shoes in one hand. He wasn't happy, or pleasant.

Her key still worked in the front door which was a slight surprise. After the last dust-up they'd had, Angel figured that her father would change the locks. She went inside and found her father sitting in the same chair as he had those many years ago. His face still wore the same scowl and he started to push himself up. "I'll get your mother."

"No. Wait. Please." Angel stepped into the living room that hadn't changed much since her childhood. A pale blue sofa with a colorful quilt thrown over the back. Family pictures marching across the mantel like little soldiers. A large framed painting of an old house in Mississippi that had been her paternal great-grandparents. Her grandmother had painted it. Not a work of art befitting a museum, but it fit here.

Angel sat on the edge of the sofa directly across from her father. "I came to see you."

"We have nothing to talk about."

"Yes, we do, Daddy." She waited for him to respond, but he didn't. He also didn't get up and storm out of the room. That was good. After a moment of strained silence, Angel became aware of movement in the doorway, and she glanced over to see her mother. The older woman just stood there for a moment then nodded at her daughter and left.

Her father folded and unfolded a napkin in his lap. Maybe from one of his favorite snacks, sliced apple with peanut butter. It was one he had almost every day after work.

Still he didn't speak.

"How are you, Daddy?"

A shrug.

"Business good?"

Another shrug.

"How long is this going to last?" She spoke with such vehemence that he looked at her directly for the first time since she'd entered.

"What?" he asked.

"This." She made a vague gesture between them. "I feel like I've been cut out of the family. And I hate it."

"You made your choices."

"Yes. But you made choices too."

He glared, then started to rise.

"Don't." The word reverberated in the room, then she softened her tone. "If you love me at all, please stay."

Slowly Gilbert sank back down, but he didn't speak.

"I've been with the people at the protests downtown."

He looked at her in surprise and opened his mouth to say something, but she held up a hand palm out to stop him. "Let me finish. Then you can say what you need to."

He nodded, so she took a breath and continued. "All along I've known things aren't black and white."

That brought a snort of laughter.

"I know. Bad choice of words. What I mean is that there aren't absolute truths on either side of the racial divide. One side isn't right. The other wrong."

"I never said they was."

Rather than contradict him, Angel waited a beat then said, "We've talked around this issue for years and nothing changes. You're dug in and I'm dug in. What if we agree that we'll always have conflicting views, and that may never change?

"Because I'm not leaving the police. And I'll probably always work with Sarah. But we can't go on this way. It's killing me." Her voice faltered for a moment, then she continued, "Do you know how many times I've driven by the house since our last fight, wishing I could come in for dinner?"

Surprise registered on his face, but he seemed unable to find words. Angel watched his mouth move in the effort, while tears made a warm path down her cheeks.

"We have to find a compromise, Daddy. We really do. I don't want to be exiled from this family. And I certainly don't want to think about my future not having you in it. Just because we're both so stubborn."

Angel waited for his response, not even wiping the tears from her face. As the seconds ticked by with nothing from him, tension squeezed her chest, and her heart thumped against her ribcage so hard she could feel it.

"What is it you propose we do, girl?"

The words were spoken softly, but with an underlying invitation.

"Step away from our differences."

"I'm an old man. Set in my ways."

She smiled. "Yeah. We all know that. I'm just asking you to try. And I'll try too."

Gilbert fiddled with the napkin some more, then placed it on the table next to his chair. "Saw on the news you caught the person what shot that officer."

"Yes, we did."

"He okay?"

It took a moment before Angel realized her father meant Ryan. "Yes, Daddy. He is. He'll come home from the hospital soon." She took a breath and added, "And home might be my place."

Gilbert glanced away.

"Ryan is probably going to be in my life for a long time." She heard a soft grunt of disapproval from her father, something she'd learned to recognize over the years. "Oh, Daddy, you have to know that I didn't set out to find a white man to fall in love with just to make you mad. Or push back on your attitude towards people who aren't like us. But he's a good man. A really good man. And if you give him a chance, I think you could even like him. Remember how you almost liked my partner when she was so helpful back when Mama was sick."

Gilbert gave a little snort at that.

"It's true, Daddy. Don't try to pretend it isn't."

Gilbert put his hands on his knees and pushed, and for a

second Angel thought he was going to get up and leave. But he didn't. He just stretched his back, and then leaned back, still silent.

"Okay. I just have one more thing to say, then I'll leave. I'm going to try to get rid of the old guard in the department that's spreading racist views from the top down. That poor young cop who shot that boy—"

"Don't tell me that was a poor young cop. That was—"

"Daddy, listen to me." The fact that she yelled stopped Gilbert cold. He regarded her with eyes wide with surprise. "Smithfield *is* a poor young cop who was trained by the wrong man. Someone so racist he should wear a white hood to work."

Gilbert almost smiled at that, but he said nothing, so Angel continued. "If I have to go all the way up the chain of command to the commissioner, I will. The department has to change the way officers are trained."

"I hope you do some good, girl."

It was spoken with an undercurrent of love Angel remembered from her childhood. When she and her Daddy were good friends. When he praised her for something she'd done exceptionally well.

There was movement in the doorway again and her mother stepped into the room. Angel guessed she hadn't been too far away this whole time. "If you two are finished, there's lemon pie in the kitchen and fresh coffee."

Angel smiled. Life was always better with Mama's lemon pie.

CHAPTER THIRTY-ONE

Monday, July 13 - Late Afternoon

S arah ordered a Rob Roy at the bar, then took it back to a table where the gang from the department was gathered. She slipped into a seat next to McGregor who lifted his glass of club soda in a toast. "To a job well done."

They all raised their drinks. "To the team," Burt said.

Sarah reached over to touch their glasses. "The best."

After everyone took a sip of their drink, Sarah asked the table at large, "Any word on when Ryan is coming home?"

"Soon," Angel answered. "But if he had his way it would've been yesterday."

That brought a round of chuckles.

Later, as the group started to break up and people headed toward the door, Sarah stood to follow Burt. Angel raised her hand. "Stay for one more?"

"Uh, okay. Sure." Sarah waved a goodbye to Burt, then sat back down.

Angel caught the attention of the waitress and motioned to their glasses. The woman gave a quick nod and a few moments later brought them fresh drinks. Sarah wasn't sure she needed another. Two was usually her limit when driving, and this was number three. But if she really started to feel it, she could finish the evening with some caffeine. And food would help mitigate the alcohol. "Want to share some fries?"

The bar had some of the best fries in Dallas, so it wasn't a difficult decision for Sarah to toss nutrition out the window. Still, she wasn't sure how married to healthy living Angel was. "Add catsup and you have two vegetables," Sarah said with a bit of a grin.

Angel laughed. "Okay."

The waitress brought the drinks and cleared empty glasses from the table. "Anything else, ladies?"

"An order of fries," Sarah said.

"Just one?" The waitress included a smile with the question.

"For now." Sarah responded with a smile of her own.

For a few moments, the waitress had been blocking the view to the television mounted in a corner of the bar, and when she moved, Sarah glanced up and saw the banner for "breaking news" scrolling across the bottom of the screen. The image quickly changed to show Bianca, the Channel Eight news reporter, standing in front of the Dallas County Courthouse. Next to her was Amelia Cummings, who wore a tailored burgundy suit over an off-white blouse. The lawyer's expression was hard to read, but it definitely wasn't happy.

"Bianca Gomez here with the latest news regarding Dallas Police officer Brad Smithfield, who allegedly shot and killed Jamel Frederickson on Tuesday, June sixteenth of this year. In lieu of a jury trial, Officer Smithfield agreed to accept a deal from the prosecutors today. The details were just released by his attorney here next to me, Amelia Cummings."

Bianca turned to the other woman. "What can you tell us about the deal agreement your client accepted?"

"He pled guilty on the charge of second-degree murder. That took the death penalty off the table."

"That's crap," Angel shouted, the outburst startling a few patrons further down the bar who turned to frown at her. "Should be murder one."

"Easy, girl." Sarah put a hand out in a vague gesture to let folks know everything was okay at the table.

"Really?" Angel drew back. "That's your response?"

Sarah considered the force of the emotion behind Angel's words. She had rarely seen her partner with this much passion and energy about anything. The woman had always been the calm one in the partnership, pulling Sarah back from some precipice or another. But if she stopped to think about behaviors in the last few months, Sarah could see how Angel had changed. Slowly at first, then gaining more momentum, especially in recent weeks.

While nobody was looking, Angel had burst out of her shell of always doing the right thing. Following the rules.

What the hell? Her partner was on the verge of becoming a version of herself. That thought elicited a soft chuckle.

"This is funny to you?" Angel pointed toward the television and the continuing news report.

"Oh, God! No! I share your anger about that shooting. And the one last year in Minneapolis—"

"Say his name."

"What?"

"Say his name." More force in the words this time and anger flashing in Angel's eyes. "George Floyd."

"Okay. Okay. George Floyd. I haven't forgotten his name."

Angel didn't respond, but the fire in her eyes could've cooked steaks. Sarah softened her tone and leaned in. "Listen. I can't begin to understand what this has been like for you—"

"Damn right you can't." Angel's voice came in a loud hiss. And Sarah held up one hand palm out.

"Can we not do this? Destroy what partnership we have?"

Angel sat in rigid silence.

"I'm angry, too. Do I really need to say it? Angry at the whole fucking mess of senseless deaths. I don't have to be Black to recognize the injustice."

Before Angel could respond, the waitress stepped to the table with a steaming plate of French fries. "Everything okay here?" She gave each of them a searching look.

Sarah glanced at Angel who gave a brief chin tuck. "We're good."

The waitress tapped the table with her fingertips. "Let me know if you need anything else."

After the waitress left, Sarah took a long swallow of her drink and watched Angel pick at a French fry. "Can we back up here a minute?"

Angel shrugged.

"Earlier when I laughed. It wasn't because of the news. Your reaction made me more aware of how different you've been acting recently. You're reminding me of myself."

Angel glanced up, her face registering surprise, but she didn't say anything. Unable to tell what her partner might be thinking, Sarah hoped what she'd said hadn't been an insult. She certainly didn't mean it that way. She was actually kind of pleased at the change in her partner. Not that Angel needed to go off the rails like she did so often, but it was good to see this new strength of purpose in her partner.

Were they partners? Truly? The lingering question that had dogged them from the first case together had never seemed to find an answer. Was the dinner the other night, and now this ... having a drink together ... was this an indication that they were finally sliding into a true and lasting partnership?

Boy. That took some consideration.

Sarah picked up a fry and chewed it before glancing back at Angel. "Why did you ask me to stay?"

Angel shrugged. "Honestly? I'm not sure. It just felt like the right thing to do."

"Oh." For once, Angel had left Sarah speechless. Was anything right in this crazy fucked-up world? In their world? After taking a sip of her drink, she asked, "Are you going back to the protests?"

Angel tilted her drink glass back and forth watching the amber liquid as it slid precariously close to the rim before slipping back down. Finally, she looked up. "I want to keep supporting the cause. It's much too important to just step away. On the other hand, I don't want to lose my job. A few weeks ago I'd been thinking about quitting the force—"

"What? Really?"

"Yeah. Really. This past year's been a nightmare. And it made me fully recognize that there's still such a huge gap between people with pale skin and people with dark skin. Within the cops and without. We can't ignore that."

"You still thinking about it?"

"At times. Then when I focus on the sheer adrenaline rush I had after what we did to help Wanda, well, nothing else could touch it."

"So?" Sarah waited a long moment, taking a sip of her drink and swallowing hard before finishing, "Can a White woman join the local BLM organization?"

Angel smiled.

AUTHOR NOTE

First, thank you to all the readers who have followed this series from the first book through this one. Readers are why writers write. Truly.

Unfortunately, due to ongoing health problems that make it incredibly hard to sustain work on a full-length novel, this will be the last installment of the Seasons Series, but it may not be the last you hear of Sarah and Angel. They are not happy that the series is over and reminded me there are such things as novellas and short stories they would be happy to star in. And in case you're wondering, I haven't taken too many meds and am not hallucinating. Characters do talk to us. Just ask any other writer.

So, this may not be the last you read about these two tough ladies.

One last thing before I leave you alone. I hope you enjoy Brutal Season as much as the first books in the series. You can do me a huge favor by going to Amazon, or wherever you purchased the book, and leaving a review. Those reviews really help. Again, just ask any other author.

Thanks,
Maryann

ABOUT THE AUTHOR

Maryann Miller is an award-winning author of numerous books, screenplays, and stage plays. She started her professional career as a journalist, writing columns, feature stories, and short fiction for regional and national publications. Now she writes primarily mysteries, including the critically-acclaimed Seasons Mystery Series. The first two books in the series, *Open Season* and *Stalking Season* have received starred reviews from Publisher's Weekly, Kirkus, and Library Journal. *Stalking Season* was chosen for the John E. Weaver Excellence in Reading award for Police Procedural Mysteries. *Desperate Season* won the top honors for mystery in the Page Turner Awards, Her mystery, *Doubletake*, was honored as the Best Mystery for 2015 by the Texas Association of Authors.

Among the other awards Miller has received are the Page Edwards Short Story Award, the New York Library Best Books for Teens Award, first place in the screenwriting competition at the Houston Writer's Conference. She was a semi-finalist at Sundance for her original screenplay, "A Question of Honor, and a semi-finalist in the Chesterfield Screenwriting Competition for her adaptation of *Open Season*. She was named The Trails Country Treasure by the Winnsboro Center for the Arts, and Woman of the Year by the Winnsboro Area Chamber of Commerce.

Miller lives in Northeast Texas with her dog and three cats. Guess who runs the household? When not writing, she enjoys reading, coloring, jigsaw puzzles, and tries valiantly not to kill the flowers in her garden or any of her numerous houseplants.

She is a contributor to *The Blood-Red Pencil* blog on writing and editing. http://bloodredpencil.blogspot.com

Follow Maryann Miller

Website – www.maryannwrites.com

Amazon – https://www.amazon.com/stores/Maryann-Miller/author/B001JP7Y1S

Twitter - @maryannwrites

Facebook – Maryann Miller (The home of mystery author, Maryann Miller)

Goodreads - https://www.goodreads.com/maryannwrites

www.ingramcontent.com/pod-product-compliance
Lightning Source LLC
Chambersburg PA
CBHW060857250626
47159CB00008B/2781